T0146458

Uncharted Waters

MICAH PERSELL

Crimson Romance
New York London Toronto Sydney New Delhi

CRIMSON
ROMANCE

Crimson Romance
An Imprint of Simon & Schuster, Inc.
1230 Avenue of the Americas
New York, NY 10020

For information about special discounts for bulk purchases, please contact Simon & Schuster Special Sales at 1-866-506-1949 or business@ simonandschuster.com.

The Simon & Schuster Speakers Bureau can bring authors to your live event. For more information or to book an event contact the Simon & Schuster Speakers Bureau at 1-866-248-3049 or visit our website at www. simonspeakers.com.

ISBN: 978-1-5072-0742-0
ISBN: 978-1-5072-0611-9 (ebook)

Praise for Micah Persell

Dedication

For all the scientists out there with two X chromosomes.
Keep slaying, ladies.

Chapter One

Bethany Morgan narrowed her eyes at her boss. Had she heard correctly? Granted, the words *flirt for results* had not actually left Dr. Dewinter's mouth, but everyone in this room had heard them anyway.

Excellent. Just what she needed a room of men to hear.

She cleared her throat and set her pencil down on the tabletop before she snapped it in two. "Just to clarify, I'm to ... get friendly"—she struggled not to emphasize the words and lost the battle—"with this Dr. Anderson to get him to hand over the schematics for our water system, even though we already own them?"

Despite the ickiness of the request, Bethany couldn't even think about the water system without a thrill shooting through her gut. In the biggest coup of her career, she had discovered the world-changing plans for a gray-water recycling system on a dusty Delaney Science computer when she'd taken a box of surplus beakers down to the basement. Even though Anderson himself was a relic who hadn't worked for Delaney since way before anyone seated at this table, he'd used Delaney equipment to create the system. Therefore, Delaney owned it. And no one would have known it even existed if it wasn't for Bethany.

She was the best in this field, but as much as she wanted to fool herself into thinking prowess in gray-water systems had earned her a spot at this table, it was the stroke of luck of finding the schematics that landed her here. And now it seemed as though her looks were the only thing keeping her here.

Dewinter, the only other woman in the room, pursed her lips, and to Bethany's right, one of her more insufferable coworkers, Jonathan, said, "But you pointed out the schematics were incomplete. And you haven't been able to figure out how to finish them. We most likely need Anderson's help."

Mansplaining was just precious. Really. "I recall that," she replied through only barely gritted teeth. Showing up on Anderson's doorstep and informing him that his water system was being legally commandeered would probably—definitely—be met with resistance. Social finesse was a necessity. "But surely there are ..." *More dignified?* "Better ways to approach this. Any of us could make overtures." She nodded toward her dearest—only, really—friend. "Mark could get friendly with him."

That lightness in her belly turned to a lead balloon in an instant. What was she doing? Had she really just offered this opportunity to Mark on a silver platter? She could be friendly!

Mark's eyes seemed to dance with light. "I'm game."

No! "I mean—" Bethany began, mentally scrounging for a way to land back at the helm of this mission in a way that afforded her a modicum of self-respect.

Dr. Dewinter held up a hand, and if she had been Evita Perón herself, she would not have gotten everyone's undivided attention faster. "We can send a team." She shrugged. "That's probably best anyway."

Fuck! She'd done it. Managed to flush away the only viable, mass-producing gray-water solution she'd come across in her career. In anyone's career. Anderson's water system was groundbreaking. Capable of solving the world's clean-water crisis. No one would have to die like Bethany's mother had ever again.

No child would ever go thirsty.

What would have happened if she'd simply said *sure* when Dewinter had asked her to sidle up to the elderly Dr. Anderson? So, she'd been asked to use her feminine wiles. It hadn't been the first time; it would not be the last. *Is your pride, your principles, worth more than human life?*

She'd made a mistake.

Dewinter opened the file folder in front of her and scanned a document. "Anderson's last known location was high in the Rockies." She closed the folder with a snap. "The Colorado Rockies, so it's a short trip."

Bethany's lips parted. A short trip high into the Rockies in the dead of winter? That was a paradox if ever she'd heard one.

Dewinter slid the file folder toward the center of the table, and all eyes locked on it as though it were a Nobel Peace Prize up for grabs. And, in all probability, it was. Bethany's hands itched to snatch it.

"A team of five seems sufficient." All gazes snapped to Dewinter, who was perusing the Delaney employees gathered around the table.

Oh, God. Pick me. The words were plainly written on each of their faces.

"Mark."

Damn it. That one was her fault. *Mark can get friendly with him.* Ugh, she was an idiot.

"Jonathan, Eric, Bryce, and ..."

A roar set up residence in her ears, and she watched Dewinter's lips moving without being able to hear what she said. Had her lips formed *Bethany?*

She darted a glance at Mark, whose subtle wink was promising. When he mouthed *She picked you*, her hearing came back with a *pop* just in time for her to hear Dewinter say as she rose, "You all leave tomorrow morning, so get packing. It's cold out there, folks." She exited the room in a waft of floral perfume.

With grumbles, those who had not been picked pushed to their feet and began exiting the room. As two men passed her, she heard one say to the other, "Like Morgan can be friendly. You hear the things she says? She's so ... crass. The old guy will be turned off in a second."

These two guys in particular could make a porn star blush with the things they said about women's bodies. And she was crass?

Bethany saw a buzzing red cloud but leaned back in her chair, projecting the professionalism that got her through similar situations several times a day. Then, like it usually did, her mouth had to go and ruin it. "You can kiss my crass, Jerry. All damn day."

Across the table, Mark coughed a laugh and covered his mouth with finely manicured fingertips, but the other three men around the table—the rest of her team—shook their heads uniformly.

They can kiss my crass, too.

But she swallowed and eyed the folder that still gleamed from the center of the table. This was important. Maybe she could reel in ... well, everything?

When Jonathan reached forward, his fingers creeping toward the folder, Bethany launched. Her hand landed first, and as Jonathan scowled, she slid it toward herself.

Bryce pushed to his feet with a sigh. "Well, I'm off to pack. We can talk plans on the way to the mountains." He nodded at the folder in front of Bethany. "Study up, Morgan. And don't forget to pack your lipstick."

Jonathan and Eric chuckled as they followed Bryce out of the room.

"Pricks," Mark muttered. "They will not be cuddling with me on that cold mountain."

Lifting her chin, Bethany smiled at him. "A terrible loss."

After a moment, Mark's answering grin dimmed. "What's your plan, Bethany? Because we both know it isn't flirting for information."

Bethany opened the folder and rolled her shoulders. "Of course, it isn't. I'll be professional. Courteous. Anderson is a smart man."

Her words drifted off as she leafed through the copies of what appeared to be every memo Anderson had sent out during his employment at Delaney. His signature graced the bottom of every page; she traced the scrawling script with her pointer finger. Like many brilliant people, his letters were barely legible.

Near the end of the stack, a new item joined his signature. Beneath his name, in exact block letters, Eugene Anderson had written *ignotumque aquas*. She frowned. Latin of course, but it wasn't any scientific term she was familiar with. *Aquas* was water, but *ignotumque*?

Unfound?

No, uncharted.

Dr. Anderson had signed this memo with the phrase "uncharted waters." She flipped through the rest of the memos; he'd signed all of them that way.

A slow grin spread across her lips. Oh, she was going to like this man. Uncharted waters would usually be a nautical term, but she knew that wasn't what he meant here. His system would take clean water to uncharted locations. Exactly where it was needed.

Eugene Anderson knew precisely what he wanted to do with this system. And it was what Bethany herself wanted to do with it: save the world.

She transferred her grin to Mark, who was staring at her like she'd been woolgathering for several awkward moments. She flipped the file folder closed. "He knows what he's created and what it means to the world," she said. "Only the worst kind of person wouldn't want to get this water system out there to save lives."

"And if Anderson is the worst kind of person?"

If she was right about him, that wasn't a possibility. She shook her head. "Then we reevaluate. But Bethany sacrificing her self-worth won't be one of the options I agree to."

"Damn right it won't be. So, when do you tell everyone else that?"

"I'll tell the guys as soon as we hit the road." As for Dewinter? Well, Bethany didn't need to be burning any bridges right now. Her place on this team was tenuous; that was more than obvious. Telling Dewinter to take her suggestion of flirting and shove it up her ass was probably a bad idea.

Bethany pushed to her feet, tucking the folder beneath her arm. It wouldn't matter. Dewinter didn't need to ever know she wouldn't follow instructions. "This is going to be quick and painless. I mean, how hard can it be?"

Chapter Two

Not a rabbit.

James stood beneath his most lucrative snare, hands on his hips.

It appeared that ... He tilted his head and narrowed his eyes just to make sure. Yep. Unless he was mistaken, instead of catching a small woodland creature, his snare had trapped a *human*.

James watched as long, silky hair swayed back and forth in midair. A slender neck led to a narrow back that tapered into an even narrower waist.

A real, flesh-and-blood woman.

He moved one of his hands from his hips, tugging at the end of his beard. There usually weren't people this high up the mountain. It'd been a while since he'd even seen a woman from a distance, and he could recognize that he was not acting logically at the sight of this one.

He couldn't seem to draw his eyes away from the way the rising sun brought flickers of blue out in her dark black hair, even though he knew his fixation could be deadly in an environment that turned hostile at a moment's notice.

He grunted and scrubbed a hand down his face to both break his gaze's hold and bring him back to logical reality.

Good thing I raised that snare.

A bear had been stealing his catches lately, and judging by the displaced snow beneath her and a few distinct paw prints, his trap had saved her life.

James pulled in a quick breath and pushed it out. He bit the tip of his right glove and jerked his hand free, quickly removed his left glove as well, and shoved them both in his back pocket. He began the process of unknotting the snare, keeping his back to the woman because it gave him a freer range of motion.

Yes, only because of that.

With the knot undone, the rope jerked in his hand, and he released it. There was a thud behind him, and James's shoulders stiffened.

He should have lowered her to the ground gently. It was a careless mistake; James did not make careless mistakes. Turning slowly, he found her sprawled in the snow on her back. His gaze zeroed in on her torso, which, after a tense moment, rose and fell. James exhaled in a rush. Then, he noticed her eyes were open. They stared blankly at the sky, and they were unblinking. No: there was one, slow blink.

His lips parted. She was conscious! Why hadn't he thought to check for that first?

He took a step toward her, then hesitated. Immediately, he gritted his teeth. *She's a woman, not a rattlesnake.*

Still, no reason to rush toward her and possibly frighten her. He leaned forward. "Excuse me," he tried to say. Instead, an unpracticed croaking sound left his mouth. He frowned. When was the last time he'd spoken? He cleared his throat and tried again. When actual words came out this time, though harsh and hoarse, he continued. "Are ... you ... all right?"

It was the most he'd said to another person in ten years. If her lack of response was any indication, she was less than stimulated. She continued to blink intermittently at the sky.

"Miss?" he grated.

Her head lolled to the side. Glassy but startling aqua-green eyes peered his way. He took a stumbling step backward, but caught himself and stood firm, waiting for her to speak. To give him any indication of how he could help her.

She remained silent, but that long hair of hers slid over her forehead and coiled in the snow. He caught sight of a shadowy mark on her forehead.

An injury.

Now, he rushed forward, kneeling in the snow beside her. He reached out an unsteady hand, and it hovered in the air between them for several seconds. He frowned at his hand. Did he plan to touch her?

Another of her lethargic blinks.

With no more hesitation, he swept the rest of her hair from her forehead. He hissed in a breath. The skin of her temple was mottled purple.

Lethargy. Limited responsiveness. If these symptoms were related to a head injury, this woman was in trouble.

Leaning over her, he blocked out the early morning light. After a few moments, her pupils expanded. When he sat back on his haunches and sunlight streamed over her face, both pupils contracted.

His shoulders fell in a rush of relief. That was good. At worse, she might have a mild concussion. So why the lack of response?

He waved a hand in front of her face. Her gaze seemed to lock on to it for a moment and then on to him. However, she still said nothing.

Something was wrong here.

He grasped her snared ankle in his hand. Even through the thick, white snow pants she wore, he could feel bones no thicker than kindling. He immediately gentled his grip.

And you dropped her from the sky like a sack of potatoes. He could have seriously injured her. Something unfamiliar and tight filled his chest, and he promised himself he'd check her for broken bones as soon as possible.

He loosened the trap and slipped it off. A quick scan proved her pants, boots, and socks were thick enough to save her leg from a painful sprain. He wouldn't be able to check her skin; for one, he wouldn't chance exposing it here where frostbite was too grievous a risk. That blank-eyed stare also made him hesitate. He could just picture her screaming if he tried to roll up her pant leg.

He placed her leg back on the ground, and when his palm remained wrapped around her ankle longer than necessary, he jerked it away by force.

He rotated, bringing his gaze with him and surveying her legs. Straight in all the correct places. No obvious broken bones there. He caught sight of her hands. Her *bare* hands in the snow.

His eyes widened, and he snatched the gloves from his back pocket with one hand while gathering both of hers into his other. They prickled with cold and were blanched white, but showed no signs of frostbite. She was lucky. Had she not been hanging in the air, her delicate fingers would have been blue and covered in ice crystals within thirty minutes. She couldn't have been in his trap longer than an hour, but her limbs did not tremble from the cold. Not a good sign.

Hypothermia.

An hour ago had been just after sunrise. The woods would still have been dim. This trap would have taken her by surprise. She would have been ... scared.

That tight feeling returned.

Mild concussion, moderate hypothermia, and probably nonmedical shock. Separately, none were cause for great alarm. Taken all together, however, they might explain her current condition. And they meant she probably needed a hospital.

He forced himself to be gentle despite the need for urgency, slipping his gloves over her fingers one at a time. They swallowed her hands, the elasticized wrists going over her jacket sleeves to her forearm.

Now what? "Miss?" No response. She wasn't walking out of the woods. His gaze darting from tree trunk to tree trunk, he searched for a solution. Nothing.

Avoiding eye contact even though she had yet to make any herself, he turned his gaze slowly back to the mystery woman.

There was no getting around it. He was going to have to carry her.

He adjusted the string of rabbits hanging over his shoulder and down his back. As he reached toward her, his hands shook. He fisted them for a moment, until the shaking stilled, then wrapped his fingers around her wrists, easily fitting them both within his grip. Just before he hauled her over his shoulder, he made the mistake of glancing at her face. For the first time, her medical condition was not what he noticed.

His lips parted. *Oh ... wow.*

That blue-black hair haloed her head, a stark contrast to the snow beneath her. Her features were—he wracked his brain for the proper word.

Full.

Her lips were plump—the top one more so than the bottom. Her cheekbones were high, and thick eyelashes brushed them. Her nose was wide but delicate. Her eyes, those startling aqua corneas, were so beautiful James found himself wishing she would focus them on him. They were large. Angled at the sides. Her skin, even in the brisk air, was a warm, sandy color.

That tight feeling in his chest traveled downward, settling heavily and uncomfortably low in his gut. His body flushed with heat, making him fight the urge to squirm. So to distract himself, he reached out with his free hand, lifted her by her nape, and adjusted her hood so her head was safely covered. Her hair was cool and slick against his fingers, and again, he jerked his hand away before it could linger.

A numbing cold began to settle into his fingers, snapping him from whatever hold her beauty had over his normally functional brain. Even before turning over his gloves, James had already been in a rush. Not only was her situation significant, but the clouds were heavy with snow. The first flake hadn't even fallen, but the storm would be bad. The only reason he was out in these conditions was to collect his catches and prepare to batten down the hatches as his father had often said while he was still alive.

With her wrists secure, he pushed to his feet, pulling her dead weight up with him. With his other arm, he caught her just beneath her bottom and flopped her over his shoulder. Her breathing audibly hitched.

He froze. Would she speak now? Scream?

When her breathing simply resumed its normal pace, he closed his eyes for a moment. She wasn't regaining her senses. He'd just jostled her. *Gently, fool.* With his eyes closed, he was overtaken by her scent. She smelled of flowers and rain. A meadow beneath a storm. It was intoxicating, and before he could even ponder why he would think something so flighty, he pulled in lungfuls of it until he swayed slightly. His eyes sprang open, and his equilibrium balanced. He shook his head to clear it and caught sight of a path of destruction through the woods. Flattened brush revealed long, smeared tracks and claw marks.

His arm around the back of her thighs tightened. She had been *chased* by the bear. Through the woods in the near dark. The culmination of her nightmare had been James's trap. No wonder she was in shock. He patted her bottom absently with his free hand, realized how grossly inappropriate such a gesture was, and jerked his hand back to his side.

Get her to a hospital.

Her clothing was fine quality. She was out here in the middle of nowhere, so she had to have been camped nearby.

People are surely looking for her.

James considered the sky: he had time. Luckily, he was close to his cabin. If the woman's campsite was not too far, he could be there and back in his cabin—minus one distracting woman—before the blizzard broke.

He needed her gone. Already, he had lost too much of himself in her presence.

Decided, he stalked forward, easily following the bear's path. When he arrived at an abandoned camp less than five minutes later, his shoulders fell. Unburdening himself of the mystery woman was an improbability.

The camp was in absolute disarray. The remains of five tents were scattered throughout, batted around as though they were inconsequential. A meal, still in the preparation stage, was strewn over a picnic table and the rest of the camp. Myriad pieces of high-tech equipment dotted the site, each bearing the name Delaney Science in a bold, black stamp. James raised an eyebrow.

Scientists?

He considered the slight weight on his shoulder. Was *she* a scientist? He quickly perused the carnage, spotting enough blood in the snow to indicate someone had been gravely injured. Most likely, whoever had remained behind after the obvious bear attack had taken the wounded for help. The woman on his shoulder may be presumed dead.

James frowned. There were obvious indications that a bear had adopted this site: scat, claw marks on a nearby tree. If they were scientists, they certainly were not biologists or zoologists—or for that matter, Boy Scouts—or they would have picked up on those clues.

A snowflake drifted past James's nose. *The blizzard will break any minute now.* There was no one here to take the woman to the hospital.

Though he knew what he had to do, his Adam's apple felt like a rock lodged in his throat when he swallowed. It appeared the woman would be coming home with him. He shoved the air from his lungs in a huff. He had no idea how to care for a woman. No idea how to care for *anything*.

There was not much time, but James made a quick circuit of the camp, finding some packs, largely intact, propped against what had once been a tent. There must not have been any food in them or the bear would have added them to its destruction. With a wary eye to the sky, James lifted a pack to his face, sniffed briefly, and then tossed it down. The second pack carried her water lily scent, and he slung it over his free shoulder. He took a moment to adjust his load to a more balanced state, cursorily eyeing the gadgets and equipment they'd brought. It was nothing better than he could make himself. He'd leave everything here for now. Perhaps after the storm, he could return for some spare parts.

He took off, leaving the camp just as the snow began to fall.

Chapter Three

As soon as James closed the door to his cabin behind them, his muscles loosened their death grip on his bones. It had taken him far longer than anticipated to get back to the cabin while loaded down with a surplus of rabbits and an entire human being on his shoulder. Though the distance had been less than two miles, by the last half mile, the snow had quickly drifted in up to his knees, and he had started to worry that they wouldn't make it.

He gritted his teeth together to keep them from chattering, one of the symptoms of early hypothermia. It was not the first time he'd suffered the condition, and, no doubt, would not be the last. The woman, however, had started off with moderate hypothermia.

He strode to the bed and lowered her to its surface—he remembered to be gentle this time, but it did little good. His muscles were a touch outside his control at present, and she flopped down harder than he'd intended.

James was supernaturally lighter without her weight. His body started to shudder in a desperate bid to create more warmth with her off his shoulder; she had been warming him more than he had guessed.

Get us warm!

He stumbled over to the fireplace and dumped her pack and his string of rabbits to the floor. With numb fingers, he loaded wood and kindling in the grate. In seconds, flames flickered. He should spend a few moments more to ensure the fire caught to its fullest potential, but the unconscious woman—she was so small.

Was she worse after being hauled through a blizzard? The gnawing worry in his gut wouldn't allow James to sit here and poke at a fire.

He made his way to the bed, snatching a thick wool blanket from the back of the couch on the way. He was pleased to find that he hardly stumbled at all this time, which meant his blood circulation was already improving after only minutes sheltered from the elements. If they were lucky, the woman would snap out of this stupor as soon as she got warm again. And felt safe. He paused at the foot of the bed. The blanket, which he used against his own skin regularly, felt suddenly far too coarse for hers, but it was the warmest he had. He clutched it in his hands and swept her with his gaze. A tad more of the tension filling his chest abated. Her skin was not riddled with splotches of frostbite as he had worried it would be. Beyond being blanched of color, her face was as ... beautiful as he remembered.

His brows drew together. *Beautiful is irrelevant. Her current condition is.* And that current condition was ... he gazed into her eyes, hoping for some glimmer of consciousness. She stared at the ceiling. "Miss?" Nothing. He blew out the breath he'd been holding. She hadn't improved. But she also didn't appear to have worsened.

He dropped the blanket at the foot of the bed. Her jacket and pants were soaked with melting snow, though they'd held up remarkably for such inclement weather.

There was no way around it. If he wanted her to get better, her clothes had to come off. And he didn't have the luxury of waiting for her to come to and do it herself.

He made a fist and released it several times at his sides. So, why was he hesitating? *This is ridiculous.* If her wet clothes stayed on, she *would* contract a severe case of hypothermia. She might die.

Forget she's beautiful. Forget she's the only woman I've seen close up since I was six. He closed his eyes. These thoughts weren't helping. *She dies if you don't do this!*

His eyes snapped open. *Right, then.*

He started with her boots, his fingers feeling uncharacteristically large and clumsy on the laces in a way that could not be attributed entirely to mild hypothermia. After an epic battle with two sodden double knots, he got her boots off. Her thick socks were dry. He exhaled slowly. That was a relief. Toes were especially susceptible to cold.

Setting her boots on the floor, he glanced at her waist and hesitated again. Boots were one thing, but pants? Medical emergency or not, could he undress an unresponsive woman?

His stomach lurched. He had to try one more time. Leaning over her, he tried to put himself directly in the path of her gaze. Her eyes didn't seem to focus, but that wasn't necessarily an indicator of whether or not she saw him. "Your clothes ..." Ah, God, even the words stuck in his throat. He cleared it. "Must ... come off." He paused. Waited for her to do or say something. Anything.

She blinked, then continued to stare. Continued not to shiver or respond. And still he waited.

This is silly! He was a grown man. A man of science. He would not shy away from taking a woman's pants off.

He swallowed hard despite the internal pep talk, and when his fingers wrapped around the elastic waist of her pants, to his utter frustration, his fingers shook. "Last chance. Speak up." When she did not move, he sucked in a breath and yanked her pants down, revealing ...

More pants.

He exhaled, tempted in equal parts to laugh and scrub a hand down his face. James took her snow pants the rest of the way off with no more hesitation; then he unzipped her jacket and eased her out of it with as little jostling as he could manage. She had dressed in jeans and a sweater beneath her winter gear. He dumped her snowsuit on the ground and placed one palm on her arm, the other on her thigh. Her clothes were damp but warm.

The snowsuit had done the best job it could insulating her body, but now *these* clothes had to come off, too, before they cooled and lowered her body temperature even more.

James wasn't going to overreact like he had over her pants again. He unceremoniously unbuttoned her jeans and, grasping the legs at the cuffs, pulled them from her body.

His lips parted.

He spun around, shutting his eyes, and, immediately, the image of what he'd seen appeared on the backs of his eyelids. He pressed both fists into his eyes until those long, toned legs and the impossibly tiny underwear—composed entirely of *black lace*—were overcome by a burst of red light.

He lowered his fists with a jerk and blinked several times, trying to dissipate the stars dotting his vision. At the same time, he reached behind him and groped for the blanket, fisted it, and dropped it over the general area of her hips.

His heart was thundering.

Logic, James!

Raising his chin, he turned. Without looking at her directly, he jerked the blanket down, covering her lower body entirely. Once it was safe again, he glanced at her face. He had an overwhelming desire to apologize. He swallowed that down, too.

Get it done.

He hooked her beneath her arms and sat her up slowly. With a series of awkward movements, he managed to draw her sweater up and over her head. He knew better than to look at her undergarments this time. Staring up at the corner of his cabin, he spread the blanket up to her shoulders.

He was just going to assume that her underclothes were dry.

With her safely covered, he dared looking at her again. He pulled his bottom lip between his teeth.

The tops of her naked shoulders peeked over the end of the blanket, appearing delicate and fragile. Her clavicle dipped gently at the hollow of her throat, creating a shadow he had the odd urge to brush his finger over. Just in case he had completely lost his senses, James curled his fingers into his palms to keep any errant digits in check. Two tiny straps looped over her shoulders and disappeared; her brazier matched her panties, if that tiny scrap of material he'd seen even qualified as panties. That she wore a matching set of underclothes was information he really did not need to possess. Despite his efforts to keep himself detached, his gaze touched every inch of bare skin he could see. She was so different from him physically.

Now James groaned. *Yes, brilliant observation.* How profound that a woman was different from a man in form. His idiocy was truly growing unbearable.

The whole purpose of disrobing her was not only to get her warm and dry but to examine her for injury, something he needed to get to quickly instead of staring at her in what was probably wide-eyed wonder.

A soft whimper sounded in the cabin. His gaze was on her face in a shot. Her eyes were still blank, but her eyebrows were drawn together. He frowned, his gaze momentarily dipping to her hand where it breached the edge of the blanket. Reaching out as though he was about to touch a hot coal, he covered her hand with his, rubbing his thumb over her knuckles. "You're ... safe now," he murmured to her as though she could hear him.

Her expression relaxed beneath his gentle rubbing, wrenching a particularly hard *thud* from his heart. Before he could stop himself, he'd brushed the backs of his fingers against her cheek. Her skin was so incredibly soft, he did it again. She turned her face into the touch with an apathetic blink.

James sucked in a breath and jerked his hand away. *What am I doing?*

Time for a break.

He gathered the bundle of her wet clothing in his arms—his own swimming head when he bent over an indication that he needed to get himself warm, too—strode over to the couch, and spread the items out to dry in front of the fire. That done, he returned to the bed. He had only been away from her overwhelming presence for a couple of minutes, but he already felt clearer. With jerky movements, he quickly passed his hands over her arms and legs through the blanket. *There. Done.* She had no broken bones. Her greatest need was getting warm. He hesitated only a moment, something he considered progress, before gathering her into his arms. Once she was cradled against his chest, the desire to tighten his arms and simply hold her scared him into moving quickly. He rushed over to the fire and placed her on the floor a safe distance from the flames.

He caught himself inhaling her scent. He abruptly retrieved his arms and stepped back, peering at her for a moment. She looked appallingly uncomfortable. He stalked to the bed, grabbed a pillow, and returned to her side.

He slipped a hand beneath her neck and raised her head just enough to slide the pillow beneath it. He lowered her head and stepped back once more.

Still not right.

He raised her head once more and gathered her smooth hair into one hand, twisted it a couple of times, and trailed it over her shoulder. Now it wasn't pulling her head back at an awkward angle.

He jerked a nod. *Better.*

He stood in the middle of his cabin with his hands on his hips. For the first time in his own home, James didn't know what to do with himself. There were things he needed to do. Oddly enough, he wanted to put them all off to stare at the way light from the fire flickered on the skin across her collarbone and shoulders.

How many times today would logic fail him?

His knees shook, and another wave of dizziness swept over him. He could no longer delay removing his own wet clothes.

Collecting his string of rabbits—hopefully enough for two people until the storm broke—he hung them on a nail outside the cabin door. In this weather, even a trip to the storage shed could prove disastrous. Though the shed was only a few hundred feet away, there was no telling how quickly the temperature would drop in the dark. He didn't need to combat hypothermia right on the heels of getting over it. He would move his catches as soon as visibility returned and pray that in the interim, a hungry animal would not wander off with them. Eating canned peaches for several days was undesirable.

Returning to the "bedroom" portion of his cabin, James retrieved a change of clothes from the dresser his father had crafted shortly after moving them out here all those years ago. He laid the items out on the bed, gazing at the indentations the woman's body had left behind on the quilt. He swallowed and looked away.

He began unbuttoning his shirt, then paused. He shot a quick glance at the woman. She hadn't moved. He stared down at the fingers on his shirt button. They were as steady as they'd ever been. The shaking that had been his constant companion since entering the cabin was absent. It wasn't a positive change. He couldn't put this off any longer. He needed to get in front of that fire himself.

Staring at the pattern of the quilt, he quickly removed his shirt, then shucked his pants and boxers.

He was just reaching for his clean pair of underwear when a piercing scream rent the air.

Chapter Four

Before she could identify she was no longer swinging above a ravenous bear, residual terror was bursting from her mouth in the same scream that had been cut off when her face met bark. Her arms jerked over her face, and she cringed, twisting to her side.

When the collision didn't come, her scream warbled and faded. She blinked her eyes open. Her cheek was pressed against a braided rug she didn't recognize. A cozy heat was at her back.

Not hanging from a tree anymore?

Her mind scrambled to find something she could recognize as thought. Was this real? Had the bear been real?

She pressed her fingers against a spot that throbbed near her hairline and grunted. *Yeouch.* This was real.

She planted her hand against the rug and pushed to a sitting position. Black dots converged and spun, and she clenched her eyes closed, gripping her temples with spread thumb and forefinger. With a groan, she strained to see her surroundings. In front of her was a couch.

Her snow pants, jeans, and shirt were spread over it.

She tilted her head to the side. *My clothes ...* Slowly, she lowered her gaze to her own body. A thick blanket pooled in her lap, and above that, her bare tummy. She sucked in a breath, tucked her chin a bit more, and caught sight of the completely impractical black lace bra she'd brought on a camping trip.

She flicked her gaze up and over the couch and locked gazes with a man standing beside a rumpled bed, eyeing her as though she were a hissing cobra.

A huge man. A huge, bearded man. A huge, bearded, naked man.

So very naked.

Whatever he saw on her face made his eyes widen, and he slowly raised his hands, palms out. Her lungs gobbled up air and spit it out again in another ear-splitting shriek.

She lurched backward, scrambling to her feet, clutching that blanket for all she was worth and trying to arrange it in a manner that hid her nearly naked body from the entirely naked stranger.

She'd moved too quickly. Her vision blanked, and she swayed, losing her balance and pitching backward, arms pinwheeling.

Her sight returned just in time for her to see the naked man move remarkably fast, vaulting over the couch and landing in front of her in what could have been no more than three steps. Just as the heat behind her began to scorch her legs, he reached out, snagged both of her arms in an iron grip, and yanked her forward in time to save her from tumbling into the flames.

Her eyes shut reflexively as he shoved her face to his chest. His breaths were harsh, and the hands that gripped her arms trembled.

Against her closed eyelids, the image of him jumping over the sofa—completely starkers—replayed. Her nose was crushed into his chest, but she quickly realized the rest of her body was crushed to him as well. The blanket was not present in any manner.

She gasped, splayed her hands on his chest, and shoved with all of her might. He absorbed the shove with a small, backward step, which meant the rest of the energy she'd invested in the move traveled back up her arms and sent her careening backward. Again.

He tightened his grip on her arms, keeping her upright. "Careful," he grated.

As her knees wobbled and she fought to avoid crumpling at his feet, her gaze poured over him, looking for details as to the threat he posed. He was so very large, standing at least a head and shoulders above her. Packs and packs of muscles covered his frame. They all seemed to be flexed, and she reflexively tried to shrink back, but his grip on her arms kept her from getting too far. Her gaze flew to his face, the features of which were almost completely hidden by a riot of wavy, reddish hair that fell to his shoulders and a beard to rival any member's of *Duck Dynasty*.

Adrenaline returned with a rush. Her arms were restrained, but her hands were free. She began liberally slapping at him, anywhere she could reach, which, it turned out, was only his chest and biceps.

"Don't touch me!" She punctuated each word with a sharp *slap*.

His lips parted, as though he hadn't realized he was holding her. His hands dropped from her skin in the next second, and as she was midswing for another slap, she stumbled with the momentum of her arm.

He reached for her, and she hit his hand away, managing to correct her stumble all by herself this time. She tipped her chin up and pinned him with an imperious glare. *See! I don't need you!*

His brows crashed over his eyes. "Move ... away from ... the fire." Though his words were unpracticed and hesitant, he still managed to make them sound like a rebuke.

Her haughtiness slipped a bit, and she looked over her shoulder at the fireplace. *Actually, a sound idea.* She took a large step to her right.

They stood several feet apart, now; Bethany crossed her arms over her breasts, and Wilderness Man jerked his gaze to the ceiling and blew out a huge breath.

Now that he was looking away, Bethany's gaze unwittingly roved the rest of his body. Her eyebrows shot toward her hairline. *Holy shit!* Mountain Man was big everywhere. A prickle of something that was not the alarm she should be feeling while naked with a stranger in a strange place skittered up her spine. Though he was currently ... at rest, he began to stir beneath her gaze.

Suddenly, he cupped his hands in front of his groin, and Bethany jerked her gaze to his face. Through all the whiskers and hair, she was sure she saw a look of pure censure as he glared at her like he'd caught her ogling him.

She pulled her bottom lip between her teeth and bit down hard. She *had* been ogling him. If she'd caught him doing the same, she'd have skinned him alive. Her gaze drifted sideways, and she stared into the flames, heat from more than the fire rushing beneath her skin.

"Pants are ... a good idea, I think," he said. His manner of speaking was so strange. Faltering and unsure.

She heard him move, and she tensed, but all he did was hold the blanket in front of her, patiently waiting for her to take it. When she did, with a small nod of thanks, he moved away. She wrapped the blanket around herself and kept staring into the fireplace while cloth rustled behind her near the bed.

Her mind rioted. Had she lost consciousness? She must have, or she would have remembered coming here, right? Wait. She closed her eyes. *Swaying over someone's shoulder. His same rough voice speaking to her.* No, she had been conscious, but she didn't remember much. Had she come here of her own volition? Clutching her blanket tightly above her breasts with one hand, she brushed the injury on her temple and realized her body was shaking. Did she simply not *remember* coming here? The way her body responded to this guy—it didn't make sense, especially if he'd threatened her.

Oh, God, *had* he threatened her?

He cleared his throat, and she spun around. He stood beside the bed fully clothed in denim and a plaid, button-down shirt.

Her gaze dipped to the rumpled quilt on the bed, and she knew beyond any doubt that she had been in that bed at some point. Why couldn't she remember? Her back straightened. "I need to know what happened. What I'm doing here."

He tilted his head to the side, and his eyes darted quickly over her face. He took a step toward her. She held out a hand, and he stopped. She raised her brows expectantly.

"You were ... hurt," he said softly. "A storm." He shrugged. "I brought ... you here."

She jerked her chin at her clothes spread over the couch. "And this?"

His gaze followed her prompting and swept over nearly every stitch of clothing she had been wearing. "Hypothermia," he said simply.

Her shaking increased, as though her body had been waiting for someone to acknowledge the cold that permeated down to her bones. Her teeth began to chatter. *Seems legit.*

"I-I need to s-s-s-s-sit down."

As she stumbled forward, she saw him snatch the rumpled quilt from the bed and rush around the couch—no vaulting this time. She sank down into the cushions, not caring that she had landed on cold, wet garments. Her teeth started chattering so badly, her vision jarred with each clash.

Mountain Man knelt at her feet, tugged the cold clothing from beneath her, and covered her with the quilt, taking enough time to tuck it around her snuggly.

She feared, if the state of her body were any indication, she was unraveling a bit. "Why were y-*you* ... n-naked?"

"Same reason."

"Oh." His hands were still on her shoulders, and they were so warm through the blankets. Would he keep them there if she asked?

"So, you didn't kidnap me?"

• • •

"*Kidnap* you?" He rocked back on his heels. She thought he'd *kidnapped her*?

Of course she did. Waking up disoriented in a strange place with a strange person—neither of them clothed.

She must be terrified. He walked to the fireplace and gripped the mantle with both hands.

Ghostly images of his father's face crumbling before his six-year-old eyes flickered through James's mind. His father placing his palm on the shiny, ebony casket of his wife—of James's mother. Of his bulky old man, a fur coat and boots swallowing up the sadness in his drooping shoulders while James wriggled in the passenger seat, bored after three hours with the same *Ranger Rick* issue, as they trundled through the mountains in an old Ford, never again to return to society.

The cabin seemed to be closing in on him, and he couldn't get enough air. Over his shoulder, he glanced at the doorway, pondering a quick exit. The wind howled outside, and James tugged at the constricting collar of his shirt. He was stuck. Stuck in this small space with a woman who feared he had or would hurt her.

People who hurt women were abhorrent. This woman had thought that about *him*?

Why hadn't he anticipated that when he'd undressed her? He closed his eyes. It wouldn't have mattered. He'd have done the same thing. He hadn't done anything the situation had not demanded to keep her safe.

You didn't do anything wrong.

He opened his eyes and turned slowly. She was huddled beneath the blankets he'd tucked around her, looking so small and vulnerable on the couch. Her aqua eyes were huge in her face, but she no longer looked scared of him. If anything, she seemed ... almost concerned about the strength of his reaction to her question.

He forced himself to drag his gaze to hers, though it felt more difficult than pulling cold molasses from a bottle. "I vow to you, I did not and will not ever hurt you." For the first time around her, he did not hesitate on any of the words.

She stared at him, holding him captive for much too long. When she blinked, his gaze slid sideways, and he nearly sighed in relief.

"I b-believe you."

His eyes slid closed, and he bowed his head. "I'm so sorry ... you even worried about ... that." *Great.* The hesitating, I-don't-talk-to-people voice was back. He swallowed. If he didn't move, didn't do something soon, he was going to go mad.

Her presence in his cabin was overwhelming in a way he had not anticipated from such a tiny person, and he twisted his neck, trying to ease the pinch between his shoulders. He hadn't shared this space with anyone since his father's passing. He shifted back and forth on his feet and dared a quick peek at her from the safety of his riotous hair. She wasn't looking at him; her eyes were unfocused, though not nearly as badly as they had been, and she still shivered uncontrollably. She was quiet again. Sitting compliantly where he'd left her. Whatever adrenaline rush she'd "woken" to had obviously waned.

She was improving, but at this point the blanket she was wrapped in was probably doing more harm than good, as it kept her skin from directly absorbing the heat of the fire. Every piece of first-aid advice in the world would say he should warm her skin-to-skin, but that was so outside the realm of possibility, he had not even considered it before she'd voiced her concerns about his integrity.

He needed to warm her from the inside out. He nodded and headed for the corner of the cabin that served as a kitchen of sorts. She didn't even glance his way as he walked by, so he started walking faster. Even though she was improved, her continuing despondency was a pressing issue he had to resolve.

The cabin had running water thanks to James's focused efforts, but it was unreliable in inclement weather. He held his breath as he turned the faucet and let it out when the water first dripped and then reluctantly sprang into action. He filled a kettle, and returning to the fireplace, set it amid the coals. In the far reaches of his stores, he found a dusty and slightly crushed canister of tea that had not been touched since his father's death. It would have to do.

He went through the motions of making the tea by rote, his eyes anxiously returning to the woman's shaking form over and over again. While she did not worsen, she certainly did not get better. When he carried the tea over to her, her gaze didn't stray from the flames; however, when he knelt in front of her, blocking her view, her incredible eyes slid lethargically to his face.

"Drink up," he mumbled, pressing the mug toward her.

She unwound her hands from the blankets, shivering anew when they hit the open air, and wrapped her fingers around the cup. She would drop it if he removed his own hands, so, awkwardly, they both held the mug as he directed it toward her lips.

She slurped a mouthful and made an odd noise in the back of her throat before taking another sip.

Good. The muscles in his shoulders relaxed a bit. This would work if she kept it up. He would make her as many cups of tea as she would drink. When she drained the mug, he pushed to his feet to make another. "Could you ... move closer to ... the fire?"

She did not seem to mark his words. "Miss?" He winced, the impersonal moniker not fitting her at all. Perhaps her pack held some clues. He hadn't studied it when he'd claimed it at the camp. Now, he grabbed it by the handle at the top and turned it, perusing the straps and anything a tag could hang off.

There! A plastic-coated luggage tag bearing Delaney Science's name on one side. Juggling the mug, he was able to free a couple of fingers to turn the tag over.

Bethany Morgan.

He turned his head toward her. "Bethany?"

Her glazed eyes snapped in his direction. Something turned over in his gut. It was a beautiful name. It fit her well. He repeated his earlier question about moving closer to the fire, and when she jerked a nod, he dropped her bag and walked back to her.

He set the mug on the floor and helped her struggle to her feet. As she stood, she swayed and seemed not to know what to do next.

"It's ... okay," he murmured. Hesitating only a moment, he scooped her up in his arms. She squeaked but did not protest as he carried her the small distance to the fire. Settling her on the floor, he said, "If you can open ... your blanket toward the flames—"

Her gaze snapped sharply to his.

"I will ... not look."

Her eyes softened. Without another word, he turned away, reclaimed the mug, and set about making her another cup of tea. Behind his back, he heard rustling and knew she was following his directive.

She would be okay. His shoulders fell, but almost immediately tensed up again.

She was healing, but she wouldn't be in any condition to leave for several hours. Perhaps even overnight.

He swayed and caught his balance with a grip on the countertop that had his knuckles bleaching.

Oh, God. A woman. In his cabin. Overnight.

How in the world would he make it through the next few hours?

Chapter Five

Bethany's stomach was tea-logged and sloshed with her every movement. She'd stopped shivering long before and was even clothed now, after James—the name he'd practically grunted at her when she'd asked—had told her it was okay to get dressed again. She was, apparently, out of the woods. Figuratively speaking, that is. Literally speaking, not so much.

At her prompting, James had told her of the state of her vacant and demolished camp in his Me-Tarzan manner. Her team had abandoned her, probably thinking she was dead somewhere on the mountain, and she was snowed in with a stranger.

She was so very screwed.

James hadn't asked what she and a bunch of scientists had been doing in the middle of the Rockies during the dead of winter, which was fortunate, because she hadn't had time to develop a lie that would suffice as an answer.

She doubted that James the Hermit would be phoning the papers or tipping off the mysterious Eugene Anderson that scientists were out to find him, but secrecy was the least of her worries. While Bethany was stuck here with these stupid injuries, Delaney would be ready to try finding Anderson again immediately. Without her!

Unfortunately—Bethany studied James from the rim of her tea cup—there seemed to be a run on mountain hermits this season. She'd found one, but not *the one*, and now she was trapped, opening the door for someone else to get her water system. Perhaps the same storm she heard rocking the cabin would keep any potential searchers pinned in place as well?

James sat in a wooden chair in a corner by the fireplace and across from her perch on the couch. Since her adrenaline-fueled accusation that he was a kidnapper, she was pretty sure he had not once looked her in the eye—though with all that hair covering his face, she couldn't be sure—and his posture, which at first had been straight and sure, had degenerated to hunched over. She had the distinct impression that if she were to move toward him or question him again, he would flinch.

In other words, she had gravely insulted the man by implying he would hurt her. For some reason—though given the circumstances she'd had every right to question him the way she did—she felt as though she had kicked a puppy. A hairy, hairy puppy.

He'd been sitting in that hard, unforgiving chair for at least an hour, and she hadn't seen him move once. He held a book in his lap—one from a countless collection that lined the walls of the entire cabin—but he had not flipped a page.

She didn't do quiet introspection if she could avoid it, and it had been a solid sixty minutes of quiet during which she'd had no other option than to introspect.

She was going stir crazy.

Well, okay, the used bookstore look did lend the cabin a cozy feel. The interior was all flame-licked light, colorful book bindings, quilts, and throw rugs. If she had to be stranded in a hermit's cabin, she had the feeling she'd scored well with this one.

A quick glance back at James showed he was the same statue he had been; she had to do something or she'd resort to what would probably horrify the silent mountain man: verbose conversation.

With a sigh, she pushed to her feet. From the corner of her eye, she saw James stiffen in his chair, but he didn't move at all, not even to look her way. Bethany was not fooled; she knew he watched her.

Gripping her teacup tightly, she strode to the nearest pile of books. James's slanted gaze burned her back the entire way.

She didn't know what she'd been expecting, but it wasn't the eclectic pile of books she found. There was the typical hermit fare: dusty, leather-bound tomes from a different era. But mixed in with those were bright paperbacks on the recent bestseller lists. James had access to some method of getting up-to-date books.

Her bet was on Amazon. They shipped everywhere.

Bethany reached out and brushed her fingers across the spine of an orange paperback: *The Immortal Life of Henrietta Lacks*. She loved that book. There were several thrillers as well, and when Bethany glanced in the corner, she did a double take.

She stumbled in that direction, sure her eyes were deceiving her until she stood right in front of the evidence. Yep. That was a guy wearing only breeches while wrapped around a woman in an exquisite red ball gown. A bona fide romance novel. She covered her lips with her fingers and swept her gaze around the corner. Mountain Man had hundreds of them.

Her lips curled beneath her fingers. *And we will be best friends.*

There was a rustle from his corner and an uncomfortable throat clearing.

Her smile turned into a grin. She reached out and grabbed a recent Kresley Cole title from the top of one of the piles. The spine was broken in several places and the pages had been turned more than once.

A favorite.

She turned around slowly. James's expression was going to be priceless.

• • •

Okay. This was less than ideal. The first woman he'd interacted with as an adult was standing in front of his cache of romance novels, a smile on her lips that made his stomach squirm a bit.

Yes, he lived on the mountains alone, but even he knew from the periodicals he received that men did not typically read romance novels. But who did he have to impress out here? One of the perks of living a solitary life away from society was that social stigmas didn't apply to him. He could do whatever he wanted.

He'd frowned at finding that first romance novel among his monthly shipment of books but eventually shrugged off the packing error. If he had the book, he should read it. The fast pace, strong characters, and—yes—sex had made for the perfect read. He'd ordered more for his next shipment and had continued to do so ever since.

Despite his stance on the matter, he felt his cheeks heating beneath her pointed stare. He couldn't tell—probably because he refused to look at her straight on—if her discovery of his reading preferences endeared him to her or made him even creepier. He gritted his teeth. With their track record, probably the latter. Oh, well. There was no hope for it. He couldn't change who he was, and he certainly wouldn't for a stranger who had invaded his cabin.

Ignoring the fact that he had hauled her in here over his shoulder—not so much an invasion—he lifted his chin and unapologetically met her gaze. His bravado stuttered a bit as he met those exotic, aqua eyes. Were all women's eyes this captivating? After that one slip, however, he raised his eyebrows in challenge.

Her smile unexpectedly broadened. "Love a man with confidence," she said, winking at him.

He felt a muscle tic in his jaw and realized he was gritting his teeth. As his gaze followed her progress back to the couch, he forced himself to relax. Then she settled onto the center cushion with a sigh, wrapped the quilt over her lap, and opened the book.

He pressed his lips together as every muscle he'd just forced into relaxation rebelled and took up rank again. There was a reason that book was his favorite. The lovemaking in it was ...

Actually, *indescribable* was probably the most apt word. He'd been in the mountains since he was six. His scientific study of the human body could only educate him technically, and his penchant for romance novels was the only sex he "had." It struck him all of a sudden as pathetic. Could he bear to watch this unimaginably beautiful woman read the pages he had read and reread a copious amount of times like a thirsty man drinking water?

He cleared his throat; she ignored him. Or, perhaps the more likely scenario, she was already enthralled in the novel.

Right, then. He snapped his hardcover shut—she didn't even jump at the sharp noise—and got to his feet.

What to do. What to do.

He scowled at the door and the wind howling beyond it. Because of the blizzard, there was no avenue for escape into the woods—woods that were more a haven to him than even this cabin. He was still freezing cold, as he had not had the luxury of basking before the fire bare-skinned. The small chills racking the surface of his skin made the idea of moving away from the flames less than desirable, but for the first time in his life that he could remember, he was being exposed to the aspect of social discomfort.

How did *anyone* live out in society? He stared at the woman stationed on his couch, pain lighting up his jaw. Was he grinding his teeth now?

The rabbits. He needed to skin the rabbits and prepare them for eating. He stomped over to the door, looking over his shoulder as he did so—still no reaction from the reading intruder on the sofa. With a grumble in his throat, he shoved at the door.

It didn't move.

A tickle itched the back of his neck; an echoing sickness swam in his stomach.

He shoved again, this time with all of his might, and was able to crack the door a fraction of an inch. It was just enough to peek out into the wilderness and see that the snow had drifted in to at least three feet.

They were already snowed in.

James never swore, but if ever there was a time, it was now. The blizzard was much worse than he'd been anticipating. Three feet of snow in a matter of hours and the storm was just hitting its stride? A wave of heat washed over him, and he brought a shaky hand to his forehead. He'd been worried about her staying here overnight? She'd be stuck here with him and he with her for potentially days.

Days!

James leaned forward, and his forehead met the door with a *thunk*. Wind swept in through the crack, and his already chilled skin protested with a riot of goose bumps. James pulled the door closed.

He should tell her.

He should really tell her.

He would tell her now.

He pulled in a slow breath and began turning toward her. He frowned when his body kept turning, his gaze roaming over her and then to the kitchen.

Perhaps dinner first. Yes. No rabbits for the time being, so he would have to get creative. Yes. Logical. Necessary. Food.

Bad news later.

Chapter Six

They'd feasted on canned peaches in awkward silence. Well, Bethany wasn't awkward—being around other people didn't bother her—but James's awkwardness over losing the solitary status of his cabin had been thick and dominant.

And adorable.

He was terrified of her, and it didn't take a genius to know that her knowledge of that would only make his terror greater. True, she could incapacitate him easily—a girl these days needed to know how to fight, and Bethany was many things, excellent student included—but he didn't know that, which had to mean he was scared of a girl simply because she was a girl.

Something about that screamed *challenge accepted* in Bethany's mind, and she forcefully shoved it aside.

She tried to focus on the book in her lap, which she was truly enjoying, but all of that tea was now taking its revenge, distracting her from the only thing that was keeping her from climbing the walls as the seconds she wasn't out searching for Anderson ticked by relentlessly. She was trying not to squirm in her seat, and it had been a while since she'd been able to focus on any of the words on the page.

This was ridiculous. She straightened, and his gaze snapped to hers, already wary. No doubt he suspected she was going to further fuck up his life.

Always a pleasure, baby. She smiled. "I have to use the restroom."

Those six simple words were met with a beat of silence, and then James's eyes widened, and she was pretty sure there was a blush beneath his whiskers. "Oh ... the latrine is not indoors."

She gave him no reaction. She had eyes in her head; she'd already deduced that the one-room cabin consisted of one room and it sure wasn't a bathroom.

He swallowed loudly enough for her to hear across the room and then said, "I could ... find you ... something—" He cut himself off and shook his head.

Bethany was pretty sure he had been saying he would find something for her to pee in, and she was game—Mama didn't raise no whiners—but without another word, James pushed up from his corner chair. He approached the door to the cabin where, instead of opening it like a normal person, he stared at it, his head cocking to the side.

"You know how a door works, right?" Bethany said after a moment.

"Under normal circumstances, yes," he said dryly.

She squinted. *Did he just* joke *with me? That* had *been what happened, right?* Granted, it had been lame, but ... this showed promise. And for once, he hadn't spoken haltingly.

James's head snapped upright, and he reached up, removing the pin from the upper hinge of the door before quickly kneeling and doing the same to the bottom.

"What—?"

He grabbed the doorknob, wedged his fingers into the crack on the other side, and yanked. The door came off in his hands with a screech of wood.

Oh, my God.

He held the obscenely heavy-looking door as though it weighed nothing, gently settling it against the wall. The show of strength was definitely ... not *un*attractive. When she could yank her gaze away from the muscles flexing in his back, she glanced at the now-open door and gasped.

Snow blocked the exit up to James's chest. Over his head, she could see it continued to fall.

"Oh, shit."

James glanced at her over his shoulder and reached for a shovel near the door. "Suit up," he said, jerking his chin at the snowsuit spread on the sofa. He shoved his stocking feet into boots and shrugged on his coat. In short order, he managed to create an impressive starting pathway from the door. He dropped the shovel to the ground, reached inside the cabin, and slid the door toward the open threshold. "I'll be back soon."

With that, he "closed" the door.

Bethany was still staring at it with her mouth open several minutes later. *Who is this guy?* "Yes, this is a much better solution than a bucket," she muttered.

Though the door had been open for only a few moments, the outside chill had penetrated the entire cabin. She shivered and walked to the sofa, donning her semidry snowsuit with jerky motions. Who knew what *soon* meant to a mountain hermit, but she would be ready for him whenever he returned. If he was going to shovel snow in the middle of a blizzard, the least she could do was what he'd requested.

She zipped up her coat, and time started to crawl. All the good the book had done in distracting her from her predicament was undone in a moment. This very second, was Jonathan knocking on Anderson's door? Was Bryce?

Her sloshing stomach lurched ominously, and she stared at the door, willing it open. How bad would it be, climbing back down the mountain in a blizzard?

Great, she was contemplating suicide now?

But my water system!

After an incalculable amount of time, the door slid back into its spot against the wall with a grinding of wood on wood. She jumped, spinning on the spot.

James stood in the doorway, limned by moonlight. Snow covered his shoulders and clung to his beard. Without a word, he extended his hand toward her.

Something in her chest flipped, displacing thoughts of water systems and ill-advised hikes. *Oh, my God. My type might be rugged outdoorsman.* She leapt into motion, crossing the cabin in seconds, but then she hesitated, staring at James's extended hand.

"You will ... get lost without me," he mumbled, the halting speech returning.

Valid point. Bethany took his hand, and before she could say anything clever, which she totally would have, James tugged her outside and set off down a narrow path as though the Yeti was after them.

She tripped along behind him until he stopped in front of another door. It was so dark outside; she could barely discern the outline of a small building.

James pushed the door inward. "Quickly now," he whispered.

He didn't have to tell her twice. She jetted into the dim room, doing a double take at the candle on a nearby table that he must have taken the time to light for her. An extraordinarily normal-looking toilet—porcelain and all—stood in the corner. Bethany quickly took care of business and then stared a moment at the handle on the side of the commode.

She tilted her head. No way that handle worked. *Come on, in the middle of the wilderness?* Maybe he just hadn't removed it from the toilet. Bethany reached out and depressed it.

The toilet flushed. With running water.

Before she could ponder the *no-fucking-way*s running through her head, the door behind her burst open, and there was James, hand extended once more.

"Your toilet flushed," she said stupidly.

He simply jostled his hand in a very clear *let's go* indicator.

Right. Talk later. She grabbed his hand once more and followed him back through the path to the cabin.

Indoors, he released her hand, turning from her to shove the door back in place, even taking the time to replace the pins in the hinges. They were secure once more.

"Thank you so much, James," she said.

He turned toward her and nodded once. Then his eyes rolled back in his head, and he hit the floor with a thud.

Chapter Seven

He'd been so cold, but *this*—this warmth. Incredible. It made no sense, and in the dawning of consciousness, that mattered to James. Things that did not make sense were not to be trusted.

And, so, the only possible solution? He was dead.

That was disappointing. But, as being dead wasn't too horribly dreadful at present, he would embrace the warmth. He turned his body toward it and encountered the source: something delectably silky and soft. *Death good*, his foggy mind grunted.

His arm moved—apparently, he could move while dead—and came to rest over more of that warm, soft thing. It moved back, fitting itself against him snugly. Something that was a paradoxical mix of firm and pliant nudged between his thighs and two somethings pushed against his chest.

Even his addled mind could connect the dots. He held a woman.

Death very *good*.

If it took dying for James to lie next to a woman, it was worth it.

He hardened in a rush, and—he was dead, wasn't he? But then the woman he held moaned against his throat and pressed into him with her hips, her stomach pushing his erection against his own abdomen, and he stopped thinking and pausing.

Instinct took over.

One arm tightened around her back, his palm finding her head and his fingers tangling in pure silk. The other hand smoothed down flawless, delicate muscles to arrive at the most plump, perfect curve he could have ever dreamed of encountering. The mystery woman's bottom was nothing less than a work of art. He flexed his fingers into the giving flesh and groaned—a sound she echoed.

Heat licked through his blood. Whatever he was doing, she liked it. His erection ached intensely at the discovery, and something warm and wet slid from the tip, causing him to slip against her stomach in a way that drove James absolutely wild.

Her, too, apparently, because she looped her arms around his neck and brushed her lips against his collarbone, arching against him.

Primitive urges he'd never experienced before rode him hard, and he flipped them: her on her back, him resting atop her. Her thighs spread and his hips fell into the valley she made. The softest, wettest thing he'd ever felt cradled the base of his erection, and he dropped his forehead into the space between her neck and shoulder as his muscles began to shake.

She raised her knees on either side of his hips and rubbed herself against him, spreading liquid heat along his arousal, and an inhuman noise erupted from his mouth, loud and animalistic.

He never knew it would feel like this. He flexed his buttocks and thrust against her himself this time, quickly unraveling.

If he'd have known it would be like this, he would have never consigned himself to a life of solitude in the mountains. He would have searched high and low for a partner.

He thrust again, and his shaking increased. The pressure in his erection grew unbearable.

He should have done this with Bethany. She had been so beautiful. Before he'd died, he should have seduced her. Wrapped himself around her instead of stalking into a blizzard with a shovel.

He froze.

Blizzard with a snow shovel. So cold.

Hypothermia.

The woman beneath him writhed in protest at his sudden stillness, but James refused to move.

I'm not dead, am I?

Memories of his ill-advised trip outside rushed back in, and one thing became very clear as his erection pulsed against soft heat: He was very much alive.

He cracked open his eyes and found himself staring at the slender, sloping neck he already recognized as belonging to Bethany the Scientist.

He sucked in a breath, panic surging through him. With a grunt, he pushed himself off her body so hard he practically flew from the bed, landing on the plank floor with a bounce.

He looked up from his graceful position sprawled on the floor to see Bethany roll over, her eyes clouded with sleep as she blinked at him. "What's going—?"

"I'm so sorry," he began to stammer over and over, intermingling *I didn't know* with his litany of an apology.

Bethany tilted her head to the side and swept her gaze over him. "Huh," she said, cutting off his babbling. "That wasn't a dream then?"

He buried his face in his hands—hands that were shaking.

"Relax, mountain man," she said.

He jerked his head up.

"It wasn't bad, actually," she said with a smile. "I was obviously into it."

Speech abandoned him.

"Look, I took your clothes off, then mine, and slept in your bed while you weren't totally cognitively aware. This wasn't your fault."

"You ... you did that?" He looked down at his body, which he already knew was nude, but seemed to see it for the first time. She *had* done that. "Why would you do that?"

"Because you fainted like a punk."

It wasn't *quite* as bad as nearly having sex for the first time while both he and his partner were semiconscious, but it was close. He groaned. Granted, he'd never really had the chance to warm up completely after hauling Bethany back to the cabin, but he'd been physically exerting himself while shoveling snow. Had been shielded by snow banks on each side as he worked. By most accounts, he should have been fine!

In his reading, he was always baffled by scientists or doctors who raved over how life's variables could completely change an expected scientific outcome. He shook his head. Only someone who wasn't repeatedly bowled over by those variables would ever say that.

Logic, James!

He had to swallow a couple of times before the words would come. "Do you ... know where my pants are?"

Bethany's eyes twinkled. "Yes, I do."

He lowered his shoulders a bit, but Bethany didn't make any move to show him where his pants might be, and the dresser was all the way across the cabin. He had not ... *recovered* from their encounter, and the idea of walking in front of her, his erection bobbing in time to his steps, made his thundering heart compete for a blood supply that was very much dedicated elsewhere.

It must have shown on his face, because Bethany finally had mercy on him. However, her mercy was suspiciously akin to man torture. He did not anticipate her getting up from the bed—in all her naked glory—to retrieve his pants for him.

He went slack-jawed as she bounded from the mattress, her breasts bouncing. *They are perfect.* Small and high and with the most mouth-watering nipples the shade of sun-warmed rock. He felt as though he'd been punched in the gut. She sauntered past him and around the end of the bed, and once her cataclysmic breasts were no longer in view, his gaze dropped automatically to the bottom he'd held in his hand minutes ago. It flexed and moved with her steps, and if James hadn't already been on the floor, that sight surely would have put him there.

She stopped suddenly and bent full over to retrieve something— presumably his pants—from the floor, her pert bottom in the air. James sucked in a quick breath and promptly proceeded to choke on it.

Great, hacking coughs wracked his ribs, and Bethany turned around, holding his pants in the air, and sauntered right on back to him as though she hadn't a care in the world.

She knows exactly what she's doing. Had probably done it on purpose.

God help him if she were set on torture. He'd never survive.

As she walked his way, his pants swayed in her hand at her side. She did nothing to block his view of her hips, thighs, and everything in between. His hacking stopped ... because his lungs lost all ability.

He knew what a woman looked like—he was a scientist for God's sake. But something had definitely been lost in translation between the clinical aspect and warm, flesh and blood woman.

She had a slight, dark patch of hair at the apex of her thighs, but as she walked, snatches of skin peeked through, and his mouth went dry. Curiosity wracked him; he wanted to see more, both as a scientist and a man.

As soon as he thought it, he knew it for the lie it was. *Scientist.* He wanted to snatch her by her hips, throw her to the bed, spread her knees apart, and look his fill—right before he finished what they'd started this morning.

Bethany stopped in front of him and cleared her throat.

With a start, James jerked his gaze to her face, where it should have been all along if he were a decent human being.

She raised an eyebrow and held out his pants. "Here you go."

Are you kidding me? Almost everything he'd read in his life had cast women as shy, retiring creatures—even some of the romance novels. Bethany didn't appear to have a shy bone in her body. Her exquisite, exquisite body. With great effort, he kept his gaze from skimming her again, and took a moment for silent congratulations on his control. He must surely be a saint, because no normal person could resist that siren call.

He didn't have to look at her again, however, to remember how perfect she was. With a body like that, "why would you ever wear clothes?"

Bethany's lips parted. He'd asked the question out loud.

Darn it. He closed his eyes and sighed.

"Well, for one," she said, causing his eyes to snap open, "you gotta wear clothes in the lab. You know: chemical spills, burns—" She stopped and wrinkled her nose. Her eyes sparkled.

His lips twitched. "Safety ... first," he mumbled.

"Indeed." She bit her bottom lip for a moment and then smiled. He found himself returning it. She was witty. That was ... nice.

She waved his pants a bit, and he returned to reality. His neck and chest heating—great, she could see that—he reached out and grabbed them. But he wouldn't be able to put them on without standing up at some point, and the discovery that she was witty on top of having a beautiful physique had not had the desired effect on his arousal.

He looked up at her through the mop of his hair, contemplating his next move.

Her smile turned a bit into something unidentifiable, except for its heavy dose of amusement. "So *cute*," she said.

He wasn't sure he liked the sound of that, but then Bethany turned around, presenting him with her bottom—he shook his head. *Back*—and he shot to his feet. Faster than he ever had before, he shoved his feet into his pants and pulled them up his thighs and hips.

He hissed in a breath when the teeth of the zipper grazed his penis. *That's what you get*, he told himself as he tried to shift his erection around so he could fasten his pants. He tried several positions and then began to panic, knowing this was taking too long, and she would turn around again any minute.

With no gentleness whatsoever, he shoved his erection downward, jostling the pants so it went into one of the legs. *Good enough.* He zipped up and prayed she wouldn't notice the very noticeable ridge on the inside of his right thigh. She wouldn't look there, right?

She turned around. She looked there.

James barely resisted the urge to groan. Things had yet to go his way with this woman.

She raised both eyebrows and pulled her gaze to his face—reluctantly? Surely not.

As she looked him in the eye, he shifted. "Sorry," he mumbled. "I'm trying to ... It won't ..." He stopped himself. He was only making the situation more awkward. "Sorry."

"Did I ask for an apology?"

James felt his own eyebrows rise. "No?"

Her smile still in place, Bethany turned from him and walked back to where his pants had been. Bending over, she began to collect her jeans, her sweater.

He turned around, affording her the same courtesy she had given him. He purposely kept his imagination dormant through the rustling of cloth, but he wouldn't be able to pull that off forever.

Luckily, Bethany spoke. "Glad to see you up and about this morning."

James nearly choked again. "Yes, well," he said. "Thank you?"

"That's right. '*Thank you,*'" Bethany said. "Do you know how enormous you are? How hard it was to get you in that bed?"

He frowned. He hadn't thought of that.

"It was like wrestling a sedated alligator into a tank." Her voice was muffled.

"You have ... experience with that?"

"What self-respecting scientist doesn't?"

"Bethany the Scientist." He shook his head. "I admit ... that's not ... what I expected."

There was a sudden silence behind him that grew so awkward, he finally turned around. Bethany stood beside his bed, fully clothed, a thunderous expression on her face.

"Hmm," she said, tapping her chin with a finger. "James the Misogynist. Well, what do you know? That fits perfectly."

"What?" His eyes widened. "No! You are muddling *fit* and *expected*—"

"Baby, I muddle nothing," she snapped. Her gaze roved his body, stopping momentarily on his rapidly flagging erection—turns out he'd only needed sharp disapproval to help his "situation"—before returning to his face. She shook her head sorrowfully. "Typical."

He drew his brows together. Unlike her determination of *cute*, he was definitely sure he didn't like this word used to describe him.

See, this *is why you live alone in the mountains.*

"Well," she said on a sigh. "Fun's fun, but I can't stay here for much longer. We should only be snowed in for a little bit more, right? When can I leave?"

Uh oh. A little bit more? Did she not realize she was stuck here for the indefinite future? He shifted his feet apart and raised his hands slightly. "You see ... I won't ..." *Be able to get you out.* He shook his head. Too many words. "You can't leave."

Her eyes narrowed, and he took a step backward. "'You won't what?" she repeated in a dangerous voice. "I know you aren't trying to keep me here against my will, because it doesn't matter how lick-worthy your cock is or how cute and shy you are, I will severely injure you and then walk blithely away."

What? What did *anything* she'd just said mean? Had he just been complimented or insulted? Both? *Lick-worthy.* An ache built in James's stomach, but before it could generate fully, he fixated on *I will severely injure you.* This tiny thing? Hurt him?

Talk about cute. He might understand all of those unidentifiable smiles she'd been casting his way all morning now. He allowed one to spread on his own lips.

It faded immediately, however, when her lips thinned and she made tiny fists at her sides. He'd just signed his own death certificate. Before he could even trace her movement, she leapt toward him, swung around, and kicked him with all of her might right in his stomach.

He would have shouted if he could. As it was, every organ in his body went into conservation mode, and he fell to his knees before crumpling to his back.

My liver. She popped my liver.

Turns out, Bethany had only lied about one thing: She didn't *walk* away. She ran.

Chapter Eight

This is what you get for teasing a mountain man.

James was oddly silent behind her on the floor as she sprinted toward the door. Had she kicked him a mite too hard? Nah. He was trying to keep her here against her will!

She grabbed the knob and wrenched the door open. The glint of morning sun on snow flashed through her eyes and straight to her brain, and she squeezed them shut and turned her face away. When the stars behind her eyelids dimmed slightly, Bethany turned back to face the outdoors and slowly opened her eyes.

Damn.

Snow. Everywhere. In places, it drifted up and over the cabin. Even the small path James had given himself hypothermia shoveling last night had been mostly filled in.

There was a groan from behind her.

Oh, this was going to be awkward. Ugh.

Pulling in a slow breath, Bethany turned around to face the music. Surprisingly, James was on his feet, though he was rubbing a hand gently over his stomach and glaring at her with all the ire of a hermit who'd had his life disrupted by a diva-like scientist.

"As ... I said," he grated, flopping a hand in the direction of the open doorway. "Problem."

She smiled at him sheepishly. His scowl darkened, and he hobbled over to his chair in the corner, flopping down onto its hard surface with a grunt.

"I suppose I should apologize," she said.

"For ... stripping me naked and ... molesting me, or ... ensuring I'll never be able to ... binge drink again?"

Bethany grinned. "Oh, baby boy, I said I *suppose* I should. Not that I was going to."

"Of course," he muttered through tight lips. A rough laugh burst from his mouth, quickly followed by a groan as he clutched his gut.

Her grin slipped, and she stepped toward him, but he cut her off with a hand held out between them. "Shouldn't underestimate you, huh?" he asked.

She planted her hands on her hips. "But you were having so much fun patronizing me! Whatever will you do for fun now?"

He looked up at her, his gaze uncomfortably astute. "*I* was the only one ... patronizing?"

A nervous giggle, of all things, slipped past her control. Okay, so maybe she'd been having a bit too much fun with the discovery that she had a gigantic, still-waters-run-deep hermit practically drooling at her feet. She seemed to remember even employing the "bend and snap" at one point ...

"Fair enough." She shrugged.

He seemed surprised by that, if his parted lips were any indication.

"So," she shifted her weight, "how do I get over this problem? I need to get out of here." And on with her job of finding hermit number two before anybody else.

He cocked his head to the side, his expression growing wary. "Bethany," he began in what could only be described as a cautious tone.

She snapped her fingers. "Sat phone." Why hadn't she thought of this last night? She strode to her pack and rummaged around, standing upright triumphantly with her enormous satellite phone in hand. She turned to James with a smirk.

He sighed, leaned back in his chair, and gestured for her to go for it.

Not the most comforting response, she had to admit. Nevertheless, she dialed the one number she had memorized—solely for this purpose—and waited.

Nothing.

"Are you kidding me? What's the purpose of a sat phone if it doesn't work!"

James stood. "Calm down," he said softly. "We're far north."

She glared at him. "What does that even mean?"

"Most satellites are ... at the equator."

She groaned. She would need to move around to find the sweet spot and get her call through. A smart girl's gamble said the sweet spot wouldn't be in this cabin that was nearly buried under snow.

"Fine. Okay. So I move around."

He raised his eyebrows and jerked his chin toward the still-open door and all the snow beyond it.

"Fine," she bit out even more bitterly. "So I shovel and move around."

He got that same, cautious look on his face again, and just before he could say her name once more, she spun around, grabbed the shovel, and attacked the snow.

Behind her, James blew out an exasperated breath. There was a rustling, and a short time later, he was right beside her in his coat, a second shovel in his hand. Wordlessly, he lent his far superior shoveling skills to hers.

Even with her thick gloves, blisters quickly formed, and when one burst painfully during a particularly zestful scoop of snow, Bethany bit back a whimper. How had James made a path, alone, during a blizzard? There was no way he was human.

As they cleared the same path, it became more and more apparent that there would be no shoveling to freedom. The very idea had been absurd. Bethany didn't know how much longer she would be able to keep this up, and the few breaks she'd taken to check the sat phone had yielded no results.

But as long as James was shoveling, she was going to be there right beside him if it killed her. And it most likely would.

The path to the bathroom cleared, James started shoveling another path. After a moment's hesitation, she joined him. It wasn't long before they reached another door nestled in an entirely new building. It was only a few feet away from the bathroom, but it was much larger. A storehouse, perhaps?

Bethany reached for her satellite phone, automatically dialed, and held it to her ear. *Yes!* She perked up, dropping her shovel at her feet.

After a moment, Dewinter picked up. "Bethany! You're alive?" The words were patchy and nearly unrecognizable through a massive echo, but Bethany had never been happier to hear her boss's voice in her life.

"I am!" she said with a laugh.

"—can't hear—"

"Hold on," Bethany said in that loud voice people used that made absolutely no difference to clarity of signal. "How about now?" she said, stepping toward James.

The echo faded with that step, so Bethany took another and then another.

"Much better. Where are you?"

"I'm still in the mountains. Where is my team?"

A sigh. "The other four are back at Delaney."

Wait, they weren't out searching for Anderson? "They abandoned the plan?" She bounced on her toes. There was still time for her to find him!

"A bear shredded Jonathan's leg, so, yes, your team has been shelved," Dr. Dewinter said, her tone terse.

Oh, shit. She swallowed down her inappropriate giddiness. "Is he okay?"

"He's ... alive."

"Okay," Bethany said. Wait, what did Dewinter mean by *shelved?* She licked her lips. That didn't mean no one was currently looking for Anderson. Come to think of it, Dewinter seemed to be choosing her words very carefully. Just what was going on here? She cleared her throat. "When can you come get me? We need to reevaluate."

"Come get you in the mountains? Bethany, are you serious?"

She gritted her teeth. Dewinter was up to something. "Uh ... yes."

"Bethany, that blizzard was the biggest one we've had this century. No one is going to be able to get to you."

"*What?*" James turned sharply and tilted his head. When she waved him away, he shrugged and resumed shoveling.

Just last week, the news had shown a story on repeat about a dramatic rescue in avalanche-ready conditions. People got rescued in these conditions all the time! "Are you in more danger than a crew would be in if they attempted to rescue you?" her boss asked.

Bethany paused. So that was how Dewinter was going to play this. Pretend Bethany was unreachable because it was "dangerous." It was an outright lie.

No, she wouldn't ... Were they cutting her out of the plan to find Anderson?

That fink Jonathan had most likely told Dewinter she had balked the plans as soon as he'd had the opportunity.

I'm grasping at straws here! And freaking the fuck out. This was crazy. Would Dewinter seriously keep her on a mountain to keep her from mucking up a mission?

Bethany pressed her lips together. Yes, she would. In a heartbeat.

She pinched the bridge of her nose. Should she let her boss know she was wise to the lie? Or play along a bit longer? "Well, when can they come get me and not be in ... danger?"

Dewinter blew a breath of air, which echoed through the phone. "I don't know, three maybe four weeks?"

"Oh, hell no!" No more playing along. She stormed toward the cabin. James didn't need to hear her screaming at her boss.

"I'm sorry," Dewinter continued, "but it's true."

How stupid did this woman think she was? "No, it's no—" Bethany froze, rocking back on her heels as sunlight glinted off something above the door to the cabin, nearly blinding her.

She narrowed her eyes against the glare. What the fuck was that? When she stepped to the right, the glare faded, and she could just make out two words carved into a sign hanging on the lintel.

Ignotumque Aquas.

Uncharted Waters. The cabin's name was Uncharted Waters!

She gasped. Spinning so quickly she almost bit snow, she scanned every inch she could see.

He's here. Eugene Anderson is here!

"Bethany? Did I lose you again?"

Oh, she'd lost all right. Bethany swallowed a giddy laugh. "No, no I'm here."

Where would Dr. Anderson be hiding? The other building James had made a path to?

She slid through the snow, nearly running in that direction. "I was just saying, no, it's ... no problem. Conditions are too dangerous. I understand."

Three or four weeks secluded with Dr. Eugene Anderson? Had she just won the fucking lottery? Let Dewinter send out a new team. Bethany had already found the prize.

"You ... understand?"

She smirked. Dewinter had expected resistance. Now that she wasn't getting it, she sounded suspicious. But what could she do? Confess she was lying and ask why Bethany was all of a sudden okay with being cut out of the deal of her career?

"Sure. I'll see you in three to four weeks. Tell Jonathan I hope he heals quickly." *Click.*

He was here! She'd dance a jig in the snow if she wouldn't risk slipping and breaking her neck. Following the sounds of James's shovel against icy snow, Bethany rounded the corner where James had disappeared and spotted him immediately.

He was leaning over and tenderly brushing snow from a small monument that stood in the middle of a clearing of white. It was a cross, and on it was carved a name: Eugene Anderson.

Chapter Nine

She stumbled to a stop. The blood drained from her face. She blinked several times, but the words didn't change.

Eugene Anderson.

He was ... dead?

Bethany's stomach cramped. Oh, God.

She moaned and twisted around the corner again, out of James's sight, so she could melt down in semiprivate.

Eugene Anderson's name on a cross. An obvious burial plot. No, there was no other way to interpret that.

Her idol was dead.

Fuck!

God, that meant her dreams of working with him, of completing his water system with him, were dead, too. Could someone's heart get whiplash?

She was curled in on herself, her stomach clenching with waves of nausea. Whatever this emotion, she didn't like it.

Thought I was being so clever. Stuck in the mountains for weeks. Dreams crushed.

She forced her posture straight. The back of her head met the wall with a thud.

Okay, so she was stuck in the woods for weeks. And finding Eugene Anderson had been a dead end.

But it was a dead end for everybody. She was just the only one who knew that.

I have the advantage!

She had weeks here to regroup. Replan. And there were worse things than being stranded with someone like James.

Bethany's eyebrows drew together. Wait ... James? And Dr. Anderson? Why the hell would they both have been occupying a cabin named Uncharted Waters?

She bit her lip. About a ... thirty-year age difference, give or take. She mentally poured through Dr. Anderson's memorized file. They were about the same height. Hadn't Anderson been a redhead, too?

Her heart began to race. "His son," she said. Holy hell. James was Dr. Anderson's son! It made perfect sense.

Her stomach roiled, and she placed a hand over it. *Steady now, girl.* She was stranded for an indefinite amount of time with Dr. Anderson's only family while everyone at Delaney futilely spun their wheels without even knowing it.

Perhaps Anderson had worked while he was here on the mountain? She straightened. James would know!

Okay. Plan. She needed a plan.

What about the original one?

She paused. Tilted her head. *It might work.*

While she was here, she could put that professional courtesy of hers into practice. When they were more comfortable with each other, she would raise the subject of his father. Put out feelers to see if Dr. Anderson had continued any of his work here at the cabin. She grinned, but it quickly faded.

It wasn't that simple. Her interactions with James thus far, the way he made her feel.

I'm attracted to him. There, I admitted it.

There was a fine line here, and she had a feeling she was already walking it. She needed the information about James's father; her body wanted James for a far different reason. Anyone from the outside looking in would amalgamate the two if they saw her going after both at once.

Not an option.

She sucked in a breath, her lungs gobbling up the air in a way that indicated she hadn't given them any in a while. Forcing a shrug, she pushed away from the building.

What her body wanted didn't matter. Not even close. All that mattered were those thirsty kids.

But, if it turned out Eugene Anderson hadn't continued his work on this mountain, and this truly was a dead end ...

Then James was fair game.

Bethany nodded once and walked around the corner of the building. The sight of James planted before his father's grave, an unreadable expression visible beneath his riotous facial hair, and his arms crossed over his chest gave her pause. Had he overheard her? What had she said out loud?

God, had she admitted she was attracted to him out loud?

"So," he said. "When are ... they coming?"

She swallowed, and her heartbeat began to slow its thunderous rhythm. "Ha, ha," she said. "You know very well they aren't."

He widened his eyes. "They aren't? Huh."

Her lips twitched. "Shut up."

"This will ... damage our relationship."

Bethany froze.

"You may have to start ... acknowledging I know things." He grinned.

Bethany rolled her eyes, but she was grinning too. They got along pretty well already. Maybe she didn't have to wait too long to bring up the subject of his father.

James seemed reasonably intelligent and rational. Hell, she'd kicked him in the breadbasket with all her might, and he'd rolled over and joked with her about it.

But the look on his face as he'd wiped snow from his father's grave. No, she had to be careful about this topic.

Damn. Why did Dr. Anderson have to be dead? The world needed him. Bethany needed him.

"Bethany?"

Her name, spoken softly and haltingly, made her skin flush with heat. He was looking at her with his brows drawn together; she'd been staring at her feet in what could only be described as a mopey fashion for far longer than was normal.

She blanked her thoughts and forced a smile. He returned it with obvious relief. "It will ... be okay," he said. "Think of it as ... a vacation. I'm sure you haven't ... taken one in a while."

Try never. Workaholic was her middle name, because her work was her everything. Every stride she made toward clean water, she felt the weight of her mother's death, the other countless deaths that occurred with each minute that passed.

"You're ... doing it again," James said.

Her gaze snapped into focus, and she raised her eyebrows.

"Woolgathering," he clarified. "Do you ... do you need to ... talk?"

She screwed up her face. "God, no."

He visibly relaxed. "Thank ... goodness."

Bethany bit her bottom lip. "Well ... *maybe* I do."

James's shoulders hiked up, and a blush spread over the parts of his face she could see despite his hair. "O-of course.

"Sucker," she said, no longer able to bite back her smile. He was just too fun. Damn, but naïve seemed to be her catnip. She let her gaze travel over the broadness of his shoulders for only a second before forcing it back to his face.

None of that. She had to behave. For now.

He was smiling again, seeming pleased with her. God, how did he survive up here alone? Didn't he realize he craved human contact? It was more than obvious to her. Well, she couldn't be his lover, not with so much up in the air. But she could damn well be his friend.

She shouldered her shovel. "Any more we need to clear?"

He looked around. "I think we're done ... for a while."

"Then, come on," she said, jerking her head toward the cabin. "We've got a vacation to start."

• • •

She's all mine. James watched the firelight dance off the lowlights of her hair from his chair in the corner. *For a few weeks, she's all mine.*

The day had started with a painful attack, reached its peak with shoveling hundreds of pounds of snow, closed with a silent meal of more canned peaches, and it had still been a good day. Maybe even the best day. He couldn't remember the last time he'd had that thought while sitting in this same chair after sunset.

Especially, his neck heated, since the day didn't necessarily start with the attack. It had started with him spread atop her, her knees hugging his hips, and his erection sliding through her slickness.

He shifted in his seat and crossed his ankle over his knee. Hopefully, that would keep his swift arousal from her view if she happened to look up from the book she was reading.

When his dad died all those years ago, James was so overcome with grief that he hadn't had the chance to realize he was lonely. As that grief had ebbed and turned into the blessed monotony of a simple life, he'd forgotten how it felt to interact with another person.

It was incredible.

How will you get on when she leaves? The thought came out of nowhere and startled him so badly, he made a retaliatory noise deep in his chest.

Bethany's head raised, and those eyes of hers raked him. She cocked an eyebrow, and he gave a pained smile that made his cheeks hurt. She shook her head, a dimple showing in one of her cheeks, and returned to her book.

How will I get on? Like I always do!

She'd been here two days. That's all. He needed to take himself in hand. There would be no getting used to her. He would never survive the loneliness once she left.

Who says you have to?

Now, this question, he was used to, and he sighed and slouched in his chair as much as the rigid seat would allow. This question had cruised through his mind at least daily since his father's death, and he'd grown used to ignoring it.

He had precious few memories of what life was like with smiles, and birthday parties, and the softest of hugs from a woman whose face he could not even remember.

He'd had less than a year at school and could not recall his kindergarten teacher's name or those of any of his classmates.

And that was okay. It was impossible to miss what one did not know. But more and more, James was feeling the strains of a solitary life. He'd been terrified to find a woman in the woods, for goodness' sake. Hadn't even been able to talk to her, not that it had mattered in her despondent state. In the few memories he did have of his life in civilization, he had been friendly. Outgoing even. Interactions with his peers had come easily. At least, he thought they had. It was entirely possible that he was misremembering things—reinventing history to paint a brighter picture against the dismal one of his current life.

Regardless of whether his memory was accurate or not, what was keeping him from returning to society? Truly: nothing. He could go back now. Live more than comfortably on the savings accounts his father left behind. Savings accounts that had continued to grow, as his dad had arranged for any proceeds from his many patents to be directly deposited into them.

So James was a multimillionaire. His yearly expenses amounted to little more than ten grand, the majority allotted for books, the costs of a post-office box, and the fuel and upkeep for the dumpy truck he kept to make limited forays into civilization for necessities ranging from canned goods to parts for his many projects. Trips he kept putting off because each time he ventured out, it became harder for him to return.

James scrubbed a hand over his face. It was understandable that Bethany's sudden presence in his life would be disruptive. He would *not* make any decisions or even consider making them under the pressure of change. That rarely worked out for the better. When he could think logically on the matter—once more variables were known—then he could think more on returning to society.

For now, he would simply enjoy the company of the intelligent, stunning woman curled up on his couch, clutching his favorite novel.

As the evening progressed, and Bethany flipped pages, getting deeper and deeper into the story, James's eyes and body grew heavy.

Next he knew, his shoulder was shaking.

His head snapped up, and his vision was blurry. He'd fallen asleep?

"Bedtime, mountain man," Bethany whispered.

He turned his gaze to her. Her hand was still on his shoulder; her other hand held the closed book.

"You ... finish it?" he asked, his voice rough with sleep.

She nodded.

"What'd you think?"

She grinned. "I'm getting a copy for my keeper shelf once I get home."

A surge of warmth in his chest cut off quickly as her words registered. The reminder that she was here for only a time was ... unwelcome.

He frowned.

"Come on, grumpy." She tugged on his shoulder once more. "You need to go to bed before that frown of yours gets frozen that way."

His lips twitched but then reverted to the frown. "You take the bed; I'll take the sofa." He pushed to his feet with a groan. His bones were already stiff from falling asleep in the chair. He wasn't looking forward to a night crammed on that thing. He was much taller than it was long.

"Don't be silly," she said shortly. "We're both adults. No way I'm making you sleep on the couch in your own cabin, and no way I'm going to do so myself. I've got a crick in my neck from simply reading on that thing."

He tilted his head and furrowed his brow. "You want ... to sleep ... together?"

Chapter Ten

She wanted him to get into that bed with her. Was he understanding that correctly? Surely not.

Bethany tipped her head back and laughed, the sound musical. "In the literal sense of the word, yeah," she said.

He was already shaking his head. "I don't think that's a good idea." There was no way he could spend the night with her again. Last night, he hadn't even known she was beside him and he'd wound up on top of her. There was no way his body would behave now.

She slapped his shoulder. "Okay, mountain man, we'll roll up the extra blanket and put it between us." He was still shaking his head when she said, "And if you try to touch me, I'll kick you in the gut again."

He stopped shaking his head. "Um ... please don't?"

She smirked. "I make no promises."

"Bethany—"

"I'm kidding, James. Come on." She pulled him toward the bed. "Don't be silly. Friends share beds all the time and nothing happens."

Was that true? Was this something she was used to in society, and now he was showing his ignorance by overreacting?

The thought made his stomach hurt, and he stopped resisting her. She made a small, adorably triumphant noise, and dropped his arm, walking quickly to the far side of the bed. As he stood by his side of the mattress like an idiot, she hopped around, taking off her boots. When she unbuttoned her pants, his heart nearly beat out of his chest. To hide his reaction from her, he spun around and grabbed the blanket from the back of the couch, rolling it up and stuffing it under the covers in the center of the bed.

"Perfect," she said.

Before he could look up, she picked up her corner of the quilt and hopped between the covers with a contented sigh.

He relaxed a bit when he saw she was still wearing a t-shirt that must have been hidden under layers of clothes. Hesitating only a moment, he took off his own boots. But that was where he stopped. It would be uncomfortable as all get-out, but there was no way he would sleep with her while only partially dressed.

Her ocean eyes watched him unabashedly as he picked up the covers and slid inside. His bones immediately showed their appreciation for the soft landing, but James in no way relaxed.

This close to her, he was overwhelmed by her cool, slightly floral scent. And the blanket between them did nothing to hide her heat.

James began to sweat, and the collar of his shirt felt like it was strangling him. He usually slept naked even on the coldest of nights. He quite possibly would be getting no rest tonight.

"Good night, James," Bethany whispered. She reached over and patted him on his shoulder, making his muscles clench in response. Then without another word, she turned to the side, presenting him with her back. Within seconds, she was quietly snoring.

A tickle rushed through his chest. *A snorer?* But the amusement quickly faded as he forced himself to lie completely still and stare at the ceiling.

Minutes turned into an hour, which turned into two, and yet, he could not sleep. He was still fully awake when Bethany flopped over violently in her sleep. She faced him now and, with her eyes tightly closed, reached across the rolled blanket. For him.

He hissed in a breath as her fingers wrapped around his biceps. *Don't move. Don't move, James.*

She frowned and made a plaintive noise. Then, through a series of ferocious kicks, she dislodged the rolled blanket, sending it fluttering to the floor on her side of the bed. With a sigh, she scooted across the space between them, wrapped both of her arms around his biceps, and rested her head on his shoulder.

James remained a block of ice for as long as he could, and then the pure pleasure of her touch became too much. He allowed himself to relax into her hold, and she must have felt it, because she sighed again and nuzzled his shoulder.

Something hitched in his chest. Cautiously, *so* slowly, he began to move his arm. She whimpered but released him, and then he was able to wrap his arm around her and pull her into his side.

She smiled softly, moved her head from his shoulder to his pectoral, and then spread her arm over his stomach. She squeezed him and resumed her snores.

It took several moments of stinging cheeks for James to realize that he was grinning down at her like a simpleton presented with the greatest of treasures. He rubbed his cheek against the top of her head, and seconds later, he was asleep.

• • •

Her pillow would not stop wiggling. She gritted her teeth, furrowing her brow. Cracking one eye, she found herself staring at flannel. A short distance away, her hand lay sprawled across a row of buttons. As she watched, her hand rose and fell.

Ah, not a pillow, then. James.

She opened her other eye and raised her head a bit, gazing down at their bodies. She was all over him, plastered against his side with her arm across his chest and her leg across his thighs.

She didn't know what had happened to James's fastidious blanket wall, but she'd probably had something to do with its demise. She craned around enough to look over her shoulder without relinquishing her hold on her lumberjack pillow.

The blanket was on the floor beside the bed.

She turned back to James. There was enough glow from the still-burning fire for her to see his features. His face was painted in golden orange, and beneath his whiskers, his lips were pinched while his eyes darted around behind his closed eyelids. Before her gaze, his brow crinkled, and he repeated the fitful wiggling that had woken her in the first place.

She propped herself up on her elbow. The quilt came up to his ribs, but she could see, obviously, that he still wore his flannel shirt, and beneath her bare thigh was the rough scrape of denim.

The man had gone to bed fully clothed beneath a quilt and with a fire roaring.

He grunted in his sleep and jerked his head to the side. Bethany flattened her palm over his heart even more and could feel the telltale dampness of perspiration beneath his shirt. James was burning up, and it was obviously affecting his sleep.

Surely, her closer-than-glue sleeping position was not helping matters, either.

Poor thing. Before she could think, she drew the quilt down, uncovering his torso.

He stilled beneath her, and in the quiet, there was the quick draw of breath. Her gaze flew to his face. His eyes were open.

"Bethany," he whispered.

His voice was rough and deep from sleep. Bethany sucked her bottom lip into her mouth and bit down on it as a chill shot through her entire body.

She was made to hear this man whisper her name in the dark.

Bad, Bethany! Bad!

Shoving her lascivious thoughts aside, she whispered, "You're burning up." She moved her fingers to one of his buttons, trying to ignore how husky her own voice was. "Let's get these clothes off you."

It was an entirely practical suggestion, but her thoughts and their close proximity twisted her words, and in the end, there was no hiding it had come out as a proposition.

James laid a hand over hers, stilling her fingers. "I ... can't," he whispered.

Bethany closed her eyes for a moment and then looked at him again. Something within her belly knotted, and she had the urge to rub her thighs together.

She swallowed. She needed to move away from him. Give him space. Go back to her side of the bed, erect the blanket wall once more, and let the poor man sleep.

Any second now.

"James," she whispered. "It's okay."

What?

His brows drew together, a mirror of her same internal question.

What, exactly, was okay? Their closeness? His nudity? Was she giving him permission to—

Good God, was she asking him to have sex with her?

Maybe.

And *that* was what got her attention. Not surprise that she wanted James—she'd wanted him all day—but surprise that she was putting aside her convictions about staying away from him. She never did that. Additionally, she was obviously more experienced than he was: Her nudity made him uncomfortable; his nudity made him uncomfortable. She was pushing him. Had their situations been reversed, she'd call him an opportunistic asshole.

With a sigh, she began to ease away from him. "I'm sorry," she whispered in the dim glow of the cabin.

He frowned and tightened his hand over hers, keeping her from moving farther away. "Why?"

She nodded at their bodies. "I'm all over you. Again." She tugged at her hand. "I'll just go back to my side of the bed."

His fingers flexed around her wrist. "I don't ..." He took a breath. "I don't mind," he whispered so softly, she barely heard it.

She looked away just in time to hide the smile that nipped at her lips. She didn't mind either. She *really* didn't mind.

He blew out a breath. "It is ... very warm ... isn't it?"

She turned to him again. "Well, you're fully clothed and wearing a midsized woman, so warm is to be expected." He might have blushed beneath those whiskers, but she couldn't be sure. Why did it have to be so dark in here? "Do you always sleep in your clothes?"

For a moment, he didn't answer her, and then he shook his head just once.

Something in her chest got tight, and though it took all of her effort to do so, she pulled away from him, extricating her wrist from his grasp, and lay beside him on her side. "I promise not to touch you if you get more comfortable, James," she said softly and firmly, more a warning to herself than anything else.

He hesitated, but she could tell he was longing to cool off. Suspecting pressing him would only keep him clothed, she stayed silent and simply watched him.

After what felt like an eternity, his hands began to move. Starting at the hollow of his throat, he began to undo his buttons one by one. Bethany's gaze was riveted, watching as more and more skin was revealed and cursing—all over again—the dark. When she took a breath, she startled herself with how loud it was.

His fingers paused at their current button, and she glanced at his face. He was staring at her with wide eyes. She was certain he wasn't breathing. In her peripheral vision, she saw him resume unbuttoning his shirt, and now she was certain *she* wasn't breathing.

God, had she ever wanted any man as much in her entire life as she wanted this mountain hermit? It made no sense; it was so intense, she didn't know if she would survive it.

He finished unbuttoning his shirt, and hesitating only a moment, he sat up and shrugged it from his shoulders and dropped it to the ground.

It had taken maybe two seconds, but Bethany had caught plenty an eyeful of flickering muscles across his shoulders in the fireplace's dim glow, and when he turned back to her, her mouth was dry. She swallowed hard in vain.

He lay down again slowly and then rotated to his side, mirroring her. The glowing embers from the fire highlighted a sheen of perspiration over the curve of his naked shoulder, and Bethany pressed her knees together.

"B-better?" she rasped.

He pulled in an extraordinarily loud breath. "Very much not," he said in a rumble.

She fisted her hands to keep from reaching for him. "I know," she whispered.

Say something, she coached herself. Talk to him. Distract. Do anything to keep herself from throwing him to his back and climbing him like a mountain. "Who's Eugene Anderson?" she blurted into the tense quiet.

She had the urge to slap her hand over her mouth and barely resisted. *That's what you come up with?* What happened to getting to know each other better before bringing up his father?

James's harsh breathing halted. After a moment, he cleared his throat, and she could see the muscles in his shoulder flex, hold, and release. "My father," he said simply. But his tone conveyed everything but simplicity.

"I'm sorry," she whispered automatically.

"I've never understood that one," he said without halting. The most he'd said to her comfortably. "Why say *sorry* when someone dies?"

A soft smile spread her lips. "One of society's expectations, I guess."

"I say *thank you*, right?" he asked.

Bethany shrugged with one shoulder. "You say whatever you want, James."

Chapter Eleven

Whatever I want? He wanted to tell her he could still feel the silkiness of her inner wrist against his palm. To ask if he could shed his jeans for the sole purpose of being naked with her. To beg for her fingertips to press into his chest.

"I don't think that would be wise."

His voice had deepened, embarrassingly so. Could she guess where his thoughts had gone? When her shadowy form stiffened, his neck heated, and he forced himself to keep talking. "He died in his sleep. It was peaceful."

"That's good," she said softly.

James nodded. It had been. His father had been a heartbroken shell of a man. James was a scientist; he didn't necessarily believe in an afterlife, but neither did he reject the premise entirely. One thing was certain, though: His father knew more peace now than he had when he was alive.

"How long ago?" she asked.

James pulled himself from his thoughts. "Ten years."

She blew out a breath. "That's a long time."

"Yes."

"I mean," Bethany said, "that's a long time to be alone."

Her words brushed along his skin as though she had dragged a silk scarf down his chest. Nothing brought home the point that he'd been alone too long like her very presence in his cabin. In his bed. "Yes," he said again, his voice a harsh rumble.

In that moment, he wanted to touch her so badly, it was a physical pain. He was achingly aroused, his erection pinched in his jeans.

"What did you two do?" she asked. "When he was alive?"

He frowned as his mind tried to place her question amid its primitive urges and drives. "Read," he said after a moment. "Hunted." In other words: "Nothing."

"Nothing?" she asked.

"My father had abandoned life," he said. "He was committed to that end until he died." Bethany was quiet, and to avoid his thoughts deteriorating into lust again, he kept talking. "He had been a great scientist, but he never worked again once we came to the mountains." It was more words than he'd ever spoken together, and he felt pathetically exhausted by them.

"Oh," she said in an odd manner. James frowned. He thought she might sound ... *disappointed.*

"It wasn't glamorous, I know," he said self-consciously. "But I do miss him."

"Of course you do," she said quickly. She sighed, and the sound carried more disappointment. For some reason, her unhappiness prodded at him. Unsettled him. He wanted her to be happy here.

Why? So she'll stay? Uh oh. That was why, wasn't it? James cleared his throat, and Bethany jumped.

This was bad. She'd been here for almost three days, and he wanted to keep her. Keep this vibrantly alive woman in his pathetic, monotonous life and cabin.

Since when did he start championing impossible causes? His logical part cringed.

"Good night, Bethany," he blurted.

She jumped again. "Oh," she said breathlessly. "You don't want to talk anymore?"

He refused to believe she was sad about that, no matter how her voice had sounded. He shook his head.

"O-okay," she stammered. "Good night, then." After an awkward pause, she turned over, presenting him with her back again.

He was surprised when his eyelids grew heavy. He'd been practically verbose with her, leaving off his usual heaviness and halting manner with words here in the dark, and it had truly exhausted him. Before he drifted off, he reached out and brushed his fingers against a lock of Bethany's hair that was spread across his pillow. Wrapping it around his finger, he slept.

Chapter Twelve

He was sleeping again, much more comfortably than he had with his shirt on if his deep breathing and lack of thrashing were any indication.

Sleep proved impossible for the rest of the night for Bethany.

She hadn't realized how much she'd been pinning all her hopes on Anderson's work. And one little sentence, whispered huskily in the dark, had erased the future she had imagined for herself.

A future based on someone else's hard work. She winced. Pathetic. Here she was, mourning the loss of something she had put zero effort into.

She didn't like herself very much right now.

James had talked to her freely in the dark, with no stuttering or halting. Fortunately, he had cut himself off abruptly and gone to sleep. He had casually announced his father's lack of work in the mountains, and she had needed James to stop talking immediately or she would have done something else pathetic: start sobbing on his naked, naked chest. Or start licking his naked, naked chest.

The night wore on and sleep continued to evade her.

Okay, so, there was nothing for her career here. Fine. When Dewinter quit fucking her over on the down low, Bethany would get back to civilization and start her own project. It would be awesome. Change the world just as much as Anderson's system would have. It didn't matter that the old man's system had been perfection and she was missing out on everything she'd ever dreamed about.

The only bright side to all this was now she was stuck here with temptation incarnate and no ethical reason to keep her hands to herself. Start corrupting the hermit now or in the morning ...? With a sigh, she started to turn over, but something snagged at the back of her head, and she paused. Twisting as much as she could, she looked over her shoulder to find a sizable lock of her hair wound around James's finger.

He held it against his lips as he slept.

Her gut jerked violently, and her eyes slid closed. What was she doing here with this man? Granted, she had no qualms about her body or her sexuality and regularly enjoyed both with the company of someone else, but James was not just someone else.

James was a man who had removed himself from society. His every interaction was open and honest, because he hadn't had to school himself to behave in the less-than-honest manner everyone in the world did to hide what they were really thinking and feeling.

With another man, stalking around naked and cuddling in the dark was totally fair game.

With James, she worried it might mean something.

She bit her lip. Okay, she *knew* it meant something. She needed to tone it down. Move slowly, if at all. They had an indefinite amount of time out here together. If she kept behaving this way, they'd be sleeping together by lunch, and then she would have done something truly horrible to another person, because without having to ask, she knew that were James to be around women on the reg, he would not be a proponent of love-'em-and-leave-'em.

She flopped to her back, reluctant to withdraw her hair from his grasp despite her personal, vehement lecturing.

She ran her tongue over her teeth and immediately longed for the toothbrush in her pack across the cabin. Her brows drew together as she counted backward and discovered it had been three days—*three days*—since her last shower.

She groaned softly, but that was all it took for James to jerk awake beside her.

She turned her head to the side, and her gaze collided with two wide-open and rapidly blinking eyes.

"Good morning," she said, her voice rough despite the fact she hadn't been sleeping.

A dreamy smile spread across his lips. He blinked again and then looked at her. "Morning," he rumbled.

He pulled in a slow breath and rubbed the lock of hair he held against his bottom lip, still wearing that smile, his eyes soft from waking.

But then he seemed to realize what he held in his fingers and what he was doing with it while she watched, because he froze in the middle of brushing it back and forth, his eyes widening.

In the next second, he dropped the lock of hair as though it had burned him. He scrambled to a sitting position, jerking the covers down to her waist as he did so. Once he was upright, he turned to look down at her, his mouth open as though he was going to say something, but then his eyes dipped to her chest, and he simply stared, mouth agape.

Following his gaze down, Bethany found her nipples thrusting against the t-shirt she wore, very obviously bra-less and affected by waking up with a man she wanted despite herself.

James was still staring at her breasts. If he had laser vision, her shirt would have surely burned away. In the "real world," James would have looked away by now. It's not like he was the first man to stare at her breasts—hello, she worked in a male-dominated field. But *they* all knew they shouldn't, and that she would have their balls if she caught them.

James didn't know any better, and the reminder was exactly what she needed when the heat flaring in his rich, brown eyes gave her ideas of inviting him to touch.

She was just reaching for the quilt to draw it up and over her chest, when James broke his gaze away with obvious effort. His face pointed at his knees, he scrubbed both hands up and down his features a couple of times, as though he were trying to erase what he'd just seen.

Do not corrupt the hermit. Do not, *Bethany!*

With his attention directed elsewhere, she slid to the edge of the bed and out from between the covers. She gave her t-shirt a tug, dismissing it as hopeless when she couldn't get it past the tops of her thighs.

Maybe he won't look.

Behind her, his breathing hitched audibly.

So much for that. His gaze carried weight, and she could feel it on her ass. It made her stomach hurt all over again. This is what she got for teasing the tiger.

As she reached for her pants, trying as hard as possible not to bend over and present him with an even better view, she caught a whiff of herself and wrinkled her nose. She'd been giving herself a whore's bath from the sink in the bathroom with mystically running water, but it wasn't cutting it. "I'd give anything," she said, shoving her legs into her jeans, "to have a legitimate shower."

"Oh," James said casually. "I have ... one."

The first thing that struck her was James's halting speech was back in the light of day. And then his words permeated her inexplicable disappointment.

Her fingers stalled on the button of her jeans, and she turned slowly, a scowl pinching her lips.

His eyes were wide and guileless, and when her scowl turned on him in full force, he flinched away. "I ... should have ... told you?"

Do not murder the hermit. Do not, *Bethany!*

"James!" she snapped. "Are you kidding me?"

He frowned. "No."

She gritted her teeth and glanced at the ceiling.

"Oh, you were ... speaking figuratively."

Frustrating man. She looked at him again and took a deep breath that did nothing to calm her temper. "Where is it?" she asked, biting out each word.

He reached for his shirt where it hung on the post of the bed and shrugged it on. Rising from the bed he said, "I'll take you ... there."

He started to button his shirt as he walked to the door, but then he caught her staring at his chest, which was oh-so-gloriously visible in the morning light streaming through the frost-covered windows.

Before her eyes, his chest flushed with color, and mouth flooding with saliva, Bethany snapped her gaze to his face to see the same flush on his whisker-clad cheeks.

Didn't I just tell you to behave? That hadn't lasted long.

"It's ... uh ... this way," James said, nodding toward the door and quickly buttoning his shirt, hiding those glorious muscles behind flannel.

Bethany jerked some semblance of a nod in his direction and tripped behind him. He paused at the doorway and grabbed her coat, holding it open for her to slip her arms into. She would have walked carelessly into the snow without it if he hadn't had the presence of mind to remember they'd just had a blizzard.

I swear to God, I'm smart!

She turned her back to him, and he helped her into her coat, his hands resting on her shoulders for a moment, their weight comforting and stimulating at once. As she zipped up, he cleared his throat and opened the door before striding out into the snow without a jacket himself. She didn't know if he was as distracted as she was or if he just regularly made the frigid weather his bitch, but that tight coil in her stomach tightened a bit more as she followed him out into the crisp air.

He bypassed the small, bathroom shack and went straight for the building they'd dug out yesterday, which would explain why she hadn't seen a shower any of the times she'd used the bathroom in the past two days.

If it wasn't in the room with running water, she was probably facing an ice-cold camper's shower of some kind that existed through a system of stored water. It was a testament to her longing for cleanliness that the idea of a frigid shower did not dampen her enthusiasm one iota.

James pushed the door inward and stepped into the building, and she followed. The light was so dim compared to the sun glaring off snow that it took several moments of blinking for Bethany to see the interior. When she did, her mouth dropped open.

Two large tanks sat at one end of the building, a series of pipes running to and from them and into the ground. They chugged with a happy drone.

Bethany's gaze swept over them, and she immediately recognized the water recycling system.

It was Eugene Anderson's project. Here in real life.

Chapter Thirteen

James smiled at the water system, running his hands over the gears and scrutinizing their gauges to make sure all was running as it should. He patted one of the tanks fondly.

If his solitary mountain life started to weigh on him, being in this room never failed to turn things around.

"What the fuck!"

James spun around and prepared for an attack of some kind. When he saw only Bethany in the room, standing in the still-open doorway and staring at the tanks with a wide-open mouth, he relaxed. But then he frowned.

"Is everything ... okay?"

She pointed at the tanks with a shaking finger. "That's a graywater recycling system."

A lightness flitted through his chest. "It is," he said with a smile borne simply of pride. "You recognize it?"

One finger still pointing at the system, she jerked her other thumb toward her chest. "Scientist," she said, the slightest frown marring her slack mouth.

He recognized that frown as the defensive one she'd sported anytime she'd accused him of underestimating her prowess.

He resisted the urge to roll his eyes. Barely. *Scientist* was a broad term. For example, a geologist would look at the system behind him and shrug, then look for some rock formations. "Is water ... your field?" he asked instead.

Her gaze switched from the tanks to him. "Water is my life."

Before he knew what he was doing, he was taking a stumbling step toward her, hand outstretched. He was going to thread his fingers through that silky hair. Cup her cheek. Ravage those lips with his kiss.

He stopped and blinked at his outstretched hand. She was staring at it with both eyebrows raised, and he let it fall to his side. *What did you think you were doing?*

He hadn't been thinking. In fact, nothing complex had been happening in his brain since hearing her words. He'd seen this woman naked. Had held her in his arms. Had thrust against her slick skin.

Nothing had turned him on as much as that simple phrase. *Water is my life.* It was a sentiment he understood; it was a sentiment he shared.

He'd somewhat regained control of his runaway libido, but his belly ached, and he had to clench his hands at his side to keep them from reaching for her again.

"This is," Bethany said, drawing his attention, "magnificent."

She moved toward the tanks, her hand outstretched in the same manner his had been toward her. She stopped in front of the output tank and pressed her palms to it, her lids sinking over those incredible eyes.

James felt his Adam's apple bob and a tingle spread over his heart, as though her hand touched him and not the system before her.

"I know," he murmured. The water recycling system was truly miraculous. It had taken years to perfect. Many tweaks to his father's plans. All of the water on his property came from and returned to these two tanks. It was cleaned and then sent out again with the barest loss of volume due to processing. He knew there was nothing like it in the entire world.

Bethany brushed her fingertips over a gauge. "This is the—"

"Intake," James supplied.

Bethany nodded and trailed a pipe between the tanks. Her fingers paused over a large piece of equipment that made most of the noise in the room. "Filter?" she asked.

He jerked a nod.

"Just one?" she asked breathlessly.

Pride swelled in his chest. "Yes."

Her breathing was shallow and quick. "My God," she whispered reverently.

He swallowed hard again, unbearably turned on by her appraisal of the machinery in front of them. "Completely self-sustaining," he said in a rumble.

Those aqua eyes traveled over to him and held his gaze captive. "This is miraculous," she breathed.

He felt like he'd been punched in the gut. "I know," he managed to get out.

"I thought you said your father didn't work here on the mountain."

He frowned and tilted his head, trying desperately to understand her words when all he could really hear was the pounding of his blood in his ears. "My father?"

A small stroke of understanding. Her field was water. His father had been a god in that field. She'd no doubt heard of him, and she assumed he'd built this system.

A primitive, masculine part of him stretched and rolled over within his chest, and he leaned one shoulder against a tank. "I built this," he said, his voice so deep it was hard to understand.

But understand it, she did, if the flare of her pupils was anything to go on.

• • •

A riot of *do nots* tumbled through Bethany's mind as she bit into her bottom lip and tried desperately to freeze her features in a mask of disinterest.

Do not show him this news has rocked you.

Do not reveal how badly you want this.

Do not jump him, take him to the ground, and grind yourself to release against his hard cock while thinking about his sexy, *sexy* brain.

Enough time passed that James straightened from his relaxed stance against the tank and looked at her with brows drawn together.

Say something. Do something!

"Y-you?" she stuttered out.

"Are ... you all right?" he asked.

She nodded a bit too quickly and made some noise that she'd meant to be in the affirmative but was truly just a jumble of consonants.

You're flipping your shit, Bethany. Keep it together. "I'm fine," she managed to say, her voice dry and brittle. "Just ... surprised. I guess."

James's face twisted for a moment, and then it cleared. He looked up and to the left. "Bethany the Misandrist. What ... do you ... know. That fits ... perfectly."

He thought she was underestimating him? A laugh burst out of her and then continued to roll when she realized he'd parroted her earlier accusation. "Trust me, baby," she said between laughs. "Misandry is the *last* thing I'm feeling right now." She brushed tears from her eyes, biting her bottom lip in a moment of weakness as she imagined kissing her way across his chest.

Under her heated gaze, he shifted, cleared his throat, and looked at his feet.

Delicious.

"I was ... kidding," he said softly.

"I know," she said. Why the accusation? Even if it hadn't been malicious, it was incredibly out of character.

Oh.

His father was Eugene fucking Anderson. That'd be like going into computers when your dad was Steve Jobs. Talk about big shadows.

No wonder her surprise at his accomplishment had rubbed him the wrong way. It would have her as well. "You're incredible," Bethany said, meaning it with every fiber of her being.

His enormous shoulders jerked, but he kept his gaze directed at his feet. Nevertheless, she was able to see the blush creep over his cheeks beneath his beard.

Knowing from firsthand experience that the blush started on his chest was doing nothing for her resolve not to jump his bones.

They stood in ever-increasing awkwardness as her mind ran riot through all the things she wanted to do to him. Like push him back against this water system from her dreams, drag his pants down, and quench her thirst for something besides water. She'd been attracted to him before, but now? When she was standing next to his brainchild?

Her attraction was out of bounds.

James cleared his throat. "The ... uh, shower," he said and then drifted off.

His gaze met hers, and he gestured to a spot behind her with his chin. She spun and saw a showerhead peeking above a wooden wall. It was crude but spacious. Beneath the showerhead and in the middle of the "stall," there was a drain. Which, she now knew, would lead back to the water system behind her, where the water would go through one freaking filtration before being clean and sent back out. The lowest number of filtrations anyone in the field had managed was two, and those systems were enormous and ungainly beside James's sleek model.

Bethany practically salivated. She would give anything to get a peek inside that filter and see what it held.

She turned again and nearly ran into James, who had followed her over and was standing right behind her. Well ... in front of her now.

She tipped her head up as he tipped his down, and their close proximity registered even more as her mind calculated the slight distance she would have to cross to press their lips together.

She raised a shaking finger and pointed at him. "I'm going to shower, and then you're going to show me how that filter works, yeah?"

Light sparked in his eyes, and his beard twitched a bit, as though he'd smiled and then quickly forced himself to relax. "Yeah," he said.

He stood there for a moment more. Was he going to leave so she could shower, or should she invite him to join her? *No, Bethany!*

With a self-conscious dip of his head, he broke eye contact with her, turned, and strode to the corner of the building where she spotted an old-fashioned tub and legitimately retro scrub board for laundry. He grabbed a bundle and returned to her, stretching it out toward her without meeting her eyes.

It was a ratty towel. She accepted it without a word, and he turned and left the building.

It was only after the door closed behind him that she realized she should have told him why she was here in the first place: that she was here for the very thing he'd created.

Fuck!

Eugene Anderson hadn't made this water system. James had. He was firmly out of her reach now.

Oh, God. She'd been flirting shamelessly. Planning his miseducation. Inadvertently, she'd done exactly what she'd vowed she would never do: flirt in a professional situation.

Her stomach roiled.

Calm down, girl. She hadn't done anything so unforgivable yet. She could fix this.

Okay, definitely can't tell him why I'm here just this second. She needed time to convince him she was a professional, not some sort of succubus out to seduce his water system away from him.

She gritted her teeth. *Good work on that one.* Because of her damn hormones, she'd have to further delay progress. Because there was no way in hell—or heaven—that if she walked up to James right now and said, "So, about this water system of yours ... feel like sharing it with me?" that he wouldn't interpret her flirtatiousness as part and parcel of her desire to get her hands on his invention

Pinching the bridge of her nose, she strode toward the shower. What a mess. Of her own damn making.

Well, at least she had time. Time to convince him she had a brain in her head. Time to convince him she had honorable intentions toward both him and his system.

And that his gray-water recycling meant life and death to countless people. Could have changed Bethany's own childhood.

Fuck. Fuckity fuck.

The worst part of this? She couldn't tell if her stomach ached because she'd put roadblocks between her and her goal ...

Or because James was now firmly out of her reach.

Chapter Fourteen

She likes it.

James smiled to himself as he made the short trek back to the cabin, but even the smile didn't release the pressure in his chest—pressure he knew was pride mixed with happiness.

When she'd discovered the water system was his, she'd looked at him differently. Like he was a man.

He may be naïve thanks to his lack of a societal rearing, but he was still able to recognize that Bethany definitely had recognized him as male before the water system. But it had been a teasing, playful recognition. There had been no respect to it, of that he was sure.

After he had confessed to creating the recycling system, however? Respect in spades flooded her breathtaking eyes. There would be no more teasing—no more bending over with her gorgeous bottom bare and in the air, no more naked cuddling—and while that made a sharp ping resound in his gut, he was thankful. It meant she no longer viewed him as a plaything that wouldn't react to the teasing. He was no longer *safe*.

He was a man. A man who would throw her to the bed and take her up on everything she was offering if she offered it again.

James paused at the door to his cabin. *Would* he take her up on it if she offered again?

He turned his head to see the water building over his shoulder. Right this second, she was standing beneath the showerhead, naked and wet.

A shiver wracked his shoulders, and he entered the cabin, shutting the door firmly behind him as the irrational idea of stalking back to her and joining her there became nearly unbearable.

Yes. If she offered again, he would take her up on it. Of that much he was sure. Because, if she offered again now—after knowing what he was capable of—she would mean it.

His eyes took a moment to adjust to the interior of the cabin, and the first thing he saw was the rumpled bed. The ache in his lower gut that seemed ever-present lately made a reappearance, and he shuffled over to the bed and made it with jerky movements, breathing through his mouth when he caught a whiff of Bethany's scent on the sheet.

That done, his idle thoughts returned to the image of Bethany in the shower. His shower. The one he had made possible through brainpower and sweat.

He'd planned to take a shower, too, but standing in that space now, he would do nothing but imagine her in it. He brushed over his beard with a shaky hand. That would be a bad idea.

He began to disrobe so he could put on new clothes, but as he did so, an unfortunate whiff of his body made him count backward. Two—no, three days since he last bathed?

His shower may not be an option, but bathing was nonnegotiable.

Sink bath it is.

He scratched his chin, his fingers sifting through his whiskers, and he paused.

His beard. His father had regularly shaved when he was alive, and when James had asked why when he was younger, Dad replied that it was just a habit from society.

It was a habit James himself had never adopted—there was no need and no past precedent—but now, with Bethany in the cabin ...

He didn't even know what he looked like. His breathing quickened. Was he ... ugly?

His boots thudded heavily against the board floor as he walked over to the dresser. He reached behind it, his fingertips brushing against what he sought immediately. Grasping it tightly, James pulled it out. Light from the window reflected off its surface and shot directly into James's eyes so that he squeezed them tightly until the burn eased.

Slowly, he opened his eyes again and stared down into his father's old shaving mirror.

A stranger stared back at him. He parted his lips—when was the last time he'd looked at his appearance? He knew for certain that the mirror had been living behind the dresser since shortly after his father's death, so ... at least a decade.

Sure, he'd caught his reflection in the window of his truck or the glass door of the Internet café he visited periodically to place orders for supplies, but he'd never given himself anything beyond a cursory glance.

He looked like the few pictures he had of his mother. Excluding the beard, of course. There was nothing of his father in him.

Feeling hollow, James bent down and opened the bottom drawer of the dresser: the place where he'd kept a few of his father's belongings. He quickly located the straight razor and gathered the other supplies before carrying his haul over to the sink.

It'd been years, but James had the routine memorized still from watching his father do it every day. He rested the mirror against the wall and adjusted it until he could see his face. Then he attacked his beard with scissors.

As his facial hair thinned, he observed the transformation in the mirror with bated breath, looking for a hint of anything that reminded him of his father. He still didn't see anything when he lathered up with his dad's shaving soap, and similarities continued to elude him as James began scraping the blade against his skin.

Least of my problems. Lack of focus on the task at hand had yielded some ... incidents.

He hissed in a breath as he nicked himself yet again, this time at the dimple in his chin. He raised his eyebrows. He hadn't known he had a dimple in his chin.

He ignored the dribble of crimson skating along his jawline; more would soon join it as he continued. He'd just clean up all at once. He raised the razor again and was about to set in once more when the door opened and Bethany stepped into the cabin.

She was scanning the room for him, blinking her eyes rapidly. James froze. Her beauty struck him like a blow all over again. Her hair was wet and straight, slicked down her back. Her cheeks had a slight flush to them; she must have taken the hottest shower she could.

She started talking even before she spotted him, walking over to her pack where it lay propped against the fireplace. "I had to put dirty clothes back on," she said, her voice carrying to him over her shoulder. "And now I feel gross." She reached down and snagged her pack. "I'm just going to go change, and then I'll come right back." She turned toward the door, spotted him at last, and tripped over her feet as she came to an abrupt stop.

James cringed, curling his shoulders inward and trying to hide. Dear God, what he must look like right now. Half of his face was scraped clean but marred with trickles of blood. The other half was covered with a ratty beard that had been hastily trimmed to uneven lengths by viscous snips of the scissors.

He looked ridiculous, his inadequacies on full display. A grown man who didn't even know how to shave. Something bitter swelled in the back of his throat.

Her eyes widened. "You're bleeding!" She dropped her pack to the floor and rushed over.

He swallowed hard and turned away from her. He should have taken time to clean each cut. He clenched his teeth. "I'm fine," he rasped, reaching blindly for the towel he kept near the sink.

Her fingers landed on his forearm; he nearly jumped from their cold, like little pinpricks from icicles. "Look at me," she said softly.

After a moment, he shook his head. "I'm fine," he said again, the protest twisting his words into the pathetic whine they were.

Her fingers moved from his forearm to his shoulder, where she exerted gentle pressure. How could he say no, even if her laughter would gut him? James allowed her to turn him.

He expected ... he didn't know, a gasp or something. Instead, she remained silent until, reluctantly, he allowed his gaze to find hers. Her eyes were large with an unnamed emotion, but he instinctively knew it wasn't pity.

The fist in his chest loosened a bit. "I don't know ... how to shave," he admitted, his gaze sliding away and fixing on the door.

He saw her shrug in his peripheral vision. "I don't know how to shave my face either," she said lightly.

He shot his gaze back to hers real quick. A startled laugh rumbled in his chest. "And it shows," he said, wrinkling his nose and shaking his head.

She patted her smooth cheek and winked at him. "All natural, baby. Don't hate."

Just when he had started to forget the horrifying position she had caught him in, she suddenly sobered. He felt his face fall.

"Why are you shaving?" she asked softly.

He jerked his gaze to the floor again. "I don't ... know."

"Well," she said, "I would hope it's for a damn good reason since you're carving your face up for it."

A touch of humor was back in her voice, and it was for that reason alone that shame didn't overwhelm him. "I only have ... good reasons."

"Of course."

He dared to glance at her face again but kept his own pointed downward. Through his rowdy hair, he saw her smiling at him softly. He'd smile back, but he had a feeling it would sting like hell's fire when it stretched all of his nicks.

"Well, I'm a semiregular leg shaver," she said. "Not the same thing, but do you want my help?"

Though the idea of her fingers stroking across his face was enticing, the idea that she thought he needed her help was another blow to his ego. He shook his head almost as soon as she'd finished offering. After he figured this out for himself, she could shave him all day long. Straddle his lap as he sat in a chair, press her breasts against his chest, and touch his jaw until they were both breathless from wanting each other.

But only after he figured this out for himself. "I'll get it," he mumbled.

"No doubt," she said. After only a moment, she leaned down and retrieved her pack from the floor. "I'm just going to change," she said, backing away from him and moving toward the door. "And maybe take another shower, because that was awesome."

With a little wave of her fingers, she turned and left the cabin, and James was alone once more. He stared at the closed door for a beat or two and then turned back to the mirror with a sigh. Might as well get this over and done with. When he scraped his cheeks again, this time he didn't cut himself, and a small thrill of victory rolled through him.

He finished shaving with only one more small cut. When he splashed his face clean, he hissed in a breath as what felt like a thousand points of fire lit across his mangled jaw. The sting vanished quickly, however, and with a glance at the still-closed door, James quickly stripped and washed his body down.

Feeling like an entirely different man, breezes he'd never felt caressing his bare face, he pulled on boxers and jeans and was just buttoning a fresh shirt when the cabin door opened again.

Bethany entered wearing her own set of fresh clothes, her hair newly wet, and when she caught sight of him, she froze on the spot.

Her eyes widened. Her mouth slackened. "Oh, holy hell," she muttered.

Chapter Fifteen

Bethany had ignored the tingle between her thighs as much as she could on the walk back to the cabin. She'd washed her hair again, trying to keep her hands occupied. It had been pointless. Within seconds, she'd been touching herself as she stood beneath James's showerhead for the second time.

It'd only taken a few frantic strokes of her fingers to bring her to orgasm. And so she'd done it again.

And ... one more time.

She'd pictured James's drool-worthy body each time she'd tailspinned into bliss.

I may not be able to touch him, but fantasies are fair game, right? Her aching stomach begged to differ.

But, now, standing just inside the cabin and staring at the angel who had taken James's place, she longed to return to that shower and repeat her mistake, this time picturing the face that made her want to weep.

This had been hiding under the mountain man's beard? Her gaze hungrily swept his features. The hollowed shadows beneath high cheekbones. The square jaw that framed the fullest, most lush lips she'd ever seen on a man. Lips she wanted to bruise and make bigger. Without the whiskers blocking most of his face, his brown eyes were enormous and full of every flicker of emotion— emotion he'd not only never learned how to hide but must have relied on his facial hair to mask for him.

Everything he felt as he returned her stare flashed in those big, brown eyes, and the tingle between her legs grew so intense, she pressed her thighs together and prayed for strength.

She must be just as obvious at the moment, however, because as his gaze locked with hers, his pupils flared. Those fucking amazing lips parted.

She moaned. Out loud.

She saw him swallow so hard, his Adam's apple bobbed several times.

His longish auburn hair, streaked with red and gold highlights from his time in the sun, was haphazardly cut and fell in ragged waves between his jaw and his shoulders, but the effect—placed around those stunning features—was something men struggled to attain in society.

If James walked, looking just like this, on any sidewalk in Los Angeles or New York, he'd be snapped up by some agent immediately. Women would fawn at his feet and proffer panties.

And he'd been hiding in the mountains for most of his life. What a tragedy.

What a treasure. And he's mine—all mine.

No! She had to be good.

"Is it ... that bad?" he asked, worry flooding those eyes.

Bethany's eyebrows shot toward her hairline. "Are you serious?" she asked, her tone sharp.

He winced and pressed a finger to a red spot by the dimple in his chin. "I know I ... look rough."

"You look like a god."

The words slipped easily from her lips, and it took her seeing the shock fly over James's face to realize she'd lost her cool in front of a man for the first time in her life.

Forget her pride, which stung a bit. What had happened to professional distance?

James's gaze slid from hers, again—he never seemed to be able to look directly at her for long—but a slight tip of his lips and a blush that she watched rise from his collar over those chiseled cheeks indicated that her careless praise had affected him.

Old Bethany would have walked right over to him, grabbed him by that lickable chin dimple, and laid the kiss of his life on him. Then she would have stripped them both and released all the steam she'd only stoked by touching herself in the shower.

Well, Old Bethany was going to have to take her knocks. The water system was more important than all the orgasms she could give them both.

Damn it, she could do this. She'd done hard things before.

She winced. That thought was counterproductive. She'd done *difficult* things before.

"Ready—" She had to stop and clear her throat. "Ready to show me the inside of that filter now?" she asked. She desperately needed a distraction, and nothing would distract her more than seeing the beauty of that water system laid bare.

"Sure," he said, glancing up at her through his eyelashes and sending another bolt of lust through her. He turned away and walked toward the door before he could see how it had affected her, which was lucky, because he therefore didn't notice her hand stretching out toward him, desperate for a touch. Any touch.

You can do this, Bethany! With a nod, she followed him back out into the cold. With a shiver that might have nothing to do with the temperature, she pulled her coat tighter and ducked her face to keep it from the wind ... and herself from being able to ogle James's ass in those jeans.

The pleasant chugging of the filter reached her ears just as he opened the door and led her inside. She was so thankful for the surge of excitement that momentarily overshadowed her insistent horniness.

This was it. She was finally going to see inside the plans she'd been unable to decipher, although—she stutter-stepped—Eugene Anderson's plans had definitely had more than one filter.

She frowned. That meant ... James had reinvented his father's plans. Improved upon them.

Damn it! Lust surged to the forefront again. This was doing nothing for her resolve.

When she was able to focus once more, she found James standing by one of the gauges, frowning.

"Something wrong?" she asked.

He was still for a moment before shaking his head and giving her a half smile. "It's running ... hotter than usual," he said.

"Probably working harder because of the weather," she said.

His face cleared. "Of course," he muttered.

"Okay, I'm dying here," she said with a couple claps of her hands. "Show me, show me, show me!"

That half smile went full blown, and Bethany's knees wobbled a bit. She gritted her teeth.

James twisted a couple of dials. From the schematics in her head, she was able to tell he was shutting off the water flow—cutting off the filter.

The whirring of water being cleansed ceased, and he moved to the large filter and opened the front panel, which swung out toward them and revealed all the glorious guts of the most revolutionary invention of the century.

In her opinion, at least.

"Hello, beautiful," she moaned, stepping forward and running her fingers over the top of the filter's casing.

God, this was stunning. In most water recycling systems, this part—where the contaminants were separated from the gray water—was the largest part. In James's creation, it was the smallest. The tanks were the largest part, meaning he could go through as much water as he wanted per day. He was also using the water for bathing and—she recollected her tea—ingesting it instead of just using it for the flushing toilet, although that would explain why the toilet was in a different building.

This was unprecedented!

She came back in focus to find James talking. Luckily she hadn't missed much, and as he explained how his system worked, she followed along. Blank parts of the original schematics she'd been struggling to fill in on her own clicked into place.

James talked and talked, and what was almost more extraordinary than his sudden attack of verboseness, he never halted or stuttered. In talking about his invention, he seemed entirely comfortable in his body and with his place in the world for the first time—in daylight at least, Bethany amended with a flush of heat. He'd had no problem talking to her in the dark, either.

James finished a particularly long explanation with a huge breath. Bethany blinked up at his angel features. Good God, this man could mentor Mensa clubs. "James," she said, "do you realize what you've done?"

He tilted his head. "Created a gray-water recycling system?" he asked uncertainly.

"You could take this to the world!" she exclaimed, grabbing his bicep and squeezing. "All you'd have to do is make it portable, and then you could eliminate the water problem in any country that needs it!"

"Oh," he said, looking at the system for a long moment and then back at her. "That's not ... why I made it."

The roaring excitement screeched to a halt in her skull. "What do you mean?" she asked with a laugh. "Why else would you make it?" She laughed again.

"To know that I ... could," he said softly.

Her stomach bottomed out. She dropped her hand from his arm, and James looked down at her hand—now fisted—and then glanced at her face, his expressive eyes wary, as though he couldn't figure out why he'd be in trouble.

"No," she said, taking a step back. "Tell me you're not one of those."

He turned his face away slightly, looking at her from the corners of his eyes. "One ... of those?"

This couldn't be happening. Not sweet, innocent James. "One of those scientists who invents just for the thrill of inventing."

His fingers spread out next to his thighs, and he flexed them as though he were helpless to see her point. "Is that bad?"

"Not if you're inventing frivolous shit!" Was she sweating? She clenched her fists at her side to keep from fanning herself. "New, improved breast implants or self-cleaning litter pans, for instance." Her hands broke from her control, and she fanned her neck like crazy. It didn't help. "But inventing something the world needs? And then withholding it?" She glared.

His eyes widened. "You're ... upset with me," he said. A cloud crossed over his features.

"Of course I am!"

"Bethany," he said, stepping toward her.

She took a giant corresponding step backward. "No, don't you dare touch me." *My mother's death.* Preventable. All those kids who died every day—how could this man stand idly by and hoard their salvation?

He bit into his bottom lip, and for the first time, the move didn't make her cream her knickers. "This is wrong. What you're doing is wrong."

Stay calm.

Fuck calm.

She jabbed a finger his direction. "And karma is going to bite you in the ass!"

His head whipped back as though her words had slapped him, and then his brows crashed down and a muscle ticked in his cheek. In a move that stunned her, he canted his head toward her, acknowledging—accepting?—her words.

Get some space before you blow everything.

With a final shake of her head, she turned from him and stalked out of the building, through the snow, and to the cabin.

She slammed the door behind her, breathing heavily. To think her biggest problem when she'd walked through this door minutes ago was keeping her vagina to herself; that was laughable.

She certainly didn't have that problem now.

The solution to a slew of the world's problems lay only feet away, and she was going to be damned if it didn't make its way out into the public.

She headed to her pack and snatched her sat phone, dialing her boss with vicious jabs of her fingers. She hadn't wanted to do this yet. She'd been waiting until she'd secured James's cooperation before reporting in.

Well, screw James and his way of thinking. If he wasn't going to change the world, she would. But getting off this mountain would require Dewinter rescuing her, which she would only do if she thought Bethany actually had information that was valuable to Delaney. Information like Eugene Anderson was dead but James Anderson had carried on his father's legacy.

So, Dewinter was willing to screw her? Fine, Bethany would screw her right back. No reason to tell Dewinter she had no intention of using what she'd learned from James.

Let him keep it. Bethany learned enough to do this on her own. She could make it better than what James had done.

She'd thought he was different. Better.

She swallowed down bile as Dewinter answered the phone. "Dr. Dewinter, there have been some developments ..."

Chapter Sixteen

Bethany had stormed out of the water shed probably an hour ago, and James had still not moved from his spot beside the tanks except for the small movements it took to close up the filter and open the valves.

This whole time, he'd stood here, his belly aching for an entirely different reason than it usually did around Bethany.

She was mad at him; he didn't like it, and that was putting it mildly.

But even that horrible, heavy feeling of being in trouble wasn't enough to supplant the tidal waves of rage that came and went in regular timing.

What did she expect him to do?

She hoped karma bit him in the ass?

Well, it had. It'd bitten hard and good, and that's why he was even in the mountains to start with. The worst thing that could have happened to him had already happened to him. A monster had raped his mother; his mother had committed suicide; his father had taken him and retreated from society.

What more did he have to fear? Life couldn't generate anything more hateful than his past, and Bethany could go to hell for wishing more of the same on him with such a flippant attitude.

Does she really expect me to help the world that killed my mother? Truly?

He stiffened.

It was exactly what his father would say. In fact, it was exactly what his father had said nearly every time he talked while they lived on this mountain together.

James rubbed over his smooth jaw with two fingers. When he'd looked in the mirror, he'd seen nothing but the mother he remembered only from photographs.

Apparently, his father was all on the inside. The realization did not bring him any comfort.

Am I being ... selfish?

He dragged his gaze over to the water system he was so proud of. The only way to answer that question was *yes*. He'd invented technology that could save lives, and he had neglected to share that technology.

But even the very thought of approaching whomever he would need to in order to mass produce this system made anxiety scrabble up his spine. Sure, James fantasized about staying out in the world each time he journeyed into it, but that was different from actively planning to leave the life he'd created here.

His father was buried here. The water system was here. He didn't really care about anything else, and he couldn't see himself abandoning either, no matter how noble the cause.

And that—he closed his eyes—*might make me a bad person.*

No wonder Bethany hated him. He might hate himself a little, too, right now.

The cold began to seep into his bones, and he shifted his weight, hoping to kick his blood flow up a notch. When that failed, he was pulled completely from his morose thoughts.

He could not spend the night out here tonight, no matter how much he didn't want to see Bethany right now.

For the first time in days, he resented her invasion of his solitude.

Okay, so, he wouldn't be welcomed into the bed with her as he had been last night. *His* bed, by the way. But she'd have to be heartless to kick him out of the cabin and into the cold, and if anything, her rage-filled reaction to him earlier proved she had a heart. A big one.

Collecting what small bits of pride he could, James forced iron into his spine and began the walk to the cabin. Anxiety filled his gut with each step, making him hesitate, despite the temperature and lack of coat, before pushing in the door.

As though she drew his gaze like a magnet, he found her immediately. She was glaring at him from the center of his bed while holding a can of peaches in one hand, a spoon in the other.

Darn it. He'd forgotten to grab more peaches from the water building. She held the last can in the cabin. His stomach growled, and he clenched his jaw. He'd be going hungry tonight, apparently, because she sure wouldn't share and he didn't have the guts to make the same anxious trip back to the cabin one more time. He really should have brought those rabbits in from the cold so they could thaw. One more failure to add to his list.

She broke her glare with a sniff and continued eating her peaches. James barely kept himself from sagging. His head started to pound. He didn't have the energy for this glut of emotion she continuously put him through.

He plodded over to the couch, settled into the cushions, and grabbed the blanket from the back. Without a word, he stretched out—or tried to at least. His legs stuck out over the side by a good bit, and his neck was canted at an odd angle.

Doesn't matter. He spread the blanket over himself, closed his eyes, and fell into restless sleep to the sounds of a spoon scraping against the bottom of a can.

The couch rumbled.

James came to consciousness slowly as though plodding through thigh-high mud. With each step toward being awake, the couch seemed to move beneath him even more.

His brows drew together, and then he pushed his eyelids open.

It was dark in the cabin; despite feeling the opposite, he must have been asleep for some time.

The couch bounced a bit, diverging from its rumbling, and an answering clack came from the dishes in the kitchenette.

"What the—"

At Bethany's sleep-logged voice, James forced himself to sit up. He looked over the back of the couch and found Bethany sitting up in bed, her silky hair a bird's nest, her face a mask of confusion.

The clacking of the dishes pitched up in volume; the couch lurched across the floor.

An explosion rocked the night.

Bethany squeaked and ducked down, but James was up like a shot and running toward the door before he could even coherently form the thought his body had already figured out: something had happened to the water system.

He wrenched open the door, caught sight of smoke billowing up into the stars, and raced into the dark wilderness.

"James!" Bethany called after him.

He didn't slow down. His heart in his throat, he placed his hand on the door, paused a moment—*Please, oh please*—and opened the door.

Smoke swarmed out, covering him and making him cough. He waved a hand in front of his face and ducked through the door, groping in the darkness and smoke to the corner.

There were no flames—who knew if that was good or bad?—but once the smoke cleared infinitesimally, he couldn't see the system and cursed himself and his urgent rush out of the cabin.

A flashlight would have come in handy.

There was a click behind him, and he turned to stare directly into a beam of light. His eyes squinted, and he held a hand up to block the painful halo. He was just able to make out Bethany's silhouette in the doorway.

She directed the beam behind him and gasped.

He spun, nearly hitting the floor in the process as his boots slid along the planks. There was water deep enough to wash over the tops of his boots. He frowned and looked in the corner. The flashlight illuminated ...

"Oh, God," James moaned.

There was a massive hole piercing the filter cabinet. The ragged metal around it was tinged black, informing him that a fire had been here at some point. Water still poured from the gaping wound, adding to the flood across the floor of the building.

"It's ... destroyed." His shoulders felt as though they weighed thousands of pounds, and the weight traveled up his neck to his head. He let it hang down. His breath shuddered out of him.

Destroyed.

There was a splash behind him and then several more. They were punctuated by tiny pants, and when James looked up again, the flashlight beam was bobbing crazily.

"Help me turn it off!" Bethany shouted, splashing past him. She arrived at the filter and struggled to juggle the flashlight, finally tucking it beneath her chin and holding it to her chest. Her tiny hands moved rapidly over the system's many knobs, and he recognized that she started fiddling with the correct one—the one that would shut off the water—but he couldn't get himself to feel or do anything.

"Shit," she muttered beneath her breath as her hand slipped from the knob without budging it. She tried again, her delicate forearm muscles straining. "Shit!" She turned her head, grabbed the flashlight, and waved it in the air. "Come on, James!" she bellowed. "Move your ass!"

It worked to unlock his joints, and in the next second, he was at Bethany's side. He brushed her fingers aside and grabbed the knob for the valve. His fingers were so numb with the cold that he couldn't feel the metal beneath his grip, but he pinched hard and turned, and the knob moved.

"Thank God," she breathed.

As James closed the valve, the gushing water tapered to a mediocre flow and finally stopped completely.

In the sudden silence, her breaths echoed through the building. He wasn't sure if he was breathing, and when he pulled in a lungful, it stung. How long had it been since his body quit working on him?

Bethany shifted next to him and pointed the flashlight beam at the water system, sweeping it from one tank to the pipes and filter, to the other tank. His gaze automatically followed it, all his hopes and dreams crashing with every inch of demolished metal the flashlight revealed.

"Wow," she said breathlessly.

He grunted. *Wow, indeed.* It was over. Everything he'd ever worked for and most of what had tied him to the cabin where he'd made his life—it was gone.

"It's not so bad," she said.

He snapped his head back and swiveled her direction. "I'm sorry," he ground out. "What?"

She nodded toward the ruined water system. "I mean, look at it."

He didn't need to. Its destruction was engraved in his memory. Instead, he tilted his head to the side and narrowed his eyes at her.

"Well, the filter is gone," she said, not heeding the warning he was throwing her. "But the tanks are still intact and most of the piping as well."

James gritted his teeth. "Exactly," he muttered. The filter was the hard part. All of the parts were custom made and had taken James years to perfect. Any fool could buy some tanks and pipes. That filter had been a work of art.

"We can rebuild this in no time," Bethany said, turning her face to him and grinning.

A terrible, half-wounded, half-incensed noise erupted from his chest. Without a word, he spun on his heel and stormed from the building.

From the splashing and sputtering behind him, he knew Bethany was following him, but he ignored her. When he got back to the cabin, he wanted to slam the door behind him. So very badly. But even at the height of his emotions, he couldn't bring himself to slam a door on Bethany, so he left it wide open, not caring if she came in or not.

At least, that's what he told himself.

Rubbing at the ache between his eyes, he sank into the couch with a huff. What was he supposed to do now? His one purpose in life lay in tatters in a rickety old building. He was as good as worthless.

Bethany would say he'd been worthless anyway.

The door closed with a quiet snick, and even though he was doing his best to ignore the woman who had invaded his home and mind, his shoulders stiffened.

He didn't think he could stand it if she started lecturing him again.

Her footsteps traveled his direction, and a knot formed at the base of his neck, tightening with each soft thud.

She placed a hand on his shoulder and squeezed gently. "I'm so sorry, James," she whispered.

It was so far from what he'd expected her to do, he blinked for several moments. Surely, his addled brain had imagined her soft touch and kind words.

"I can only imagine how much that system meant to you." Her hand moved up into his hair, her fingers stroking across his scalp. Every follicle on his head stood up at attention. The goose bumps traveled down his neck and to the rest of his body so quickly it should have been a physical impossibility.

In the wake of this oddly devastating grief over the loss of his father's water system, the touch of her fingertips—even as innocent as it was—set his blood to boiling. Without any warning, his penis jerked and stiffened in a rush, pinching behind the fly of his jeans.

He hissed in a breath and squirmed a bit, alleviating some but not all of the painful pressure. This was bad. This was very, very bad. He did not have control of himself right now, not by a long shot. He needed her hands off him, and he needed to go to sleep. Forget about everything that had happened.

"I'm—" He had to stop and clear his throat. "Tired," he finished in a rough voice.

"Okay," she whispered. Her fingers combed through his hair once more, and then her hand left his body. He refused to look at her but heard her moving away.

He relaxed for a moment, ready to swing around and stretch out on the couch, but then he heard her move again.

"Come sleep in your bed, James," she said.

Chapter Seventeen

A hoarse sound, half cough, exploded out of him. Then he couldn't seem to catch his breath, sucking it in through a loud, conspicuous gulp.

"What?" he asked brilliantly.

"You need rest, and you won't get it on that couch."

Neither of them would get it if he moved to that bed. He shook his head.

Bethany sighed. "You're going to make me say it?"

James frowned and turned his face to the side a bit. He was able to see her through his peripheral vision but didn't have to suffer the devastation of viewing her beauty head on.

"Fine," she said in a huff. "I'm sorry for yelling at you." She paused. "And you better appreciate the rarity of a Bethany-issued apology, mister."

The lump in his chest unfurled the tiniest bit, bringing with it a rush of warmth that momentarily rendered him even more stupid, because James pushed to his feet before he could stop himself. When he turned to face her, he grimaced.

Why was he doing this?

No, James, no! Return to the couch. Go to sleep.

Bethany stretched out her hand; her fingers were splayed and waiting for his. Like a fool, he stumbled forward, skirted the couch, and took what she offered.

Her palm was hot against his, and she interwove their fingers, giving them a squeeze. His jaw slackened.

She turned and tugged him over to the bed, and he stumbled behind. When she stopped next to his side, she faced him again and released his hand. She nibbled her bottom lip, her usually clear eyes clouded with ... something.

Was she still worried he was mad at her?

No, it wasn't quite that. Whatever it was, he half expected her to step back. Put distance between them. Before he could mourn this loss, her tiny fingers rose and alighted at the top button of his shirt. By the time she'd unfastened it, he was breathing so hard, Bethany's hair was fluttering in the breeze.

He tried desperately to stop it. To be normal, for God's sake. But holding his breath for a count or two only heightened his senses, so that when he finally had to breathe again—right around the time she was undoing another button—his air exploded out of him, carrying with it a sound akin to a moan.

Her fingers stalled; her gaze rose slowly to his. She maintained eye contact as she undid the final buttons, no hint of her earlier reticence present in her eyes. Instead, something resembling resolve appeared in the firm set of her delicate jaw. *Resolve to behave or resolve to continue touching me?* By the time she pushed his shirt from his shoulders, his entire body was trembling.

He wanted her so badly, he couldn't see straight. But even through his hazed vision, he could see that her eyes were dilated, that gorgeous aqua diminished to a ring. Her breasts rose and fell shallowly beneath her shirt, and when she lowered her arms to her sides after baring his chest, she squeezed her fingers into fists.

Does she want me? God, he hoped so. But she needed to say it. He was so clueless when it came to women; he didn't want to make a mistake.

She blew out a shaky breath. "In you go," she said softly, gesturing to the bed behind him with her chin.

She doesn't want me. He pulled his gaze away from her, and when he swallowed, it hurt. In fact, everything hurt, his throbbing erection topping the list. He nodded—too curtly?—turned away from her, and got into bed. He pulled the covers up to his chin, his eyes following her as she moved around the bed.

She unbuttoned her jeans, and James squeezed his eyes shut and forced himself to focus on his breathing. Focus on anything but the sound of her pants hitting the floor and the rustle of the sheets as she slid into bed beside him.

"Come here," she muttered.

When his eyes snapped open, it was to find her holding out her arms to him. He didn't know what to think, what to do, but after a couple of awkward moments of her holding her arms open, he warily slid over.

As soon as he was within reach, she wrapped her arms around him and pulled, directing him to lie within her embrace with his head over her heart. Once he was settled, she threaded her fingers through his hair with one hand; with the other, she stroked his back shoulder to shoulder.

His muscles slowly unclenched, and he reveled in this closeness. In her care for him. It took several minutes, but his racing heart began to slow, and his erection went from full to half-mast. His eyes even grew heavy.

She kept stroking his back. "Everything's going to be okay," she whispered into his hair, her lips fluttering against him.

The desire to sleep vanished, replaced, instead by a glut of conflicting emotions. His fingers curled, digging into her as he clutched her around the ribs. His next breath was ragged, and horror of horrors, his eyes grew wet. He buried his face into her chest, just above her soothingly beating heart, and fought for control.

As his mind scrambled through all of the things he'd lost, she held him tight, murmuring nonsense into his hair, into his ear. Simply hugging him while he struggled with tears.

No one had ever held him like this. Or if anyone had, it was probably his mother before his memories started sticking. His father had certainly never coddled him—emotionally or physically. But Bethany did.

It was the most amazing thing he'd ever felt, and any efforts he made to maintain a modicum of dignity were worthless. Bethany's arms were stronger than anything he could fight against.

It may have been only minutes that he silently cried, but it could have also been hours. He'd never had a reaction like this before, and time ceased to exist in any recognizable form. When the sorrow started to abate and he became cognizant once more, Bethany's shirt damp beneath his cheek made him cringe.

She must have felt him stiffen, because her fingers paused on his back and in his hair for a short moment before they resumed their stroking, and she said, "Don't go all macho on me now, baby."

It was the first time she'd called him *baby* with any semblance of affection, and the husky endearment shot straight to his groin. He'd had no room for lust among the glut of other emotions he'd been feeling, but now that they'd been purged ...

The soft scrape of her nails across his scalp shifted from being soothing to stimulating. And the fact that his leg was looped over one of hers and he was cradled knee to ankle between her thighs became suddenly and glaringly apparent.

He needed to move a bit—and quickly—or she'd be able to feel him stiffen against her leg. He tried as subtly as possible to cant his hips away from her. He released a relieved breath when he succeeded.

But she was still stroking him, apparently blissfully unaware of what her touch was doing to his body. He needed to distract himself. Now. His mind scrambled. *Get her talking. Say something, James!*

"I worried I was being selfish."

He closed his eyes. Great. He'd said something all right. The very last thing he ever would have said if he had one complex thought in his head.

Her hands froze. "Selfish?" she asked in a tone that could only be described as careful.

In for a penny ... He sighed. "About the water system." Why was it he was always able to talk to her like a normal man when they were in this bed? No stopping and starting. Just talk. His body liked the direction of these thoughts very much, so he forced himself to continue. "I'd never thought about it the way you did."

He could feel her struggling for something to say beneath him and was surprised that she didn't just burst out with what she was thinking as seemed to be her normal operating protocol. Did she care what he thought? That was ... new. And stimulating.

Interesting. Definitely not stimulating.

In the end, she didn't say anything; rather, she hummed. The sound reverberated through his temple, and he nuzzled his cheek into her, tempted to turn his head a bit and press a kiss to her breastbone.

"I suppose it doesn't matter now," he muttered, his eyes focusing on the wall.

"Why is that?" she asked softly.

He drew his brows together. "It's destroyed," he said slowly.

She stiffened beneath him. "Then you rebuild it," she said, employing the same, insulting, slow speech he'd used.

He sighed. "Why?" he asked bitterly.

"Why?" she repeated, clearly not understanding his problem.

He'd built the system to know he could. That accomplishment remained, even though the system itself did not. Still, he frowned. It didn't sit right. It was logical and made perfect sense, but a part of him—a *big* part if the feelings were any indication—wanted to rebuild the system anyway.

"To help people," James whispered, unclear until the words left his lips that he was going to speak out loud.

"Exactly," she said. She began rubbing her chin on the top of his head, momentarily distracting him.

"But I don't know the first thing about helping people." His pulse thudded in his throat, making it difficult to swallow.

"Baby," Bethany said, "you think way too much."

He felt himself smiling against her soft T-shirt. "That's a bad thing?"

"When it makes you stupid, yes."

His smile faded. "Hey."

She shrugged, the movement dragging her t-shirt against his stubble—an entirely new sensation, and one he loved. "James, helping people isn't hard."

He definitely disagreed with her there. There'd been no help for his father. There was no help for him. He stayed silent.

She must have taken that as permission to continue. "You've already done the hard part. You made the most badass water recycling system in the universe."

Okay, so maybe he loved ego stroking almost as much as skin stroking. He arched his back into her touch and said, "Go on."

Her laugh was light and musical and traveled through his body. "Just take it one step at a time," she said. "Build it and they will come."

After several awkward moments, he was able to figure out that she'd made some sort of reference that he should understand but didn't.

"Ugh, hermits," Bethany said, giving his hair a little tug. "We'll just rebuild the system, and then we'll go from there, okay? We'll find a way. This will all work out."

His throat was suddenly dry. "We'll?" he asked hoarsely.

"Well, obviously, you'll need my genius expertise." She patted his shoulder. "You've got the system down, but I'm the expert in making things tiny and portable so that sucker is useful where it's needed most."

Working with Bethany on something. Wow. He really, really liked that idea. Images of them huddled over a table, heads bent together as they constructed something out of nothing—

He cleared his throat. "That could work," he said casually. *Do not to rub your erection against her flank!*

Her hands stopped moving. Every muscle he was in contact with tightened on her lithe body. "R-really?" she asked breathlessly.

James frowned and lifted his head. "Why wouldn't I be serious?" he asked, meeting her eyes.

They were wide. "No qualms about working with a woman?"

James turned his head to the side. "No?" he said, drawing it out for several extra syllables and turning it unintentionally into a question. Why would her being a woman make any sort of difference? "I'm confused," he confessed.

"Never mind," she said quickly.

James narrowed his eyes. He hadn't seen her ever actually work. He'd heard some of her intelligence in their conversations, and she never hesitated to tell him how capable she was, but ...

"You are able to pull this off, right?" he asked.

Her signature sass made a very quick reappearance across her face. "Yes," she snapped.

"Then, what's the problem?"

Her eyes shifted away. "I guess nothing," she said in an odd voice.

"Okay then," he said softly. "Looks like we're building a portable water recycling system."

"Okay then," she parroted back. She was quiet for a moment and then: "Holy shit."

James only had time to raise his eyebrows before she grabbed him on each side of his face and pulled. She met him more than halfway, pressing her lips to his roughly and quickly; it was over before he even realized what had happened.

She'd kissed him.

His lips parted as she pulled away. She was sporting the biggest grin he'd ever seen, and it did funny things to his stomach.

She'd kissed him.

My first kiss.

He wished he'd known it was coming. He would have paid better attention. Memorized the texture of her lips. Her taste.

He slid the tip of his tongue along his bottom lip and caught the vaguest hint of her flavor: mint and something else.

Delicious. He moaned softly and closed his eyes to savor it better. It was gone too quickly, and he opened his eyes, trying desperately to keep disappointment out of them.

When he focused again, it was to see Bethany staring at him as though she'd been struck dumb, that incredible grin of hers nowhere to be seen. As he knew he was losing the battle of keeping his face emotionless, he was able to recognize she was having the same problem.

Something flashed in her eyes, hot amid the cool color. He didn't know much, but he would guess it was hunger. It seemed to be warring with another emotion, however. Something that made her seem on the verge of calling this whole thing off.

Desperately do not want that.

He bit into his bottom lip and slowly—*so* slowly—raised his hand. When she didn't shove it away or scoff at him, he grasped her chin gently between his thumb and crooked finger and drew her forward. Her eyes widened, but instinctually, James knew it wasn't because she wanted him to stop.

It was the opposite.

He paused a fraction away from pressing their lips together; a flash of doubt rode through him. He didn't know what he was doing. Would probably be horrible at it, and she deserved someone who would be able to please her.

But then, her lips parted, and she exhaled. Her breath smoothed over his own lips and carried the scent of his toothpaste. Just like that, the doubt vanished.

He closed the distance, settling his lips on hers. His eyes slid closed, and his bottom lip fit into the grove below her top lip, putting their mouths together like a puzzle piece. It was magnificent the way nature had designed them to fit together, even in something as simple as a kiss.

He drew his brows together; he couldn't taste her very well as is. So, he parted his lips slightly and stroked her top lip with the tip of his tongue.

There it is. Her minty, spicy flavor. It was amazing. He needed more. When he tilted his head to the side and opened a bit more, he was preparing to lick her again, but she shocked him when she mirrored his action and touched the tip of her tongue to his.

He jumped, to his shame and horror, but the feel of her tongue against his was anything but what he'd been expecting. When he'd read about this type of kiss, it had always been about heat and passion and moaning.

The first thought that popped into his mind, however? *That's weird.*

He froze, not knowing what to do next. Luckily, she didn't have the same problem. She slid her tongue past his lips and lapped at the roof of his mouth. Instinctually, James closed his lips around her tongue and sucked softly.

That was when she moaned.

I made her create that sound.

And that was when he got into it. Really into it. He wanted to hear it from her again. And again. In varying volumes and pitches.

He shifted, laying his upper body across hers and becoming immediately distracted by the feel of her breasts thrusting up against his chest.

Is that—?

God in heaven, were her nipples hard? He could *feel* that?

He sucked on her tongue again—*hard* this time—and flattened himself against her, wanting more than anything to touch more of her luscious breasts and erect nipples.

Her breath whooshed out of her in a rush, ending up in his mouth, where, like an idiot, he choked on it. He coughed a couple of times, and she pulled away.

"Heavy," she murmured, her lips brushing his as she spoke.

Heat rushed up his neck and cheeks. "Sorry," he muttered, shifting back to where he had been, leaving her chest with reluctance.

But when he moved, she came with him. She pushed him onto his back, then proceeded to crawl on top of him. He stared in wonder as she settled herself between his legs, giving them a shove with her knees when he failed to widen them to accommodate her.

She settled her hips against his, and he hissed in a breath. The pressure was exquisite, but it was also just as equally torturous. He squirmed a bit, trying to create space between their bodies where there was none. He so desperately didn't want to offend her—

Bethany shushed him, pursing those lips together. She then pushed herself up, dragging her pelvis along his erection in the process and nearly causing him to die of pleasure on the spot. She pressed a soft kiss to his lips. "It's okay," she murmured against them.

She then wrapped her arms around his shoulders and began kissing him with soft sweeps of her lips against his.

He tentatively began moving his arms. When she didn't stop kissing him, he wrapped his arms around her back, placing his open palms upon her delicate spine.

She responded by licking her way past his lips, and—this time—the intimate kiss felt like he was drinking fire, her kiss devouring him like tinder. Not weird at all.

He opened to her and pressed his tongue against hers. He wanted into her mouth. When he got there, she moaned, and just like the first time she'd done it, it lit him up.

She made the smallest movement with her hips, a fretful circle, and before she could do it again, his palm in the small of her back shot downward and grabbed her bottom, stopping her.

The feel of her warm, firm curve covered by thin cotton in his hand did the exact opposite of what he was hoping for when he'd stopped her in the first place. Her movement had felt too good. For a moment there, he thought for sure he was going to do something horribly appalling, like ejaculate in his jeans. But now that he held a part of her he found so utterly titillating, he was no better off. Maybe even worse.

Against every ounce of force he was exerting on himself, his hand squeezed. His eyes nearly rolled back in his head, but her reaction stunned him. She bucked against him, pressing into his erection and then thrusting her bottom more firmly into his hand. She also nibbled his bottom lip and then sucked it into her mouth.

"Again," she commanded around her hold on his lip.

He whimpered. *Whimpered.* And he was so horrified by it that every muscle in his body stiffened.

She released his lip only to press a kiss to the corner of his mouth, then a couple across his cheek. "Come on, baby," she whispered into his ear. "Squeeze my ass again."

Like she'd whipped him, he obeyed, bearing down and grabbing her flesh in an unforgiving hold.

She bit his earlobe, and he grunted, just barely keeping himself from crying out.

Her fingers threaded into his hair, and she began trailing those kisses down from his ear to the tendon of his neck. As she did so, she began to move within his hold. He could feel the flex and pull of her muscles beneath his palm, but his entire world soon narrowed down to the points of pressure between their bodies.

She's thrusting against me!

The realization rocked him, and his balls tightened, drawing up into his body. He had to grit his teeth and hold still or lose himself in a moment. He tipped his head back as she continued kissing down his neck, his breaths exploding out of him loudly.

"I'm going to," he began, his words heavy with panic. "Bethany, stop or—"

And she did stop. Immediately. And he was so relieved, he almost didn't notice how devastated he was by that fact. Almost.

She pulled back and looked into his face. Whatever she saw there must have been drastic, because her eyes widened. "Hey," she said, rubbing a palm over his chest. "It's okay. James—"

"I just don't"—he paused, hating himself—"know what I'm supposed to do." His hand stroked over her bottom to her flank, and he halted himself through sheer will. "It feels so good, and ..." He managed to shrug with one shoulder. "I just can't do anything you don't want." His gaze locked with hers. "Please, Bethany."

Something clouded her eyes. She bit into her bottom lip for a moment, then said, "You're not doing anything I don't want. I promise." Her eyes skirted his. "Am I doing anything you don't want?"

He snorted, and her eyes shot back to his. A half smile tipped her lips. "Is that a *no*?"

"That's an emphatic *no*." The majority of his worry was alleviated, but still ... "What are you wanting right now?" James asked. "I need to hear you say it. And be clear."

"Not sex," she blurted quickly.

"Okay," he said easily.

There was a moment in which Bethany looked shocked into silence. She blinked her eyes several times. "Not sex, but can we ... touch each other?"

The faintest pink hue lit Bethany's cheeks, and James didn't know much, but he knew sexual situations didn't make Bethany blush. Why now? "Touch where?" he asked.

Her gaze held his. "Anywhere you want," she said, her voice husky.

"Okay," he said. But when it came out garbled, he cleared his throat. "Yes, we can do that." His fingertips burned where they pressed into the smooth skin on the back of her thigh, right below the curve of her buttock. He wanted his hand back on her ass, but there was one more item of business. "You tell me to stop at any time."

"James, I'm not going to—"

"Say it," he demanded, cutting her off.

Her eyes widened for a moment. "I'll tell you to stop if I want you to stop," she said softly.

He pulled in a breath and then nodded. Right. Now, he could enjoy it without thinking. Which was a good thing, because he wasn't doing much thinking when his hands were on Bethany.

"Kiss me," she whispered, leaning in toward him.

Chapter Eighteen

Everything else boiled away, and he narrowed in on her lips, which were still redder than normal and framed by cheeks that were scraped raw from his stubble.

"Yes, ma'am," he whispered back.

She cut him off effectively by licking into his mouth. When she whimpered as she slid her tongue along the top of his, he did what he'd been dying to do the entire time they talked: returned his hand to her glorious bottom, squeezing with more confidence this time.

And just like last time, she began moving her hips against his erection, which had never gone away, even when he'd momentarily panicked about consent and the ghosts of his past.

Though the thin cotton of her panties felt wonderful, it would be nothing like the silk of her skin, and he skated his palm slowly up toward her waist, moving the fabric of her t-shirt up along the way until his fingers brushed across the skin at the small of her back.

She moaned into their kiss, and he dimly heard himself moan back as he found the elastic of her panties and dipped his fingers inside.

Immediately, his fingers encountered what had to be a dimple right where her back started sloping into her bottom, and in curiosity, he spanned his hands and found a mirroring one right above the other cheek.

Oh, God. His deepened their kiss, images of her matching dimples dancing in his head. He'd give anything to see them.

To dip his tongue into them. They would be nothing short of life-changing.

He traced soft circles around one and then the other, making her squirm against him. He sucked in a breath as her pubis bone ground against a particularly sensitive part of his erection near the head, and he was so distracted by the flare of pleasure that he didn't notice her hand drifting across his chest until she scraped a nail across one of his nipples.

He pulled his mouth from hers just in time to keep from biting into her lip. Hard. Instead, he bit into his own and groaned, his head tipping back.

"Mmm," Bethany moaned through closed lips. "You like," she said, seemingly speaking to herself.

James nodded his head vigorously, so desperate for her to do it again, he was willing to beg if need be.

"Stop teasing me with tickles then. Grab me again, and I'll do what you want," she whispered.

He immediately obeyed, reaching down and palming one luscious cheek of her bottom, squeezing hard—probably *too* hard, honestly.

But Bethany moaned again, and what was even better, she flicked his nipple with her thumbnail, making his back shoot straight, a chill sweeping his flesh.

Through his hazy vision, James saw her smile at him, and then she wiggled down, shoving her ass into his hand in the process. He curved his fingers over her bottom, and his hand was big enough that the tips of them drifted over the crease between her legs. The heat there alone was so unexpected, it almost made him come.

Bethany leaned down and covered his nipple with her open mouth. It had been so cold a second before from her teasing, and now the contrast of liquid heat and the soft flicking of her tongue nearly drove him mad.

His other hand wove into her hair, palming the back of her head to keep her from moving. With a breathy chuckle, she set in to licking his nipple again, and now, James couldn't keep his hips still. They began to move with hers, and the friction between them began to feel so good, he didn't care if his jeans were giving him the worst case of rug burn that had ever existed on earth. It would be more than worth it.

He started to explore with the fingers wedged in her panties. He traced the seam between her legs with his middle and ring finger until he suddenly encountered something so very wet. He froze, and then he realized what it was.

He'd found her vagina, and—*Oh, God*—she was so wet, his fingers were sliding against her.

A word he'd never said in his life broke through his lips; simultaneously, Bethany thrust back into his fingers, taking the tip of his middle finger into her body.

She bit his nipple sharply once, and as he hissed in a breath, she lifted her head and started shimmying her hips. "Take my panties off," she breathed. "Now." And then, instead of waiting for him to follow directions, she pressed rough, quick kisses to his lips as she grabbed her underwear with both hands and yanked it down far enough that she could begin kicking it off the rest of the way.

"God, Bethany," he muttered, holding as still as he could while she writhed all over him. "Keep moving like that and—" He cut off and groaned as she settled over one of his thighs, spreading her legs wide and giving him unlimited access to her slick, incredibly soft lips.

"Fuck," he groaned, saying that word for the second time.

"Inside me," she commanded between those kisses she was still raining on his lips. "Put a finger inside me."

He snaked his hand farther around her waist to obey, gained a precious few extra inches and rubbed his middle finger down her center. She coated him with her arousal, and he bit back another groan as he gently pressed in.

"Oh, God," they said simultaneously as her body willingly accepted him.

He wasn't moving fast enough for her, apparently, because she didn't wait for him to press deeper on his own. Instead, she shoved her hips back, taking his middle finger into her body until he was pressed as far as he could get.

"Shit, James!" Bethany cried. She buried her face in his neck, her panting breaths rushing over his skin. "I'm so close."

He was sure he couldn't breathe. "From just this?" He was barely touching her.

"God, *move*," she begged, her nails digging into his pectorals, and her ass rising, pressing into his palm and wrist.

He wrapped his arm around her, cradling the back of her neck in the bend of his elbow. Grabbing tightly to her bottom with his other hand, he spun them to the side, keeping his finger inside of her the entire time, until they were lying on their sides, facing each other. Her legs still straddled his thigh, but at this angle, he had much more movement.

He eased his finger out of her and was amazed as her body spasmed, trying its best to hold him inside.

She whimpered, her sharp little claws digging into him a bit more, so he claimed her mouth in a searing kiss as he moved his hand to her front and smoothed his fingers down from her belly button.

She anticipated the direction he was heading and hitched her leg farther up his hip, opening herself to him more, but he was momentarily stalled. He'd found—he hissed in a breath—she was so *smooth* between her legs. All except for a strip of hair directly down her center. He thrust his tongue into her mouth over and over as he trailed that hair with his fingers, following it down, down until his ring finger passed over a small, swollen bud.

Bethany jerked from the kiss, throwing her head back and crying out loudly. She grabbed a handful of hair at his nape and tugged. "James!"

His brow furrowed, and he panted so hard he grew dizzy, but he focused all of his energy on stroking that bud again, and when he did—

"Coming!" she breathed, hugging him tightly.

He watched, mouth agape, as her eyes squeezed shut until she looked like he was hurting her. But before he could panic, her face cleared and then morphed into that of an angel, the most beautiful smile spreading across her lips as she moaned long and low, her body trembling in his arms.

It seemed to last forever; it was over far too soon. He could have watched her orgasm every second for the rest of his life, and he immediately wanted to do it to her again, but before he could start stroking her once more, her eyes fluttered open.

"Shit," she said. She nibbled on her bottom lip, and then her hand was at his fly, popping the button and lowering his zipper. "I'm going to make you come so hard for that."

He moaned, his erection kicking at her words.

She shoved at his jeans, lowering them just enough for his penis to bob free between them. The head brushed against her soft, soft stomach, and James gritted his teeth and started reciting prime numbers in his head, barely avoiding ejaculating.

Her fingertips brushed along his arousal, and they were surprisingly cool against his hot skin. His hips involuntarily thrust, seeking a stroke from her hand as unimaginable pleasure flooded his entire system. She wrapped her hand around him and squeezed tightly, while, with her other hand, she hefted the sac between his legs.

A loud noise escaped him. "Bethany," he blubbered. *Begged.* "Stroke it. God, stroke me hard."

"Oh, shit," she breathed. Immediately, she moved her fist down his length and then just as quickly back, and stars lit behind his closed eyelids.

This is going to last no time at all.

"Want you to come with me," he muttered, trying his best to focus. He grabbed her knee as she continued to stroke him, his hips helplessly thrusting into her movements, and pushed her to her back with her legs spread wide. With a complete and unusual lack of patience, James tossed the blanket off them with such energy that it went flying off the bed.

And Bethany was laid bare to him from the waist down. He was able to recognize how delicate and beautiful she was—how the little light there was in the cabin gleamed off her slick, aroused skin—and then he was lost. Had to touch.

He went straight for the center of her, thrusting his middle finger inside and stroking along the tight passage there. Her hand tightened on his erection in response, and she tossed her head back and started moving it restlessly side to side.

"Oh, don't stop," she begged.

But she started stroking him faster, and he had no idea if he could get her to finish before he did.

"Never," he vowed. He'd touch her here as long as she'd let him, whether he'd already come or not.

An idea struck him, and while he thrust his finger inside her, he reached up with his thumb and brushed the bundle that had driven her crazy moments before.

And just like that, she shot off like a rocket. She cried out his name as her back bowed. Her nipples were hard and thrusting through her shirt; her hand tightened almost to the point of pain around his erection. And when her face went into angel mode, James lost himself.

His balls drew painfully up into his body and the most unbearable pressure climbed his shaft. He groaned in agony and pressed his face into her hair where it was spread over his pillow. Then—

Release.

The first, hot spurt of semen shot from him, wrenching a strangled moan from his chest. And then he shot again. And again.

And he kept coming until his voice grew hoarse, and he became aware that Bethany was holding him again, the slightest bite telling him her nails were digging into his back.

"So fucking hot," she was murmuring over and over into his hair as shudders wracked his body.

With one final spurt, all of the tension left his body, and he collapsed, bone weary, into her arms.

He'd made a mess out of Bethany, but ... *Can't move.* With a grunt, he finally pushed himself away and groped blindly over the side of the bed until he found his shirt. His cheeks heated as he used the flannel to wipe his orgasm from her stomach, but she sighed as he tended to her, and raised her fingers to brush through his hair. Finished, he pressed a quick but soft kiss to her soft belly, pulled her t-shirt down, and wrapped his arms around her to tug her sharply into the curve of his body, pressing her clothed chest into his naked one and her naked sex into his clothed one. He pulled the blankets over them and focused on getting his breathing and his heart rate back to normal.

"When can we do that again?" he was able to ask several minutes later. He squeezed her tightly.

A light laugh filled the night, just as he'd expected, but then Bethany's breathing hitched unusually.

With a flare of panic, he tried to pull back, to look at her face, but she shushed him. "Everything's okay," she said in so normal a voice that it actually convinced him he'd misheard that little hitch. "Just hold me until we go to sleep."

"I'll hold you forever," he mumbled into her hair.

"What?" Bethany asked.

"Good night, honey," he said a little louder this time. An endearment felt good. Natural. Not at all the awkward roll of syllables that he'd expected.

She sighed. "Good night, James."

• • •

In no time at all, his breathing evened out and grew heavy, and she knew he was asleep. She turned her head and looked at the ceiling of the cabin, her eyes stinging suspiciously.

That had been—

The best sexual encounter of my life?

Bethany winced, but, yes, James was the best lover she'd ever had, and they hadn't even officially become lovers. She'd made sure of that, blurting *no sex* like a perfect idiot because, hey! If they didn't actually have intercourse, she wasn't violating her hands-off rule.

But she'd violated it. She'd violated the ever-living hell out of it, and now she knew exactly what James sounded like as he came for her. What he looked like as he touched her, which just so happened to be an expression similar to "I'm the luckiest man alive."

And she'd ruined everything. Things would be different now. Even more stupidly, she wanted them to be different now. After one epic lay that wasn't even a lay. Like she was in high school and had just been fingered by the captain of the football team and started doodling his last name next to her first on all her notebooks.

She'd just orgasmed away all her professional understanding with James. Again.

She shifted her gaze from the ceiling to the corner where her pack lay. As though she had X-ray vision, she could see her sat phone where it lay at the top of her clothes inside. In her mind's eye, it glowed red hot.

She really shouldn't have called her boss. Dewinter hadn't taken the bait like Bethany had planned anyway. Instead of stepping up a rescue, she seemed to have given Dewinter more ammunition for keeping her on the mountain. With James. With the water system.

James shifted in his sleep. He pulled her close, and the tiniest smile lit his face. He sighed contentedly and drifted back into deep sleep.

And now, everything was at stake. How James thought of her. How Dewinter still seemed to think she would do exactly what she had done.

What James had done to her body clouded all her judgment, and now she was having asinine thoughts like, *is it so bad to flirt with him when I'm legitimately attracted to him? It's not flirting for professional reasons.* And *no one will really have to know anyway, right?*

Thoughts that not only went against all logic, but violated every code of integrity Bethany held dear.

And she couldn't really bring herself to care.

Fuck, she was so screwed.

Chapter Nineteen

As Bethany's closed eyelids started to glow an obnoxious shade of bright orange, she closed them even tighter, clinging to sleep with all her might. But she couldn't squeeze her eyes this tightly for long without causing her forehead to ache. With a sigh, she opened them.

And immediately hissed in a breath as a white-hot shard of morning sun seared her retinas.

"Balls," she muttered, throwing her arm over her head and flopping to her side. Her hand automatically smoothed over the sheets, headed to the other side of the bed. When her palm felt nothing but cool cotton, she woke up.

James.

Last night came rushing back in, and she closed her eyes again and groaned. "What did I do?" she asked herself in a whisper.

Immediately, her eyes shot open, and she scoured the inside of the cabin. Indeed, she was alone, and James hadn't heard her talking to herself. She blew out a breath.

She pressed her knees together and winced at the sticky feeling between her legs from her intense arousal last night. When she ran her hand across her stomach, she also discovered that James hadn't done the best job of cleaning her up with his bone-dry flannel shirt last night.

Ugh. She needed a shower. And about a gallon of coffee if she was going to face this day without losing her mind. God, she would kill for Starbucks.

Oh yeah. The water system had gone boom last night. No shower. No coffee unless she melted snow.

"Fucking wilderness." She threw back the covers and stomped from the bed, scooping up her underwear and jabbing her legs through them before pulling on her jeans. She scowled as she thudded her way over to the kitchen and scrounged around for something big enough to heat up enough snow for a sponge bath. When she found a big soup pot, she grunted in ill-tempered victory and made her way to the door, flinging it wide.

Bethany immediately found James. He was walking from the water shed toward the cabin, flipping his collar up to cover his neck. She froze, but her pot clanged against the doorframe, filling the morning air with a resounding gong.

James's head shot up, and the moment he saw her standing there, he beamed.

Bethany found it suddenly difficult to breathe.

"You're up!" He added speed to his gait and was in front of her in seconds. Without hesitation, he slid an arm around her waist and hauled her into his considerable chest. Her pot bounced against his thigh, but he ignored it, swooping down and pressing an ice-cold kiss to her lips.

When he pulled back, he was grinning again, but she was pinned in shock. *The morning after.* She'd never done one before. She and her partners had parted ways in the night: either he leaving her apartment or she leaving his.

James's grin slipped and then faded. "Uh," he said. "I'm allowed to kiss you, right?"

"Yep," Bethany answered. *Yep?* Damn James and his expressive angel face. She meant *no!* No kisses that made her cease to think.

His smile made a reappearance, but it was a ghost of its former self, as though he knew her *yep* hadn't been heartfelt. He swallowed and looked down. His brows drew together. "What's the pot for?" His tone was a little distant, but he still had his arm around her waist.

"Snow," she said. *Not a real sentence, Bethany!* She forced her thoughts away from how warm James's body was against hers. "To melt snow for a bath."

His gaze shot back to hers. "Oh, I already made you a bath."

Her lips parted. "What?"

"Melted some snow a bit ago, and it's nice and steamy hot in the old-fashioned tub." He jerked his head behind him toward the water building.

"Huh," she said brilliantly. Inside, however, everything within her was clanging as loudly as the pot had against the doorframe.

"And we'll get that shower up and running for you soon, so don't worry. Together, rebuilding the filter will go even faster."

We'll. Together.

She dropped the pot to the snow. With both hands, she grabbed fistfuls of James's shirt and jerked him forward. His mouth opened slightly, but before he could say anything, she was kissing him. *Dirty* kissing him.

She nibbled at his lips and sucked his tongue into her mouth where she flicked hers against it a few times.

James groaned harshly. He tightened his arm around her waist and threaded his other hand into her hair, then literally bent her backward like they were in some black-and-white movie, and kissed her until she was breathless.

Almost too quickly, it was over. James straightened them, pressed one final kiss to her lips, and pulled away. "If you don't hurry," he said, his voice and breathing ragged, "your bath will get cold." He dropped his hands and stepped to the side. "And we've got work to do."

Bethany pressed the back of her hand against one of her flushed cheeks. "O-okay," she stuttered, setting off toward the water building but not quite remembering why. Oh, yes. Bathing.

It wasn't until she closed the door to the water shed behind her and saw the steaming tub by the shower that she realized James had talked to her this morning. *Really* talked to her. The way he did at night or when he was discussing his work. And she'd kissed him again!

With a groan, she let her head fall back where it *thunked* against the door. Damn it, this situation had spiraled desperately out of her control.

James could return any moment, and if he came in while she was naked, much nastiness would ensue. She forced herself to put a hiatus on thought for a bit. She stripped and slid into the water, sighing as its warmth enveloped her.

James had set out her toiletries in a row within easy reach, and with a smile and a touch of warmth in her chest from his thoughtfulness, Bethany went through her bath as quickly as possible, even though she wanted to relax and enjoy it.

She was toweling off when the door creaked open. She held her towel in front of her body, but James only reached in and deposited her pack inside the doorway without even taking a peek. Maybe he knew he wouldn't behave any more than she would if he saw her naked.

"Brought your clothes," he called through the partially open door. "How do you take your coffee?"

"Oh, fuck me, you made coffee?"

It was quiet from the other side of the door for a moment. "I needed some extra energy today," he said finally. "Thought you might, too." Another pause. "Is that ... okay?"

His first hesitating question. She wanted to slap herself. She cleared her throat instead. James likely would make mountain-man coffee strong enough to make her grow testicles. "Lots of sugar, please," she called.

"Got it." He closed the door.

She waited until his footsteps faded before jetting across the building and grabbing her pack. When she opened it, her phone was still sitting directly on top of everything. Her gut lurched, and she shoved the phone down the side as far as it would go until she couldn't see it anymore. With a shaky hand, she spotted a clean change of clothes and began to pull them out. Before she did, however, she caught sight of a small bag she'd forgotten she'd packed.

She paused then held her breath as she pulled the coin-purse-sized pouch from her pack. Inside, she found the two condoms she always carried with her when she was going out of town.

Two condoms. Two times James could fuck her.

Shit, shit, shit. She really could have done without finding these right this second.

She shoved them down by the phone, grabbed her clothes, and while she dressed tried desperately to avoid thinking about the ways James's body would move and flex as he drove himself into her over and over and over …

She'd just finished dressing when the door opened, pulling her from her imaginings with a startled gasp and a rapid spread of heat across her cheeks. By the time she spun around, James was already walking toward her looking like sex on a stick. Or maybe that was just the two cups of coffee he carried that were getting her all hot and bothered.

Keep telling yourself that.

"Those both for me?" she asked, pasting a smile to her face.

He laughed. "Do you need both? There's plenty more in the cabin; I can just make myself another."

He held out a mug to her, eyebrows raised as he waited for her answer. He was seriously offering his coffee to her? She couldn't think of anyone she would offer her coffee to. "I'll get a second cup in a bit." She took the mug he offered and raised it to her lips, closing her eyes and inhaling its awesomeness. Just before she took a sip, her stomach growled violently.

She glanced up to find James slipping his hand into the pocket of his jacket. He pulled out a wrapped square and handed it to her.

Wary, Bethany accepted it. It was warm and soft in her hand, and when she opened the wrapping, two pieces of bread were inside. *Warm bread.* "Did you bake this?" she asked, raising her eyes to his.

He shrugged. "I had time."

She vaguely recalled the sight of a bowl with a towel over it sitting in the kitchen when she'd undergone her search for a snow-melting pot. He'd legitimately baked bread. Just how late had she slept anyway?

"I hope jam is okay," he said, jerking her attention back to his face. When she didn't say anything, he nodded toward the bread in her hand.

She glanced down and saw a thin line of something purple between the slices of bread. "Jam's perfect," she said, her voice sounding funny.

"Good." He clinked his mug against hers, making her jump. His eyes smiled at her over the rim of his coffee as he took a sip, then walked past her toward the water system where he promptly grabbed a few parts from the filter and sat on the ground.

A contented clanking ensued while he got right to work. Bethany, however, stood by the door, coffee in one hand, bread in the other, and stared at him like an idiot.

Who was this guy? How did one even make bread without perishables? James was like an even hotter version of freaking MacGyver, for God's sake.

She stared down into her coffee. *I think I like the morning after.* If this was what she'd been missing out on—a man catering to her needs before she even expressed them—then she wanted to go back in time for some do-overs.

Although, as she mentally cataloged her past lovers, there was no one she was even tempted to do a morning after with.

"Hey," James said.

She turned to find him still working away.

"I need my partner to start pulling her weight," he called over his shoulder.

That kicked her out of her little funk. She took a sip of her coffee, bracing for it to singe her nose hairs off, and was pleasantly surprised when it was the perfect strength. She walked over to James, taking a bite of the bread as she went.

As soon as it hit her tongue, she moaned.

James's head snapped up, his gaze landing on her with lascivious interest. One night together and she had him trained to her moans like Pavlov. She swallowed her bite with a smile.

"What is this?" she asked, holding the bread aloft and sitting next to him on the ground.

His gaze was narrowed in on her lips when he answered. "Just some Amish bread. Very easy."

She had a feeling he would term literally everything he tried to do as *very easy*. "Uh-huh," she said. She took another bite and closed her eyes in bliss as she chewed. When she opened them, James was still watching her, his eyes dilated.

Bethany swallowed. Unable to stop herself, she leaned forward, and gave him a quick peck on the lips. "Ready to pull my weight, sir," she said only a breath away from his mouth.

He grunted and seemed frozen on the spot. After a second, he blinked, and then his eyes seemed to focus. He blew out a breath and turned his attention back to the parts on the floor in front of him.

Sand was strewn all over the floor from when the filter had lost its guts in the explosion and ensuing fire. Half of James's filter had been a conventional gray-water filter consisting of bark and sand to separate waste. It was the second half of the filter that they were going to have to work so hard to replace. It consisted of a system of boiling water and then routing and collecting the steam until it recondensed and flowed—toxin-free—into another reservoir. All of the parts for that half of the filter, of course, had been custom made by James.

"Okay," she said, pausing to take another gulp of her caffeine. "I can easily re-create the sand filter. What do you need to be able to make some of your parts?"

"Hmm." He scanned the debris on the floor around them. She continued to eat her Amish bread and jam and added her eyes to the hunt. If they could find big enough pieces of scrap from the originals, they could work on creating smaller versions of the parts from that.

Her gaze lit upon a particularly promising piece of junk. She bent forward.

"Could you hand me that—" James started to say.

Bethany held the piece toward him, their eyes met, and they both smiled. *On the same page.* Nice. That was rare in a lab setting, even though no one would really term a rough building in the wilderness a *lab*.

He opened a toolbox next to him; even some of the tools seemed custom made.

She was going to have a sciencegasm at least twice today. She just knew it.

Throughout the morning, they collected the scraps they could: she for the sand filter, he for the steamer. It wasn't until her stomach growled again that she realized they'd been working solid for several hours.

"Lunch break," she said, setting down the broom she'd been using to sweep together the scattered sand—a water filter the only reason she'd ever pick up a broom. "You got peanut butter?"

James looked up from the gadget he was fiddling with. "And honey, as a matter of fact."

"Peanut butter and honey sandwiches it is." Bethany dusted off her hands and headed toward the door.

"Oh, you wanted them for a sandwich," he said.

Her lips parted, and she spun around to find him staring at her, his lips pressed tightly together and his eyes practically dancing. Was he—he'd just *teased* her?

Mental images of her drizzling honey all over James's body flashed through her mind. "Hmm. For now," she said. "We can repurpose them later."

The mirth vanished from his face in a heartbeat. His mouth opened, but before he could say anything, she waved her fingers at him and shut the door behind her. She had to bite her lip to keep from giggling. Giggling—which was not something she did. Ever.

My resolve is slipping. Right through her fingers. She really liked James. Personally and professionally. Why, again, was it so important she keep the two separate?

She made a few sandwiches, focusing on the menial task with more mental acuity than it actually required, then took them back to the water building where she set them down between them next to some bottles of water James had taken out of storage while she'd been out.

They started eating in companionable silence, side by side, their backs propped against the wall.

"God, that must have taken forever," she said, gesturing to the tanks with her sandwich. "All the piping you had to place. The digging. Actually inventing the thing." She took a bite of her sandwich. "How long have you been here?" she asked off-hand.

He took a swig of water. "Since I was six. So, plenty of time."

Her bite of food hit her stomach with the grace of a grand piano dropped from a crane. "Six?"

James's expression grew guarded. "It's not a big deal."

The hell it's not. "You grew up in the wilderness?" She was screeching. She could tell. Unfortunately, there didn't seem to be anything she could do to rectify that situation. The idea of a tiny, impressionable James being raised as a hermit made her chest ache.

He glanced down at his hands and screwed on the cap of his water bottle. "My dad didn't feel like he had a choice," he said softly. "I don't blame him for the decision, all things considered."

She was squeezing the honey out of her sandwich. *Calm down.* "What things considered?" she asked in a perfectly executed impression of a sane person.

"My mother's rape and death."

She paused with her sandwich halfway to her mouth. James simply looked at her, and her hand dropped back to her lap. "Oh, my God," she said. "James, that's terrible. I'm so sorry."

He ducked his head. "My dad loved her a lot." He took a deep breath. "After she ... killed herself ... my dad needed to leave." He paused. "I really think he only meant for us to be here a little while. But the years added up, and we never left." He shrugged.

"She killed herself?" Bethany asked in a whisper.

James nodded sharply. "Dad says ... said ... I was the one who found her."

Bethany sucked in a breath.

"I don't remember it." He jerked a shrug. "I don't remember her hardly at all."

That probably doesn't matter. Something like that—it left scars, whether people knew what caused them or not. She reached over and pulled one of his hands away from its death grip on his water bottle. She threaded their fingers together. "What do you remember about her?" she asked quietly.

"Hugs," he said immediately. He touched his nose absently. "She smelled like roses." He smiled. "She was beautiful, like all moms are."

"So, the important things," she said, squeezing his fingers.

"Yeah," he said, squeezing back. "I guess so."

Bethany pulled in a deep breath and held it. Was she really going to do this? She exhaled. "I lost my mama, too."

He made a sound deep in his throat and set his water bottle aside. He then pulled her hand into his lap where he cradled it between both of his, and he slouched a bit against the wall, as though he were settling in to let her talk as much as she wanted.

And she suddenly really wanted to talk about her mother, the person she hadn't told anyone about since—God, since high school at least. "I was eight. She was in the Peace Corps, which wasn't something my dad really understood, but he supported her wholeheartedly while she was alive. It wasn't until she'd died from malaria in Kenya that he started hating dangerous causes."

"Malaria?" James asked in an odd voice.

"I know," she said. "It's a vaccinated disease, but there had been a temperature glitch in transportation, and Mom's vaccine didn't end up working." She swallowed. "The water there was so bad, mosquitoes ran the place."

He stiffened, and out of the corner of her eye, she saw him glance at the water tanks next to them, obviously putting together two and two when it came to a few things.

"Dad was ..." Bethany drifted off then breathed a humorless laugh. "The rest of my childhood, all I heard was there were some risks not worth taking. But I had way too much of my mom in me, and that went in one ear and out the other. I think I actually thrive on being told not to do something. Like, automatic motivation overload."

She tipped her head back and stared at the ceiling. "Then I got into my career and the shouldn'ts I started to hear shifted away from danger and toward my gender."

"Your gender," James repeated as though the words couldn't mean what he thought they meant.

"Women shouldn't be scientists. Women shouldn't be in the lab. Hell," she said, tossing her free hand into the air, "even a Nobel laureate said women only caused trouble in the lab. Crying and making male scientists fall in love with them."

"A Nobel laureate said that?"

"A biochemist," she said negligently. "So, obviously not that great of one." If someone was making gross, stereotypical judgments of an entire population when he knew as part of his studies that those judgments were not scientific, then fuck 'im.

James snorted, and after a second, Bethany actually cracked a smile. "Anyway, I am doubly motivated to do something badass in my field." She gestured to the debris around them.

James hummed, and then they were both quiet for a bit. She'd just started eating her sandwich again when he asked, "You remember your mom?"

She nodded. "A lot."

"That must be nice."

She shrugged. It was intimidating, not exactly *nice*. "My mom ... was like a superhero," she said softly, looking down her stretched-out legs to her boots. "It's hard to live up to. I guess. But when I finally do this"—she gestured to the water filter in parts around them—"I'll have made a difference. Lived up to her."

"Who says you have to live up to her?"

Me. "It's my dream," she said in a small voice. *And I will achieve it. No matter what the cost.* Even if the cost was any sort of fling with this gorgeous, brown-eyed man who held her hand while she told painful secrets. Who worked with her like she was an equal.

She pulled her hand from his and finished the last bite of her sandwich, not quite able to meet his gaze, which she felt burning a hole in her cheek. She needed some distance. Needed to remind herself of what was important. If it was a choice between saving lives or her potential happiness with a man, it was no question what would win. But for the first time in her life, she thought, *And doesn't that just suck ass.*

• • •

James loved talking to Bethany; too bad she had been strangely quiet throughout the rest of the afternoon. And not the I'm-focused-on-my-work kind of quiet James was used to. This had been more along the shut-up-and-don't-get-closer-to-James type of quiet. He was impatiently waiting for her to break the silence, dying to talk to her more about her dream. When she'd confided to him her desire to go around the world, bringing people clean water, it had ... resonated with him. If he had Bethany's courage, he'd want to do that, too. Go help people in a way that only he could.

Ludicrous, of course. He couldn't even leave his cabin.

A little bit ago, James had retrieved the rabbits he'd snared right before the blizzard, and thanks to the far-below-freezing temperature up here, they were still good. He was attempting to clean them, which wasn't going as smoothly as he'd hoped given their frozen state. He was making slow progress as Bethany put the finishing touches on the sand filter.

They would both finish about the same time, it looked like. The rabbits and the sand filter, at least. Not the steamer. That would take a couple of weeks.

Which, if she continued to give him the silent treatment, would be a very long time.

Bethany sighed and leaned back with her hands on the floor behind her, scrutinizing her work.

It was an amazing job; in fact, her sand filter looked a lot better than his had in the original. He'd always cared more about the steamer since that had required more ingenuity. Bethany apparently put effort into everything she did, even the menial stuff, which in his opinion, put her a cut above him.

If only he could just open his mouth and tell her that right now, but he wasn't sure what his reception would be, and he wasn't so delusional that he didn't realize his ego was a little delicate around her right now. Their little bare-the-soul session earlier had left him vulnerable, and it was a feeling he wasn't a fan of.

Bethany shot to her feet with surprising speed. "Well, I'm ready to turn in," she said. "You?"

His eyes widened. She was talking. *Say something, James. Say something!* "Uh ... yep. Uh-huh."

Brilliant.

He got to his feet and leaned down to gather his rabbits, taking the opportunity to roll his eyes at himself. When he was upright again, Bethany was already walking to the door.

James slung the rabbits over his shoulder and followed her, thinking up and just as rapidly discarding potential conversation starters that could get them past this awkward hump.

They walked through the snow quietly until she gasped about halfway to the cabin.

His head shot up, and he found Bethany frozen solid, staring at something off to his left. A spot on the back of his neck tingled, and he turned to see what she was looking at.

Bear.

Like a shot, James was in front of Bethany. He wrapped his left arm behind him and around her and held her in place. He strained his eyes as hard as he could at the animal, which was standing on its hind legs and observing them with great interest.

"Black bear," he murmured to himself. An adolescent even. It was a fantastic stroke of luck that meant they may not be dying tonight.

Just then, the bear flopped back to all fours and started walking toward them, becoming clearer and clearer as it closed the distance.

He shoved Bethany back. "Get to the cabin," he ordered.

"What? I'm not running away and leaving you!"

"You're not leaving me, and definitely don't run," he whispered urgently, the bear getting closer. If it took off, it could capture Bethany as she made her way to the cabin if she didn't start moving now. "Walk slowly. Don't turn your back. Get a pot. Something to make noise."

She still hesitated.

"*Right now*, honey. Please."

Something in his voice must have convinced her, because she actually followed his pleas. She pulled away from him and started backing toward the cabin slowly. He watched her avidly with his peripheral vision, keeping tabs on the bear at the same time.

The bear's head cocked to the side, and it was obvious its attention was on the moving target.

Shit. Not taking the time to think, James thrust his arms into the air, fingers splayed. "Hey!" he shouted at the bear.

Success. The bear turned its head, paused midstride, and then began walking toward him.

"What are you doing?" Bethany hissed. She was only a few feet from the cabin door.

She's almost there. Almost safe. He ignored her question, waiting for the moment Bethany ...

She opened the door. *Safe enough.*

The bear was closer now. One hundred feet and counting. James reached for the rabbits over his shoulder and, rearing back, launched them with all of his strength. They made it pretty far, and the bear arrived at them quickly.

It stopped, sniffed them, then raised its head and stared at James.

Take them and go. Just take them and go.

The bear tossed its head and belted out a roar toward James. Snow flew up in arcs in the bear's wake as it charged, and adrenaline coursed through James's system.

"James!" Bethany screamed.

He dimly heard several crashes in the cabin as he widened his stance, waved his arms, and bellowed at the bear. The bear kept coming. Twenty feet and counting.

Damn it! In a last-ditch effort, hands still raised and waving, he sprinted toward the animal, yelling at it all the way.

The bear hesitated now. Then stopped. Took a step back.

James kept running, and when he was only a couple of feet away, the bear jerked to its hind legs and roared warily.

James covered his head with his arms and ducked, just missing the swiped paw that had been aimed for his skull and nape. He plowed into the bear's chest with his shoulder, the impact nearly knocking him breathless and getting him almost nothing in return: the bear swayed but didn't even step backward.

James snapped his arm back, made a fist, and brought it down, hammer style, on the bridge of the bear's nose.

Now the bear stepped back. Its eyes darted. James had managed to cow it. "Get back!" he shouted in the bear's face, raising his arms again and lunging at it.

It obeyed but was still eyeing James. It hadn't given up the challenge yet.

Suddenly, from behind them, a terrible, loud clanging ensued. The bear flinched and, with one final, long look, turned and jogged back toward where it'd come from, pausing to grab the string of rabbits in its jaws before taking off completely.

When the bear disappeared, James's knees wobbled. "No. Please no," he muttered. He didn't think he could bear to fall to his knees as his adrenaline ebbed away. Not with Bethany watching. By some miracle, he was able to stay upright through sheer force of will.

He sucked in several breaths, eventually getting them to slow, and when he could walk without hitting the snow, he turned and headed back to the cabin.

Bethany stood on the open doorway, the soup pot in one hand, a metal ladle in the other. As he got closer, he could see that her face was ghost white, but other than that, she looked more solid than he did.

He stopped right in front of her, his arms itching to wrap around her body. "Thanks for the assist," he said, his voice only trembling a little.

She stared at him, lips parted and eyes wide, for several seconds. Then she stepped to the side, making room for James to enter the cabin.

He ducked inside and closed the door behind him. "I can't believe he took my rabbits." That's what he decided to say? *Well, that was asinine.*

"You fought a bear," Bethany said in an odd voice.

He turned toward her. "That's a ... generous description."

"Why are there so many bears on this mountain?" She blinked. "You fought a bear," she said again.

He narrowed his eyes and did another quick sweep of her body. Her hands clenched the pot and ladle until they were bleach white, and her shoulders were trembling. "All right, honey," he said gently. Stepping toward her, he reached out and took hold of her noisemakers. "Let me just take these, okay?"

She stared at her pot and ladle as though she didn't know why she was holding them. She pried her fingers apart one by one, and James took the items back to the kitchen, leaving them on the countertop.

When he stood in front of her again, her trembling had increased so that he was sure her teeth were clacking together by now. "Let's get you warm," he mumbled.

She nodded—or her trembling was worse, he wasn't sure—and allowed him to lead her over to the sofa where he helped her ease down onto the cushions. Once she was safe there, he rushed over to the fireplace.

He added logs, fumbling them as he went, but when he tried to strike the flint, he had his own trembling problem to contend with. The need to get Bethany warm was able to eclipse whatever adrenaline drain was currently ravaging his body, and after only a few tries, he was able to get the logs to flame.

Not trusting his knees to hold him any longer, he shuffled over to Bethany on all fours. Thank God it was only a few feet and wouldn't look *that* weird. It didn't matter anyway. She wasn't looking at him but was staring blankly at the wall.

A lock on his brain creaked open, and the full import of what had just happened flooded his system.

A bear attack.

God, so many things could have gone differently. Gone wrong. His gaze roved Bethany's face, and he scooted forward until his chest was pressed into her knees. His mathematical brain calculated all the variables.

If it had been a grizzly instead of a black bear. If Bethany had stayed behind him instead of going inside to get the pot. If the bear hadn't been intimidated by James's weak, human blows. If he hadn't had the rabbits to offer it a distraction.

He reached out, his hand wobbling, and cupped Bethany's cheek. She jerked as though zapped, and her gaze flicked to his. "I'm so thankful you're okay," he breathed.

Her eyes were wide, her breaths ragged.

She didn't hear me. And that was okay. All things considered, he was feeling some pretty intense reactions to almost losing this woman, and if she heard the sentiment he wanted to blather, it could be a real embarrassment once this all wore off—

Bethany suddenly sucked in a hard breath that sounded like a cry, and then she launched from the couch. Her entire body hit his chest with such force, James's breath *oof*ed out of him. She sent them flying backward, his shoulders taking the brunt of the impact, and his head—luckily—missing the hearth by a matter of inches.

His mouth flopped open as his body tried desperately to pull in air.

Bethany was scrambling over his body, everywhere at once. It took her a matter of heartbeats to straddle his hips with her thighs, planting her knees on the floor. She stretched out on top of him belly to belly, and he'd just regained the ability to breathe— gasping—when she thrust her hands into his hair and crushed her mouth against his.

His eyes widened, and he blinked several times in a row, but her tongue was insistent in his mouth, pressing and retreating desperately, harsh little moans streaming from Bethany's taut-as-a-string body.

It took all of five seconds for the heat to take James over, too.

With a harsh groan, he threw his arms around her. He flipped them so quickly, he would have been dizzy if his eyes hadn't been open.

Her back hit the floor, and he thrust his hips between her thighs. As his erection ground against her, she broke from the kiss, crying out.

Oh, no. None of that. He cupped her cheek roughly and turned her back into his kiss. She could make her noises into his mouth, but he couldn't bear to be not kissing her right now. He moaned as he thrust his tongue past her lips and, at the same time, thrust himself against her.

Her nails scraped down his back, biting into his flesh even through his shirt, and she scrambled beneath him, spreading her knees even wider and canting her hips until—

He must have moved right against her clitoris, because she bit down on his tongue while keening into his kiss. The bite was hard enough to bring stinging tears to his eyes, but he couldn't care less.

Her hands moved from his back to his ass, and she gripped him. She tilted her hips up and ground her pelvis against him frantically.

Both their breaths billowed loudly in the quiet amid the cracklings of the fire.

It felt so good. It all felt so amazing.

We could have died.

Planting his hands beside her head, he raised up on straightened arms to get more leverage for his thrusts. It forced their kiss to end, but the new angle was so good, he was distracted as intense pleasure that made his eyes roll back poured through him.

As he thrust against her faster and faster, Bethany reached up and fisted her hands into his shirt. "James," she cried, her head moving back and forth against the rug. "*James!*"

He tilted his head back and squeezed his eyes shut. The way she said his name—

His climax came so swiftly, there was no way for him to pull back before it was too late. With a shout to the ceiling, he started ejaculating in his jeans, his thrusts rough and short between her thighs.

As his orgasm started to fade and he could blink down at Bethany during his waning thrusts, it became apparent that, by some miracle of the universe, he'd managed to make her come, too.

Her eyes were tightly closed, but that angelic expression she'd given him last time when his fingers had pulled an orgasm from her—that expression graced her face, and James shuddered as it pulled an extra shot of semen from him.

He groaned, stilling against her.

They both panted, staring at each other with wide eyes. His cheeks heated as he tried desperately to figure out how long he had lasted. Because he was pretty sure it had been less than two minutes, and that was horrifying.

"I'm ... I'm sorry ... I—"

She shook her head, cutting him off. "No, don't talk."

He frowned down at her. He guessed he deserved that, but it stung a bit. She wasn't quite looking him in the eye anymore, and while his breathing was starting to slow, hers still sped along. Perhaps even quickened.

She gritted her teeth, and her breaths whistled through them. Her cheeks reddened.

"Are you all—"

"*Don't talk*," she begged, her voice catching. "Don't—"

She sucked in a wobbly breath, and as she blew it out, a tear slipped from the corner of her right eye, tracking down her temple and into her hair.

I'm going to be sick. It was the only thought he was capable of as he stared in dread at the trail left behind by Bethany's tear.

He'd done something—hurt her, taken advantage of her—that much was clear. And now she was crying.

He looked frantically around, the possibility of him losing his lunch very real.

"You ... could have ... *died*," she said, causing him to snap his gaze back to her. She was wailing by the final word, and a torrent of tears streamed from both eyes. "We could ... h-have died!" By this point, she was sobbing so hard, he had trouble understanding her words.

Wait. He hadn't done anything wrong? He peered at her through wide eyes. He wasn't 100 percent confident, but these tears might not be because of what they'd just done.

"You fought a bear!" she cried.

Not totally because of me, then. "Okay, honey," he murmured, propping himself on his elbows and framing her face with his hands. He brushed her tears away with his thumbs, but they just kept coming. "It's okay now."

"I *h-hate crying*!" She hiccupped. "I never cry. What the f-fuck is this?" Her sobs kicked up a notch, and James bit his bottom lip hard to keep from smiling.

It was true—she wasn't a crier. If anyone was remotely weepy in nature, what Bethany had gone through lately—that first bear attack, waking up naked and injured with a stranger, being snowed in by a blizzard—would merit tears. "I know you don't cry," he whispered, continuing to use what he hoped was a soothing murmur. "It's just adrenaline, honey."

"Fuck adrenaline!"

Oh, God, the pressure of the laugh that wanted to escape was going to cause his lungs to rupture. Surely.

She met his gaze with her tear-logged one, and her brows drew together. "I didn't want to see you die," she confessed in a small voice.

The desire to laugh vanished, but the pressure remained. Grew sharper. "Bethany," he whispered. "I didn't want me to die, either. Not just when I'd—"

Found you. It'd been on the tip of his tongue, and he'd caught it just in time, thank God.

But the way Bethany's gaze shifted, she'd heard it anyway. A look of panic flashed across her eyes, and James thought she would shove him away. He was certain his heart wouldn't be able to take her rejection. But, then her aqua eyes softened in a sort of resigned acceptance. "I think I like you," she whispered, almost horrified. "A lot."

A punch to the gut wouldn't have stolen his breath as quickly. Her words traveled from his brain straight to his chest and then even faster to his groin. "That's good," he managed to say in a choked voice. Because he was an idiot: He was falling in love with her. After a handful of days. He knew normal men didn't do anything so unadvised, and the fact that she liked him a lot made his tenuous position out there on the ledge in Idiot Land a lot less dangerous. For him.

And, honestly, her position on the ledge wasn't dangerous for her either. Because he was crazy about her. There was no woman in the world more secure in liking a man than Bethany was in liking him. He suspected he'd follow her to the ends of the earth if she gave him the chance.

"That's *really* good," he amended.

But her eyes flooded with tears again, and she widened them and blinked rapidly. A tear escaped anyway, and she wrinkled her nose. "So many ... feelings."

Tell me about it.

"It'll be okay," he murmured. He could make sure it was okay for her. "I'd never hurt you, Bethany." He'd die first.

She relaxed beneath him. "I know," she whispered.

But her eyes still looked haunted, and she broke from his gaze, peering over to the left.

Want her eyes back on me. He was also dying to taste her lips. "That would do it," he muttered.

Like he'd planned, his cryptic words brought her gaze back to his. Whatever she must have seen in his eyes made her part her lips, and he dipped his head.

She made a noise that was part whimper, part groan, and then she lifted her head and met him halfway.

Her kiss was salty, and the further evidence of her tears tore him up inside. He pulled back from her lips only enough to say, "Shh," and then he was back, slipping his tongue into her mouth and stirring it languidly, putting all the tenderness he was feeling for her into this mating of mouths.

She opened wider for him and clutched at his shoulders, moaning around his tongue, and, God, her moans ... he wanted more of them.

Her hips were making restless circles against his. She wanted him again. The knowledge rocked him, and he stiffened in a rush. With a soft groan, he moved with her, thrusting against the spot that had quickly taken her to orgasm, along with him, a few minutes earlier.

Immediately, he froze. *God, just how hard* did *I grind against her?* The simple movement had sent a sting zipping along his length.

He had carpet burn—or jean burn. On his penis.

His eyes widened, and he pulled from the kiss so sharply, it was just a hair away from being a jerk.

Had he hurt her? Did she sting like he did?

Bethany raised her brows in silent question. *I'm killing the mood.*

Okay, so, grinding probably shouldn't be an option. But what about ... He had to bite back a grin at the surge of excitement.

He allowed himself a soft smile that was just a fraction of what he was feeling inside, and then he pressed a kiss to her lips. As soon as he did, she parted for him again—so responsively—but he had a different place in mind for his mouth.

He nipped her bottom lip and then moved down a bit, nibbling on her chin and kissing his way down her neck.

She threw her head back and moaned to the ceiling when he licked over the place where her pulse threaded in a racing rhythm, and he memorized the spot. He would return here later. And often.

He kissed down her chest until he reached the top button of her shirt, and though he'd been planning to simply continue down her stomach to get to his prize, he paused as he caught a glimpse of her shadowy cleavage.

Bethany had extraordinary breasts. Those tawny tips that stiffened so enticingly. Their perfect size. His mouth watered at the idea of tasting her there, and he couldn't resist a small detour in his plan.

Pressing an open-mouthed kiss over the hollow of her throat, he worked at her buttons with one hand while keeping himself from crushing her with the other.

With a sigh, she threaded her fingers through his hair and held him against her as he languidly licked his way down her breastbone. He finished with her buttons, and he spread her shirt wide.

The sight of her body hit him with the grace of an anvil, just as it had the other times he'd glimpsed it. But this time, the overwhelming rush of lust and adrenaline was accompanied by something different and new. He felt possessive of what he was gazing at. Felt that it belonged to him. And that possession triggered a surge of pride.

Mine.

The finest, most beautiful woman in the world lay spread out before him, and she allowed him to do delicious things to her. He was the luckiest man alive.

Her bra was lacy and wickedly small. And he could see through the pattern of the lace that her sweet nipples were already hard and straining against the fabric.

His erection leapt within the hot confines of his pants, and he planted both hands on the floor at her waist and leaned down. He nuzzled the valley between her breasts first, breathing in her scent, his eyes closing in bliss.

"James," she breathed. Her hands were in his hair again, tugging. Trying to move him over to her left breast.

He was successfully tempting her. Teasing her. Driving her crazy. And it felt incredible.

Following her lead, he moved over her left breast and opened his lips over her lace-clad nipple, pressing his tongue against the stiff flesh and sucking.

A startled cry erupted from her, and he jumped, his heartbeat kicking even faster. Sure he'd done something wrong—something she didn't like—he stiffened and tried to pull away, an apology already rising to his lips.

But her fingers clenched in his hair, and she wrenched him closer, arching her breast against his mouth and whimpering plaintively.

She likes.

James groaned and sucked her nipple into his mouth once more, the rasp of lace against his tongue boiling his blood.

Despite how much he loved the texture, he quickly became desperate to taste her skin. With one shaky hand, he eased beneath Bethany's back, his fumbling fingers searching for the clasp of her bra.

How did the men in novels unhook this contraption so easily? After an appalling amount of time, during which he tried desperately to keep Bethany distracted from his lack of prowess by sucking her nipple until she keened, he was finally successful: the bra unhooked, loosening around her ribs.

He kissed his way back to center, bracing himself better with his knees so he could reach for her shoulders with both hands, snag the elastic there, and begin to draw it down.

He didn't get very far. The bra straps met resistance, and his passion-hazed mind took several long seconds to inform him that he'd forgotten to remove her shirt first.

He must have tensed, because Bethany was suddenly there, murmuring, "It's okay," into his ear while shifting beneath him and tugging off her shirt. "Take yours off, too, baby."

He obeyed, his gaze never leaving her body as, with another tug, her bra joined her shirt on the floor. She was panting so hard, her breasts heaved beneath his gaze, and longing punched his gut while her nipples tightened even further.

She reached up, cupping a breast in each of her hands and brushing a thumb over each nipple. "Come and taste," she rasped in a whisky voice.

James's lips parted. Out of a fantasy. He could not be luckier. Forcing himself to ease down upon her once more instead of flopping like he was bellying up to a trough like a pig, he rested his hips between her thighs, planted his hands on the floor, and leaned down to take what she offered.

Deferring to the right breast this time, he closed his lips around her nipple and flicked his tongue twice along the peak.

She hissed in a breath. "Shit."

He barely heard her. *Skin as sweet as honey.* With a harsh groan, he lowered himself even more, his bare stomach meeting her naked belly. He sucked her nipple harder, his hips reflexively thrusting.

That same, searing sting wrenched a gasp from him, and he remembered—he was supposed to be sucking and kissing elsewhere.

Torn, he allowed himself to linger a few moments more, but then with a light nibble that made her fist his hair, he began kissing downward, taking time to press his lips and tongue against every rib along the way.

By the time he'd reached the end of her ribcage, it must have become obvious what he was planning, because Bethany's panting breaths hitched, momentarily ceased, and then kicked back faster than ever.

Her tight hold on his hair shifted slightly, and she began pushing him toward his destination. The next time he pressed a kiss to her skin, this time right above her navel, his lips were curled.

God, she was amazing.

He kissed lower.

Lower.

• • •

What the hell am I doing?

Bethany's hands flew from his hair to fumble with the button and zipper of her jeans.

Stop this right now!

His full lips brushed her fingertips as she struggled with the jeans that would ... not ... cooperate. His blunt fingers tangled with hers, and as the sound of her zipper going down rent the air, she raised her hips for him.

They both shoved and pulled at her pants, getting them down her thighs until she could kick them away. They went flying somewhere off toward the corner. Kneeling between her spread thighs, James's gaze clapped on the apex of her thighs, his lips parting.

Her gaze dipped just in time to see his erection kick behind the front of his jeans, but then it roved slowly and reverently up from there. Her eyes found each and every dip of his stomach, the ridges upon ridges of muscle that carved his abdomen into a work of art. Following the dip up the middle of his abs, her gaze landed on the massive pads of his chest. On his tight, dark nipples.

How could he be so beautiful? She made an embarrassing noise deep in her throat.

James's head snapped up, his heat-filled gaze meeting hers. His throat bobbed beneath a swallow. "You match." Reaching out a hand that trembled, he dragged one finger over the lace covering her hip as he nodded toward her discarded bra beside them. "I like it," he said reverently, his gaze dipping to her panties once more. "A lot."

She swallowed a moan, rolling her hips into his touch as his finger traveled along the sensitive skin where her leg met her torso.

Baby, I'll show you matching. At home, she had a drawer full of lingerie that would blow his mind. *Imagine his face when he sees—*

Whoa. Just ... whoa.

At home? What the fuck was she thinking? She wasn't. She was crashing with adrenaline. Stupid from yet another deadly situation. She was better than this. He deserved better than this. She pushed up on her elbows, her mouth open, and a *stop* perched on the tip of her tongue.

But, James's face as he continued to touch her ... His eyes were alight, brows drawn. He licked his top lip as his fingertips deviated from the bend of her leg to the lace covering her opening, and her stomach clenched. The light drag of his fingers traveled upward, over her clitoris, and her head nearly fell back. Locking the muscles of her neck, she watched as his fingers continued to travel up and over her pubic bone. They curled around the waistband of her panties. He flicked his gaze to hers, licked his lips again, and raised an eyebrow.

Now her head did fall back. She swallowed down the *yes* she was desperate to mutter.

I resolved not to do this very thing only hours ago!

She couldn't do this. She wouldn't do this. James was a colleague. Thanks to her rash phone call earlier, everyone at Delaney now knew that.

But they won't know what I do here.

Slowly, she raised her head. When she looked at James's face again, his expression was unchanged. His chest, however, billowed with barely contained, frantic breaths. He wanted her with a passion she'd never had the privilege of being the focus of.

I want him just as badly.

Oh, God. She was slipping. Because, it was true: Everyone she worked with wouldn't know what she and James had done on this mountain. But they'd suspect. They'd suspect no matter what she did. If she kept her hands to herself, they'd just know she'd lifted tail.

What she did, or for that matter didn't do, made no difference at all.

Her breath whooshed out of her along with the very last shred of her resolve.

She met his gaze again. Slowly, she nodded.

His grin was sudden and devastating. Her belly ached with renewed arousal as, with both hands, he dragged her lace panties over her hips and down her thighs. He bent down, his abdomen rippling in the firelight, and pressed a kiss to her upraised knee as he wadded her panties in one large hand. He rubbed the soft lace between his thumb and fingers for one quick moment before dropping them to the floor. Looking up at her, he pressed another kiss to the inside of her knee, then just above it on the inside of her thigh.

She couldn't look away; his gaze held hers captive. Her breaths felt shallow as she tried to swallow them down. To clear her head.

James's doorframe crushing shoulders began to push her knees wider apart as he continued to kiss his way toward the center of her body. His hands planted on the floorboards and made the muscles of his arms, shoulders, and back ripple.

She was helpless not to touch him.

Skating her palms over every part of him she could reach—his clavicle, his neck, and finally his shoulder blades—she leaned back, relishing the flicker of his muscles beneath her fingertips as he shoved her legs as far apart as they could go. As he pinned her wide open as a butterfly on a display board, his fingers brushed along her sex again. In the next instant, he was filling her with them, sliding first one, and then two fingers deep into her body.

Her eyes nearly rolled back in her head, but she forced them open. Forced them to stay locked with his. His eyes flickered with intent, and when he broke their connection, looking down at where his fingers played, she was momentarily adrift.

She swallowed quickly, her fingers curling into the pads of muscle stretching across his upper back, but without even a pause, his head dipped.

His lips parted, and the tip of his tongue darted out, barely flicking against her clitoris before he drew it back into his mouth and closed his eyes.

She held her breath, every muscle in her body tensing. *Would he like it?* Some men didn't—she'd found most of them herself in her dating life.

He swallowed harshly, his brow furrowing.

"Baby," she whispered. She stroked his back. "It's okay. You don't have to—"

With a groan, he lunged for her. His next lick was with the flat of his tongue, and the sound he made deep in his throat as he gave her a desperate third lick vibrated through her body.

"Oh, God." She fell back on her elbows again, but her head snapped upright immediately, her gaze searching him out once more. She watched as the tip of his tongue made an appearance at the very top of her sex before it dove down again.

He began to thrust his fingers in time with his licks, and though she fought to keep herself upright, to keep her sight on him, she lost the battle.

Her back met the floor, and her hips rolled into his next thrust as she clenched her eyes closed against the rush of pleasure. *How did he know to do that?* "James." She moaned, her fingers searching for his hair and then weaving into it.

Another thrust. Another lick. Her fingers tightened; she had to be pulling his hair, but he groaned harshly and licked her with even more enthusiasm.

"Oh, fuck." She arched her back. "God ... James. I'm going to—" It was too fast. Felt too good. What was he doing to her?

Instead of the lick she was anticipating—needing—he parted his lips over her clitoris and sucked.

God damn! Her ears seemed to clog as she lost her mind, undulating against his mouth. Her head arched back and her mouth fell open around a cry that had to be shaking the rafters. As she started to come down, she found herself yanking James's mouth against her in time to the frantic movements of her hips, using the grip she had on his hair.

"Shit," she moaned, forcing her fingers to loosen. "Shit, sorry," she babbled incoherently, raising her head and cupping his cheeks with her hands instead.

His gaze was focused on her, his mouth still locked on her clitoris. His fingers lazily thrust in and out of her as her hips began to slow.

With one last shudder, she went completely boneless. Her thighs hit the planks with a *slap*, and she struggled to catch her breath, blinking up at the ceiling.

Can you die from orgasm? Had anyone conducted an experiment on that yet? Because things were a bit iffy right now. Her heart was about to crash right out of her chest. She placed one open palm over it, willing the beat to slow.

James crawled up her body, and she tilted her head to the side, unable to lift it, but wanting to see him move. She was not disappointed. His shoulders rolled as he lowered himself until they were chest to chest, but he kept most of his weight off her and on his elbows.

Framing her face with his hands, he brushed a light kiss across her lips.

She could taste herself on him.

Against all medical odds, her hips rolled into his.

He gazed down at her, smiled lazily, and gave her another small kiss.

"Your turn?" she asked, her lips brushing against his as they moved.

His gaze darted away from hers, and he jerked his head in an approximation of a *no*.

She frowned. "You don't want me to—?"

He cleared his throat. "I ... already ..."

She widened her eyes. *Again?* Something warm tingled in her chest. How a man could be as sexy as James while being equal parts adorable had to be impossible.

Her arms somehow found the strength to wrap around him. She pressed his face into the crook of her neck, sighing with unmitigated pleasure when he sagged against her, as sated as she was. "Probably a good thing," she murmured. "I'm having trouble moving."

A warm, rumbling chuckle reverberated through his back and into her palms as she stroked lazily up his spine. "I'll put you in our bed." With a groan, he pushed away from her, scooping her into his arms before he'd even gained his feet.

He definitely had no trouble moving. She nuzzled her cheek into his impressive chest as he carried her across the cabin.

But then his words hit her. *Our bed.* Before she could stiffen and tip off James that something was wrong, she sagged intentionally into his hold.

He laid her between the sheets as carefully as though she were hot glass a second away from shattering, then crawled in right behind her. Her mind ran riot over those two words as he kissed her shoulder, wrapped his arm around her waist, and drew her back into his body.

Within seconds, he was asleep, his deep, even breathing wafting over her skin with each of his exhalations.

She closed her eyes, but sleep was the last thing on her mind. She had very few regrets in life. None when it came to men.

But what she'd done earlier on the phone with Dewinter ...

Bethany had barely gotten the words out that Eugene Anderson had passed away, but James Anderson, his son, had continued to improve upon the water system. Dewinter had nearly bowled her over with questions about details.

Her stomach uneasy about the direction the questions had taken, Bethany had lied and said James hadn't revealed anything pertinent to her.

Which had led Dewinter to stick to her story that it was too dangerous for a rescue yet. Maybe even for longer than Dewinter had originally predicted.

Trifling bitch.

But that wasn't what Bethany was upset about now. Telling Dewinter about James hadn't felt like a betrayal at the time, fresh from discovering he planned to hoard his work from a needy world. Besides, she hadn't told Dewinter anything about the water system. Certainly not that she had memorized the complete plans and could replicate them in her sleep.

But now? After his change of heart? After thinking he was going to die and then finding the most life she'd lived in his arms? Beneath his mouth?

Bethany wasn't sure, but she thought that, perhaps ...

I made a mistake. Maybe one she couldn't forgive herself for.

Chapter Twenty

Bethany watched James's back flex beneath his shirt, absently rubbing the tip of her pointer finger back and forth along her bottom lip.

Damn, but that man can move.

Today, they would be able to run a test on the water. It was possibly the most exciting day of her career, if not her life, and yet she couldn't drag her gaze away from the wide expanse of James's shoulders long enough to pay attention to anything else.

In the days and nights since the bear attack, Bethany had felt those muscles move beneath her fingers in myriad ways. Had come to recognize when he was close to orgasm by the way his breath sounded in her ear, hitching right before he started to come.

Her lips curved beneath her fingers. She had indeed returned the favor he'd given to her, going down on him for the first time the very next morning. He was insatiable for her mouth on him, begging for it at least once every day.

She was helpless against that begging, her lips now in a constant state of swollen bruising.

She'd put off actual intercourse, unable to stop thinking about her maybe betrayal, but each time they were together, she wanted him even more. They were going to finish their work today, and she knew she wouldn't be able to stop herself from having him— really having him—for the first time.

The wrench James held in his hands slipped off a bolt with a screech and a thud, and he cast her a sheepish look over his shoulder. She bit into her bottom lip and let her gaze rove over him until his cheeks flushed and he turned back to the pump with a clearing of his throat.

He could feel it, too. All day, he'd been making little mistakes that proved his mind was occupied elsewhere. They were both strung so tightly, despite the daily orgasms, as they'd gotten closer and closer to actual sex without crossing the line.

He tossed the wrench aside, leaning back on his hips and swiping a burly forearm across his forehead. He looked at her again, his eyes flaring as he quickly perused her entire body.

She could have him out of those clothes in two seconds. She'd done it before. With him strung just as tightly as she was, he would be inside her before she could even say his name.

She took two steps back. "I'm going to make lunch!" she blurted.

James's heated perusal of her body stopped. He frowned. "Okay."

She groped for the doorknob behind her. "Yeah," she said. Her fingers closed on the knob. She wrenched and pushed back with her ass. Immediately, the cold winter air shot through her clothes, dotting her skin with goose bumps. "Be right back."

With that, she fled.

I can't do this. Not yet. That phone call she'd made stood between them, more stalwart than a fifty-foot fence.

James just didn't know it existed yet.

She frowned as she leaned over the counter in the kitchen. *Do I want that wall gone?* Nothing between her and James? She couldn't be serious. That sounded ... dangerous.

No, she didn't want the wall gone. She just wanted honesty between them.

Rolling her shoulders, she reached for a loaf of James's bread.

She couldn't do something like take James's virginity with this secret between them. She'd never been somebody's first. She swallowed around a tight throat.

I couldn't stand for him to regret it. She was going to tell him.

Like all the other times you had the opportunity to tell him, and you didn't? There'd been dozens of opportunities. She'd let each pass.

"You really are a heartless bitch, you know that?" she muttered.

"Uh ..."

With a gasp, Bethany turned around, her butter knife clattering into the sink.

James stood in the open doorway. "Did you just call yourself that?" he asked.

Her cheeks stung, and she didn't answer. It was obvious that's what she'd done anyway.

He frowned. "I don't think I like that."

She forced a laugh. "That I talk to myself?"

A small shake of his head. "That you're mean to yourself."

Her heartbeat skipped and then picked up again faster than ever. *No, don't say stuff like that to me.* "What if I deserve it?" she asked in a whisper.

"What was that?" he asked, stepping toward her.

She whirled around, grabbed the two sandwiches, and said, "Lunch is ready!" in an overly enthusiastic voice.

When she turned around again, she nearly plowed into James's chest. He touched her upper arms with light fingertips before wrapping his hands around her shoulders, brushing his thumbs across her clavicle. "You make me so happy," he muttered. "Have I told you that today?"

He'd actually told her some variation of that each day this week. The back of her throat tasted bitter. "James—"

Tell him. Maybe he'll think it's no big deal.

"Yes, honey?" he asked, his gaze traveling over the swoop of her hair.

Now was the perfect time.

The moment passed.

He tucked a strand of hair behind her ear. "Do you want water with your lunch?" he asked.

It took a moment for her to catch up. Not boiled snow. Water. Their water system. "It's done?"

"Just tightened up the last bolt."

Excitement edged out all of the self-loathing for a few blessed moments. She thrust a peanut butter sandwich at him, grabbed his free hand, and turned to the door. "Come on!"

She could have sworn he chuckled a time or two as she hauled ass through the snow to the water shed.

It took a few seconds for her eyes to start adjusting to the dimness, but she knew from memory where she'd set up the testing equipment earlier today. Dropping James's hand, she headed there, blinking her eyes desperately.

Taking one bite of her sandwich, she snagged a beaker and joined James at the water system.

"Do you want to do the honors?" he asked with a smile.

He didn't have to ask her twice. She took another huge bite and shoved her sandwich at him.

Her fingers easily flipped through the valves, releasing the water they'd loaded in the reservoir this morning. She knotted her fingers together as the filter kicked on, and after only a minute or so, James said, "I think there should be enough for a test now."

Bethany twisted a knob on the second tank and held her beaker beneath the small outlet pipe.

Clear, clean water trickled into the container. It took all of her strength not to break into a happy dance.

"Looks promising," he said.

She nodded. When she had enough for the many tests she had to run to deem the water safe enough for drinking, she turned off the valve, grabbed her sandwich from James, and tromped back over to her testing table.

She quickly got lost in the comforting hubbub of lab work, her mind occupied with movements big and small that were as ingrained in her as breathing.

She barely noticed as the light started to wane, and James eventually brought her boiled snow to wash down her sandwich.

After she finished the final test, calculating her results, she came back to awareness as though rising from a fog.

She blinked her eyes several times to find James sitting at the end of the table, watching her raptly.

"Done?" he asked, his voice husky.

That brought her a moment's pause. Did he like watching her work as much as she liked watching him?

Nice. "Done," she said softly, tightening her lips against the emotional reaction already rising within her chest.

He got to his feet. "And?"

She looked at her latest equation one more time to double-check. "It's safe," she said, raising her gaze to his. "Cleaner, actually, than water from most kitchen taps."

With a whoop, he wrapped his arms around her, swinging her around in a circle before planting her back on her feet and laying an enthusiastic—if short—kiss on her lips. When he broke off, she smiled up at him.

"Ready for a taste test?"

4Dream man.

She shook her head to clear it.

Moments later, James was returning, a mug in each hand. He handed her one, his eyes twinkling. "Bottoms up, honey."

With a soft clink of their mugs, James lifted his to his lips and took a huge, noisy gulp.

Now that was confidence.

She took a sip of her own, her fingers tightening on the mug. She'd done the tests correctly but that didn't mean it would taste good ...

They locked eyes at the same time, and slowly, matching grins spread across their lips.

"It's perfect," she said.

"Yes, it is."

There was something in the way he said the words that directed Bethany's attention away from the cup she held to focus solely on James.

He set his mug down on her table, reached forward, and took hers as well. Their hands free, James twined their fingers together and gave her a gentle pull, bringing her chest against his ribs. "Nice work, partner," he said in a rumble that traveled from his heart to hers.

She swallowed hard. "Th-thanks," she stuttered. "You, too."

"I could get used to working with you."

Oh, God, I could get used to everything *with you.* She wanted to recoil from the words—draw back and guard herself—but they'd already wormed their way into her, forging a new, deep path as sure as a raging river.

"Bethany," he said, leaning down.

He said her name like a question—as though he were going to ask her something. She waited for him to continue, but he didn't speak again. At least, he didn't speak with words.

He breathed out slowly, and then he fitted his lips over hers.

Longing unfurled in her belly, and she opened to him.

With another of those deep exhalations, he swept his tongue over hers. Letting go of one of her hands, he cupped her cheek so tenderly she knew she would remember it forever. Their other hands still bound, he moved her arm backward, keeping their fingers locked as he wound their joined arms behind her back, using their fists to push against the dip just above her buttocks and bring their hips flush together. She splayed her free hand over his heart, measuring each solid *thud* in an almost covetous manner.

He hardened against her, and his erection against her belly made her go a little weak in the knees.

"Let me make love to you," he murmured into the kiss.

And there it was: the point of no return. The one she'd been craving and avoiding since that first encounter. And the truth was, there was no way she was going to say no. She wanted it too badly.

And she'd tell him. Before things went too far, she would tell him.

"Please," she whispered.

His fingers tightened in a rush around hers, and just as quickly, he released her hand. Pressing a kiss into her hair, he swooped her up, cradling her against his chest.

She sucked in a breath of surprise, and next she knew, he was carrying her to the cabin so quickly, he bordered on running.

Her mind blanked. Thought fled as the feel of his body around hers overwhelmed her. His heartbeat was quick and excited against her ribs, and she wrapped her arms around his neck, kissing his cheek once. Twice.

He stumble-stepped as she kissed him a third time, and she was smiling against his cheek as he wrestled the door open while holding her.

Once inside the cabin, James kicked the door closed behind them. They were at the bed before the resounding *boom* had faded into silence.

Her back met the mattress. He pulled away from her, and she made a disappointed sound, but he was kneeling between her legs, unbuttoning his shirt with near frantic fingers.

He's wanted this as badly as you have.

His shirt went flying. When his hands moved to his belt, his pecs flexed in ways that made her mouth go dry.

Things are about to go too far.

"Hold on, baby," she said, putting her hands over his.

His head snapped up, his eyes questioning.

Her mouth dried out. Words were impossible.

Not yet. I can't do it yet.

"Be right back," she said, swinging her legs out from around him and getting to the floor. "Hold my spot."

She toed off her boots, leaving them where she stepped, and hurried over to her pack. She riffled through the contents until she located the little pack of condoms she'd hidden, though out of sight, out of mind had definitely not worked in this case.

She pulled out the condoms, discarding the little pouch back into her pack, and then she spun around, ready to walk back to the bed.

No more delaying. She had to tell him everything.

She made it only two steps before she froze in her tracks.

James was spread out on the quilt like a buffet of sexy man. His arms were bent behind his head, elbows wide, and the effect on his wide chest was breathtaking. The big pads of muscle flickered beneath his skin, putting on a display that made her mouth drop. His torso narrowed, the small spattering of hair on his chest condensing into a thin line that crawled down the center of his abs, the muscles flexed tightly to help him hold his partially upright position against the pillows. Below his bellybutton, that trail darkened and thickened slightly until it disappeared behind his unbuttoned, but still zipped, fly.

That track of hair made her gut clench in need.

She couldn't bear to ruin this.

Okay, no sex. The condoms burned in her palm in protest. *No!* Not until she could tell him. Be honest with him. She'd have to distract him. Distract them both the same way she had over the past days to avoid going all the way.

Get him so hot we both lose our minds. Forget the plan had been sex at all.

She squeezed her knees together as heat swept through her, and she nearly flooded her panties.

His eyes lighting with internal fire, he held out his hand, fingers curled upward. "Come here, honey," he said, his voice a husky rumble.

That was a command she could get behind. She started a slow saunter in his direction, shedding her shirt as she did so. His gaze zeroed in on the bra that she knew was his favorite.

James was nothing if he wasn't a breast man.

He licked along his bottom lip, his gaze rapt, as she walked his way. Fisting the condoms that would go unused with one hand, Bethany flicked open the button of her jeans with the other and unzipped her pants.

His gaze traveled slowly downward, obviously reluctant to leave her breasts, so as she walked, she shimmied out of her jeans as sensuously as possible to reward him.

When his breath hitched and he unconsciously palmed his erection through his jeans with his right hand, she added a little spring to her step.

Like magic, his gaze shot to her breasts again. With a moan, he canted his hips and opened his arms to her. "Faster, honey."

She was at his side in an instant, clad only in her bra and panties. She slid into his arms as though coming home. Their hearts aligned; her hips were cradled between his spread thighs, and she could feel the blood pumping through the insistent erection pressing into her belly.

He wrapped one arm around her waist, bringing their bodies flush. "What's this?" he asked, uncurling her hand with his.

The firelight glinted off the foil packets as Bethany ceded them to him. He frowned down at them for a couple of seconds; then realization lit in his eyes followed closely by frustrated consternation and then relief. "I'm lucky," he said simply. "Hadn't even thought of this. Thanks for being prepared."

James tucked the condoms under the pillow he reclined on.

Where they'll stay.

Her gaze flickered over the way his muscles flexed as he wrapped his arm around her. He slid them down until he was flat on his back. Then he grabbed her by her hips and lifted, hooking her thighs with his knees. With a lift and a spread, she came down straddling him, his dick pressed right against her clit. It was a remarkably smooth move for a virgin, and she was momentarily struck dumb.

When his big hands covered her ass, a cheek in each palm, one hand started to knead her ass, but the other skated up her belly, causing her to suck in a breath. His fingers on her ribs drew goose bumps over her body in their wake, and when he cupped her breast, squeezing it in time with her ass, Bethany arched her back and moaned.

The motion rocked her clit over his erection, and after only minutes in James's bed, she was right at the edge of orgasm.

He chuckled, leaning up to lick the hollow of her throat. "Not so fast," he murmured.

"No," she whispered plaintively as his firm hand on her ass kept her from rocking atop him. *Just one more time. That's all it would take.* They'd both be too far gone to think of waiting to explode for even one more second.

He kissed up her neck, across her cheek, and to her ear. "How badly do you need it?" he asked, his voice wicked and low.

"Bad," she moaned.

He squeezed with both hands again. "We can get this one out of the way, don't you think?" He nibbled on her earlobe.

"Please." She sagged against him. She'd done it.

Now enjoy him. She may never get the chance to again.

With a soft kiss below her ear, James released his hold on her bottom, shifting his fingers to curl over her hip, more than giving her permission to writhe on him until she came.

Oh, thank God. Digging her fingers into his biceps, she rocked once.

She sucked in a breath as sensations zinged through her entire body.

He made a noise akin to a growl against her neck. "Do it, honey," he commanded, his fingers flexing on her hip and breast.

She rocked again ...

And teetered over the edge. "James," she breathed, unable to keep control of her hips as they ruthlessly ground against him while pulses lit through her empty vagina, clenching against nothing when they desperately wanted to be clenching against his dick.

A slight tremor wracked his upper body, and he groaned along with her moans while he held her through the waves of her orgasm.

When the pleasure ebbed, Bethany stilled and buried her face in the pillow beneath James's head. Heat streaked her cheeks. That had been embarrassingly quick. *I mean, I'm not one to look the multiple-orgasm gift horse in the mouth, but ...* It'd be nice to get five minutes into a sexual encounter with this guy and not blow the top of her head off.

He abruptly rolled them, settling between her thighs and gazing down at her face with an expression nothing short of adoration. "The sounds you make," he said roughly. He shook his head, almost in disbelief. "So sexy, I can't breathe."

She was caged beneath him, and she took full advantage of the position, palming his pecs and running her hands lovingly over the bulging muscles.

His head dropped down, hanging from his shoulders low enough that some of his hair brushed over the tops of her breasts, eliciting another spike in her desire, even right on the heels of the sweetest release.

"Don't ever stop touching me," he implored, rocking his hips gently against her.

"I promise," she whispered, skating her hands down his pecs, his abs. When her fingers stopped at his unbuttoned fly, he pushed himself farther back, giving her room to maneuver.

She unzipped his pants and began pushing them down his hips, biting her lip as his erection sprang free, falling heavily to her belly.

With a hiss, he stirred his hips, dragging the sensitive skin of his cock against her.

She was growing desperate again. Already. That first orgasm hadn't been nearly enough, as it never was.

He pushed himself away, ogling her breasts as he finished the job of removing his pants, tossing them over his shoulder and to the floor.

She held her arms open to him, as he had to her minutes before, but before he accepted the invitation, he reached down and divested her of her bra and then panties, so much more practiced now than he had been the first time he'd tried—a memory that still make her chest tighten.

He fisted her lacy underwear in one hand and dropped it gently over the side of the bed. Then, as he always did, he took a moment to sweep his gaze over her entire body. He never seemed to get enough of her, a feeling as familiar to Bethany as her own hungry gaze poring over James.

He knelt between her spread thighs like a virile god: fully and proudly aroused, every muscle on display. The firelight licked over his chiseled face—his incredible good looks still enough to make her sigh every time she looked at him.

When her gaze made it to his eyes, she found him already staring back at hers. "I never thought I'd get—"

He stopped. Swallowed hard enough for her to see.

Never thought he'd be with a woman. A swell of her own emotion crowded her throat, making her swallow just as hard as he had.

Oh, God. She was slipping. "Come here, James," she whispered, her words thick. She'd wrap her mouth around him. She could still salvage this—

He gave a partial shake of his head, as though he were too distracted to refuse fully. His gaze dipped to her breasts for a moment before he visibly forced it back to her eyes. "Have to say something first."

The earnestness in his expression made her wary. She licked suddenly dry lips. "Okay."

"Bethany," he began. He reached down and stroked a hand over her hip, then frowned and glared at his hand as though it had disobeyed him. He gripped his thighs and leaned down, making sure their gazes were locked. "I wouldn't do this with anyone unless it was real," he said solemnly.

Her lungs ceased their function. A burning started up around her heart.

"Hell." He shoved a hand through his hair. "That's not what I meant to say," he said, frowning. He took a big breath. "I love you." The frown disappeared, a light tipping of his lips taking its place: He'd said it the way he'd planned, apparently. And he liked it.

The corners of her eyes started stinging, and James's form wavered a bit as tears edged along her bottom lids.

"That was it," he said, shrugging with one shoulder. "I wanted to make sure you knew, before—"

She nodded. She could tell by the way he parted his lips and took a breath that there was more. Not that he was going to ask for her to say it back—his expression and posture held no expectation. He wanted to say more. Open his heart to her.

She would never survive it. Her resolve would never survive it.

"James," she whispered huskily, playing a little dirty by spreading her knees even more.

His erection kicked between his legs, and his lips parted.

"I need you," she said, not too ashamed to beg. "Please."

This time, the distracted shake of his head was affirmative. She held her arms out again, but he ignored them. Instead, he slid backward, laying on his belly and guiding her thighs over his shoulders.

She shuddered out a sigh. That had been so close.

He wrapped his arms around her hips, sprawling one huge hand over her belly. The other he wound around tighter, traveling over her pubic bone, his fingers spreading her wide.

He made a sharp noise deep in his chest. "Already so wet," he whispered. Then he leaned down and licked her, long and hard. His tongue flashed at the top of her sex before he closed his lips, swallowed, and gazed up at her.

Shit. Goner.

As though he could see her falling even harder for him, he smiled softly, and—keeping their gazes locked—began undulating his tongue over her clitoris.

With a gasp, she arched beneath him. She cried out his name and threaded her fingers through his hair tightly.

He groaned and scooted in closer, his wide shoulders spreading her thighs even more. As he licked faster, she felt two fingers probe her entrance before slipping inside as far as he could get them.

"*Oh, God.*" Her fingers tightened. Her back bowed. She was going to do it again: come minutes after he started touching her.

"Come on, love," he murmured against her slick flesh before giving her a slow, deliberate lick.

Detonation. Her eyes flashed wide as she started to tremble, her thighs clenching tightly around his ears as she ground herself against his face. She cried his name over and over as waves of pleasure crashed through her.

When it grew to be too much—when even the softness of his tongue sent jolts throughout her body, she pushed fretfully at his head and fell to her side.

Glancing up at her with hooded eyes, he dashed his forearm across his lips, and then he prowled toward her on his hands and knees, his shoulder muscles rolling, with promise written all over his face.

He caged her in, arms on each side of her shoulders, legs braced wide and keeping her legs spread far apart. "We need one of those condoms," he rasped. "Now."

She was still shaking after her orgasm, and the blatant sex in his husky voice set her limbs trembling even more. With unsure fingers, she groped beneath the pillow until she found one of the packets. Like an idiot, she extended it toward him.

No!

He looked at it for a moment; then his gaze flicked back to hers, unapologetic but slightly abashed. "Put it on me, honey."

She nearly closed her eyes. *Virgin.* The word repeated several times in her mind, echoing off in the distance until it faded.

What are you doing, Bethany? This—James's virginity—was not something either of them could take back. Undoubtedly, he would wish to once he knew what she'd done.

She hesitated, condom clutched tightly in her palm. "James ... in the morning ..." She broke off. He raised his eyebrows.

Yes, where am I going with this?

She swallowed. "In the morning, we have to talk."

What? That's not good enough.

No, I'm not good enough. Not to withstand this.

What I did isn't that bad. He'd brush this off. He had to.

His brow relaxed. His eyes softened. "Yes, we do." He cupped her cheek with one hand.

She turned her face into it and nuzzled his palm.

"Please, Bethany," he said softly, his voice shaking. "I want you so badly, I—" He broke off, gazing down at her with an imploring look.

I'm going to hell. She tore the packet open. When she fitted the condom over the crown of his cock, it jerked, slipping out of the latex.

She glanced up at him. His teeth were gritted, his struggle to gain control of his body visible. She grew impossibly slicker between the folds of her sex. Her muscles clenched, desperate to have his body inside of hers.

She glanced down at the condom only long enough to place it correctly again, and then she watched his face as she rolled it down his length. His eyes widened slightly, and he bit into his bottom lip as his breaths quickened.

Once she was done, his gaze searched hers, seeming to find a hint of the turmoil she was struggling with.

Shifting his weight to one arm, he reached up with the other, cupping her cheek and stroking his thumb along her bottom lip. As always happened when he did this, her lips parted.

"Don't forget," he rasped.

I love you. The words were as clear as they would have been had he spoken them aloud. This time, an overwhelming sense of luck—that she had such a man as James feel so strongly for her—pervaded her chest.

She pressed her hand over his and stroked the back of his thumb with her own. Turning into his hand, she kissed his palm softly, closing her eyes for only a moment before looking back up at him.

His gaze was intent as he lowered his hips. The head of his erection found her clit and then slid downward, nestling right against her entrance.

She sucked in a breath, holding herself still with all her strength when everything within her called out for her to cant her hips slightly—the small movement that would bring him inside of her.

The hand he held against her cheek trembled, and with one last piercing glance, James looked down at their bodies, his expression focused and intense.

With the smallest flex of his hips, he breached her entrance. He drew a quick, shuddering breath and blew it out slowly as he continued his thrust, filling her with exquisite deliberateness until his pubic bone ground against hers.

Seated to the hilt.

He blinked down at their joined bodies, then raised his gaze to hers. His face was rapturous.

She needed to speak to him. Make sure he was ... "Okay?" she managed to ask.

He didn't answer for a moment. Finally: "It's so ... tight." He stirred his hips, making a small circle against her. The movement ground his body so perfectly against her clit, and her eyes nearly rolled back in her head. She bit back a moan, but it escaped anyway.

Unease flickered across his expressive eyes. "I'm hurting you?"

She shook her head.

"You're just so small," he whispered. "I didn't know ..."

"I promise it doesn't hurt," she bit out, allowing herself the small pleasure of putting a hand on each of his hips.

He lowered his arms, lying atop her and balancing his weight on his elbows. The hand cupping her cheek shifted, fingers weaving through her hair. His gaze skittered back and forth as he looked at first one eye and then another. "So hot," he whispered. "Like a forge."

He moved his hips again, this time withdrawing a bit and then pushing back home before circling and grinding against her clit.

Her eyes closed, and this time, her moan was filled with complete abandon.

"Oh, Bethany," he murmured, his voice impossibly deep. "I like this."

"Me too," she whispered back, her eyes still closed.

He thrust again, and—how in the world did he know to grind against her clit each time he moved? Men who'd had many lovers still hadn't figured that one out. "James," she said breathlessly. Her hands shifted, moving to his glorious ass.

This time when he thrust into her, she felt his muscles flex against her palms, and she curled her fingers, digging her nails into them on pure instinct.

He groaned sharply, withdrew, and thrust into her with more power. The bed rocked with a creak, and Bethany tipped her head back and cried out as pleasure wound through her like a tight coil. "Don't stop that," she begged, her words so distorted by lust as to be almost unrecognizable.

But James understood them. He pressed hot lips to her throat and did it again, groaning as she gasped.

She raised her knees, surrendering her grasp on his ass as she wrapped her legs around his lower back and locked her ankles, her heels digging into those flexing muscles.

The move sent him even deeper inside of her, and he buried his face in her hair and gripped her ribs almost too tightly as he shuddered over her. "So deep," he groaned, withdrawing his hips to deliver another jolting thrust.

With that, she grabbed handfuls of his hair—half cradling his head against her neck, half holding on for dear life as she barreled toward orgasm. "Faster," she begged. "You have to ... go ... *faster.*"

He muttered her name and obeyed.

The bed cried out in rhythmic protest as James fucked her hard and fast. Her cries grew sharper, turning to near sobs, as his heart thundered against her breasts and his breaths billowed over her neck.

He covered her breast with one palm, kneading her flesh as he kissed up her neck. In her ear he panted, "I'm not ... going to last." A shuddering breath.

"Bethany."

The headboard banged against the cabin wall as he thrust with even more power, and she crashed over the edge.

She crushed James to her, hugging him as tightly as she could. Her back arched, and she screamed as wave after wave of white-hot pleasure seared her straight through to her heart.

He muttered words she couldn't comprehend into her ear, and then he stiffened in her arms. He moaned brokenly, his hand flexing on her breast, and with one final thrust that was much softer than the others, every muscle in his body went lax, and he collapsed atop her.

As she fought to regain her breath, she held him just as tightly, not wanting him to get up and move away. His tongue fluttered over her racing pulse as he licked his lips, and then he blew out a shuddering breath.

Pushing himself up on his elbows, he forced himself to take his weight off her, the effort of such a move visible in his expression as he met her gaze. Since he gave no indication he would be pulling out yet and getting off her, Bethany loosened her hold a bit, skating her open palms over his shoulders and down his biceps. Leaning up, she pressed a soft kiss to his lips. When she pulled back, he was smiling softly.

He shifted to his side, his semihard penis slipping out of her in the process. She took a moment to mourn its loss, but James quickly tucked her into his chest, folding her within his arms. She listened to his heart as it continued to race.

James was not necessarily a shout-to-the-rafters lover—though in a couple of her best moments, she had gotten him to do so. But he'd always been very vocal—almost chattier in bed than he was out of it.

"You were so ... *quiet*," she whispered. Had something gone wrong and she hadn't picked up on it?

There was a rumble in James's chest. "I ... had to be," he said, his voice a mixture of amused and slightly embarrassed. "All those equations I was doing in my head required focus."

"Equations?"

"Don't ask me to tell you which ones. I don't remember."

She pulled back to glance up at him. "You were doing math?"

"Considering I almost came from you putting a condom on me," he said, "you bet your gorgeous fanny I was doing math."

He squeezed her and grinned. "It's the only reason I lasted longer than a minute."

Something panged in her chest. "You didn't … enjoy it?"

James frowned down at her. "Is that what I said?"

She frowned back. "Isn't it?"

He shook his head. "You're underestimating the sexual thrill I get from mathematics."

She tilted her head to the side and stared at him from the corner of her narrowed eyes.

His lips twitched. A chuckle rumbled in his chest.

She smacked his arm. "Don't say shit like that yet!" Against her will, she found herself giggling. "You've gotta wait at least a few more months before joking about your sexual proclivities."

His chuckle faded.

Shit. She'd spoken about the future. As though it were a foregone conclusion. It was the first time either of them had done such a thing.

James cleared his throat. "A few months, huh?" He shrugged casually—too casually. "I can manage that."

Her gaze skated away from his; she wasn't quite up to the intensity of his expression at this moment. "I think I'm sad that you didn't let loose," she said, bringing their topic back to what, for her at least, was safe: sex. "I was expecting spontaneous orgasm after initial penetration."

A strained laugh. "You almost got it."

She yawned. "Promises, promises," she said, nestling into his chest. "We're scientists, remember. I'm going to require proof."

He squeezed her tightly. "I'll see what I can do about that in the morning."

She murmured against his warm skin, his scent filling her senses and bringing her closer to sleep. He sighed into her hair and stroked a palm up and down her back.

Just before she slipped into slumber, he whispered, "I love you, Bethany."

Her eyes popped open, and she fought with all her control to keep herself from stiffening and letting him know she hadn't fallen asleep yet. After a moment, though, she didn't have to fight to relax. His warm embrace, his love for her, the amazing sex they'd just had—

In the morning, she would be telling him everything. When they both laughed at how circumstances had brought them together, and all of those things—his love, the sex, their partnership—continued ...

Would it be so bad?

Chapter Twenty-One

James hadn't been able to sleep from the surfeit of excitement that had flooded him, no matter how tired he'd been from a hard day's work and a night in bed with his first lover.

His demanding lover. She certainly had no qualms about telling him what she wanted from him.

Harder. Faster.

His dick distended against her soft belly as he remembered her whispered, desperate orders.

She worried he hadn't enjoyed their first time together? He'd been overwhelmed, every touch and new sensation clamoring for attention. Sure, he'd been quiet. He'd been focused: wanting to commit every moment to memory. Wanting to make sure he made it good for her.

He wouldn't lie, though. Her invitation to let loose held appeal. A lot of it.

What had started off as a semi-erection now went full-fledged. His cock pressed against her, and she was so damn soft, he groaned, pressing his lips against her hair. He'd been stroking her back since she fell asleep, but now he indulgently allowed his hand to travel farther. His palm cupped one luscious cheek of her bottom, and he gave her a squeeze.

In her sleep, she sighed softly. She shifted, turning into him so that she was almost lying on her stomach, and he leaned back, propping himself on his elbow so he could stare down at her.

She wanted to talk in the morning? Well, so did he.

Ask her to stay here with me. The moment he had the thought, it felt right. Waking up next to her for the rest of his life? His heart thudded quicker.

She was so beautiful. Her arms were curled beneath her, and her face was turned to the side, her nose inches away from brushing along his chest. Her lips parted around her deep breaths, and every time she exhaled, warm air washed over his nipple—a caress she didn't even realize she was delivering. Her hair flowed out behind her on the pillow, and dim light from the moon streamed through the window and washed over it and her gloriously naked back.

He would do it. He'd ask her to stay. She'd be all his.

Hand still on her bottom, he used his forearm to nudge the covers down until he could see what he held: gorgeous curves that made his mouth water. He gave another possessive squeeze, and in response, she spread her legs.

His gaze shot up to her face; she was still sleeping. Responding to him instinctually. His erection jerked. It was dim in the cabin, but there was enough light for him to see the curve of her buttocks wind down to the place cloaked in shadow between her legs.

With a barely suppressed groan, James moved his hand. His fingers caressed down one curve, down the inside of one thigh, upward until ...

Wet heaven.

He sucked in a breath as she coated his fingertips, so aroused in her sleep that she was dripping with it. Holding that breath, he explored farther, tracing the seam of her opening and then finding her clitoris swollen with need. He brushed it with his ring finger.

She woke with an arch of her back. "James?" she asked in a voice laden with sleep. She peered up at him, blinking those gorgeous eyes and lush lashes.

He froze. "Yeah, honey?" he asked in a rough whisper, not at all close to pulling off the casual air he'd tried to effect.

"Mmm." She arched again, moving her sex against his fingers, causing him to lose all his air in a noisy rush. "It's morning," she said. "I'm sure of it."

As though she'd plucked the words from his very head. But her voice was still sleepy; she nestled her cheek against the sheets. She needed her rest. "It's the middle of the night."

A siren's smile spread her lips. "It's morning somewhere." And then she splayed her hands next to her shoulders, bent her knees, and lifted her ass in the air, pressing her sex into his hand.

While most parts of him froze in the face of such blatant invitation, his heart raced quicker than could be healthy, leaving him a little lightheaded as seemingly every drop of blood in his body rushed to one location. He groaned, cupping her fully.

Heat poured over his palm as more of her arousal filled his hand. He crooked two of his fingers, pinching her clit between them, and she gasped loudly. Had he hurt her? Before he could chastise himself over the idiocy of pinching a woman's most sensitive flesh, she moaned long and low and begged, "Again," in a throaty voice.

Moving quickly, almost scrambling, James shoved to his knees awkwardly as he managed to successfully keep his hand full of her. With his new height beside her, a shadow from the light behind him fell across her body, blocking his view of the sweet spot between her legs.

Not acceptable. He shuffled around, rubbing her clit gently while doing so. When his knees bumped into hers, she spread hers wider, making room for him to kneel between her thighs.

He rewarded her with another small pinch, and then settled into his place. When he looked away from what his hand was doing long enough to glance down at her body, his lungs seized.

She is ... From this angle ...

His thoughts were riotous, and he couldn't catch one long enough to examine it. If he'd ever read about a woman in this position before, he'd shrugged past it, finding it as stimulating as could be expected from such descriptions but not life-changing in any way.

Now, he knew the appeal. Bethany's long, sleek back caught and held the moonlight in the dip of her arched spine. Her fingers clutched at the sheets by her breasts, and her sweet, plump lips were parted around her shallow breaths as she stared up at him heatedly from the corner of her eyes.

But her gorgeous ass—that was high in the air, perfect and round and begging for his hands. Helpless to resist that pull, James momentarily abandoned her weeping sex. With reverence, his palms moved to hover, one over each firm globe, until he allowed himself to lower them slowly—so slowly—until he could squeeze.

She gasped, and his eyes nearly rolled back into his head at how good she felt to him. When he squeezed again, watching how his fingers plied her generous curves, she groaned and rolled her back, arching for him even more.

If she didn't stop, he was going to show her that abandon she had asked for in the morning without a second thought.

He leaned down, wanting to press a kiss to the delicate curve of her shoulder blade, but as he did so, her bottom pressed into his hips, and his erection nestled in the sweet dip of her opening.

They both froze, he with his lips inches away from the skin he'd set out to kiss. After a moment, Bethany rocked her bottom against him, wetting the tip of his cock with her arousal.

An animal sound rumbled in his chest, almost a snarl, and he abandoned his hold on her ass to keep himself from falling on her desperately. With arms locked and fingers splayed over hers, he muttered incoherent pleadings, only barely managing to keep himself from thrusting into that welcoming heat.

As he pressed reckless kisses down her spine, she slid one of her hands out from beneath his. He licked one shoulder and then nipped at her nape as she reached under the pillow and emerged with their other condom.

"Yes," he breathed, so excited she wanted him inside her he could barely stand it. She held it up for him, and he snatched it from her fingers in a way that would probably make him wince when he wasn't in the throes, but all he cared about in that moment was that he would be with her again.

He tore the packet open, tossing it God only knew where as he shoved upright and jerked his hips back enough to roll the latex down his length. Then he was back, pressed against her entrance, hands atop hers once more.

He wove his fingers through hers and brushed his lips over her shoulder. "Kiss me, honey," he whispered roughly.

She raised her head and met his mouth with hers, sucking on his top lip until he went wild from it. Squeezing her fingers, he pushed forward with his hips. She gasped as he filled her, and he thrust his tongue into her mouth as he seated himself as deeply as he could go.

And—dear, God—was it deep. Deeper than he could ever have imagined two people could be joined.

His heart rocked within his chest. He released one of her hands so he could wrap his arm around her belly. Reaching up, he palmed one of her breasts, making her moan and arch.

He instinctually thrust into that arch, and they both sucked in a breath.

Abandon, it is. Hardly able to control himself, James bucked his hips. Back, forth; back, forth.

"Yes, James," she breathed, joining him in his bruising rhythm.

In the next second, she was pushing up, kneeling between his spread thighs and pressing her bottom into his lap. Reaching up and behind, she wrapped her arms around the back of his neck. Her pert breasts thrust toward the ceiling, and the sight of her and the feel of her ass against his groin—

He was undone.

His lips crashed to hers, his tongue thrusting inside. His arm wound up between her breasts and he clenched her jaw—none too gently—to keep her still for his claiming. With his other hand, he gripped her hip, and then he *thrust*.

She bounced, over and over, in his lap, her breath catching and then releasing each time he shoved into her as far as he could go.

His eyes open, he drank her in—everything he could see stimulating him to the point he was a razor's edge away from coming. Her breasts bounced with his thrusts. Her eyelashes fanned over her cheeks. Her hand skated down her belly. Dove between her legs.

His eyes widened, and he broke from the kiss to ask, "You touch yourself?"

The delicate bones in her hand worked as she stroked her sweet sex. "Yes," she moaned.

He abandoned his hold on her hip. Swatting her hand aside, he pressed his fingers against her clitoris and rubbed a hard, tight circle. "My job," he grated.

"Oh, God," she sobbed, winding her hands around his neck again, her fingers delving into his hair. She writhed in his lap. "James—" She took a shuddering breath. "I'm going to—" She cried out.

"Me too," he moaned desperately. His seed climbed his shaft, his balls tightening in pain. "Bethany—"

She threw her head back against his shoulder and screamed his name to the rafters. Her clitoris pulsed against his fingers, and in a wet rush, she came around him.

"Done," he groaned. Biting into her shoulder, he shook violently as he started to come, lash after lash of semen filling his condom as she bucked in his hold, chanting his name over and over as he joined her in the most intense pleasure he could have ever imagined.

She collapsed against him, sagging in his arms with a sob. Finally able to gentle his hold, he wrapped his arms around her, cradling her against his body as he kissed over the mark he'd left with his teeth.

He stared at the clear indentations of his teeth in her sweet skin with wide eyes. "I bit you," he said, aghast.

She sighed happily. "I remember." She turned her face and nuzzled his neck.

His eyes slid closed as he focused on the soft press of her lips against his skin.

"Told you it'd be better if you lost control," she said, her voice smug.

He exhaled quickly through his nose. "That wild lack of finesse was better?" He stroked her soft belly, eliciting another sigh from her.

"God, yes."

He paused. That had been ... "I loved it," he confessed in a whisper. *Almost as much as I love you.*

"Sleep," she muttered, her eyelids already fluttering.

A tender smile spread his lips. With a groan, he separated their bodies, pointedly ignoring the fact that he was still semihard. Apparently, he had a lot of celibate years to make up for, and his body was going to remind him of that constantly.

She pushed from his arms and flopped to the bed, limbs splaying. After a moment and with visible effort, she held her arms out to him. "Sleep with me," she whispered.

"Anything," he whispered back. He now understood the danger men could get into after mind-blowing sex. If Bethany asked for something right now, he would give it to her no matter what.

He settled down next to her and then pulled her against his chest. When she nuzzled him and drew her knee over his thighs, he sighed in bliss. This was perfect. She was perfect. For the first time in his life, James was ... happy.

Just as his eyes had slid shut, they popped open. He was happy.

Shit. His mind scrambled in panic. He could lose her. He could lose this feeling. He could become his father. When he asked her to stay, she could outright refuse. Why wouldn't she refuse?

Hey, baby, come be a mountain hermit with me. I'll snare all the rabbits you can eat.

His heart rate no longer sluggish, James blinked up at the ever-lightening ceiling, unease stealing through his entire being and robbing him of all his joy.

He gripped her with both hands, subconsciously trying to keep her from leaving him even though she was right here.

After an hour, when his panic had not abated at all, James gave up. He'd just had his first sleepless night. As he eased Bethany to the bed, brushing her hair from her eyes and pressing a kiss to her forehead, he wished his sleeplessness could be solely attributed to the vigorous sex.

He pulled on his clothes with a heavy heart, and trying to ignore the feeling of impending doom, he trudged through the snow for a shower. Surely, everything would look brighter once he was clean and clear-headed.

Chapter Twenty-Two

Whomp, whomp, whomp.

Something pulled Bethany from her sleep, slowly and sweetly, as though she were taffy. As the beginning glimmer of reality intruded upon dreams, a smile spread her lips.

James made love to me.

She stretched; tiny twinges lit through the muscles in her thighs and groin, and she moaned in the deep satisfaction of a woman well loved. She wanted to wake this way every morning for the rest of her life.

Well, perhaps just a slight difference. Every other morning of her life, she wouldn't be facing telling him some news he may reject her for revealing.

She reached out for James, her eyes still closed. If she got the secret-telling part over with, maybe she could entice him to make love to her again before they got out of bed.

No more condoms.

She frowned. Okay, then, she'd give him one hell of a blowie instead of sex. And, maybe, not having a condom wasn't the worst thing ever.

Bethany's fingers encountered cold sheets, but it was her thoughts that startled her eyes open, not the realization that James wasn't in bed with her.

Not the worst thing ever? You want to get pregnant? Her mind worded the question the same way it might have asked, *You want to be hit by a Mack truck?*

Sun streamed through the windows, igniting floating dust specs in the brilliancy and beauty of little stars, but her morning-after glow was fading fast.

Whomp, whomp, whomp.

"The fuck is that?" she grumbled.

She slowly sat up, letting the sheet and quilt pool in her lap.

Whomp, whomp, whomp.

It was getting louder.

Bethany's eyes widened, and she snatched the sheet to her chest. "Helicopter!" she cried to the empty room.

Empty?

"James?"

His name echoed through the cabin, even over the constant thrum of an approaching helicopter. She winced. That desperation in her voice could be attributed to waking up wonky more than being broken at not finding her man in their bed.

WHOMP, WHOMP, WHOMP.

Okay, that helicopter was definitely landing. Bethany sprang from the bed and began the frantic search for her discarded clothing. She shoved limbs through clothes, nearly hitting the plank floor several times in her haste.

It took her less than a minute to get fully dressed, but James was still nowhere to be seen. "Where are you?" Her teeth were clenched as she stormed toward the door.

Someone was invading their peaceful love nest, and James was nowhere to be found. She was equal parts frustrated with him and frustrated with herself that she seemed to expect him to come to her defense if things got dangerous.

"I don't need a man to defend me." She grabbed the cast-iron frying pan from the stove on her way to the door, hefting it in her hand. *Good enough.*

She wrenched open the door. Her mouth dropped.

There was a helicopter, all right. It'd landed a few feet away from the water shed, and the morning sun caught and glimmered on the Delaney Science emblem emblazoned on the metal bird's side.

"Oh." The hand holding the frying pan dropped to her side. The helicopter was here for her.

She mentally counted backward. Her eyes widened. Had she truly been here with James for three weeks already?

A familiar, ebony head of hair peeked out from the sliding side door, and then Mark bounded to the snow in full snowsuit regalia. He spotted her right away and threw her a cheery wave, as though he landed on snow-covered mountains in helicopters to rescue stranded scientists on the reg.

She didn't realize she was scowling at him until he visibly flinched backward before walking in her direction.

A vicious and sudden sweep of agony robbed her of breath, and she covered her gut with her free hand, rubbing in a slow circle. It had not occurred to her at any point that the sound she woke up to was announcing the end to her time here with James.

Acid churned in her stomach. When Mark was only a few feet away, a movement over his shoulder caught her attention—James, his hair sopping wet and shirt wide open as he bounced on one booted foot while pulling on the other boot—standing in the doorway to the water shed.

His normally placid eyes were harried and flooded with panic, but he quickly took in the scene. She knew when he comprehended what it meant, because his body visibly jolted.

He planted his still-bare foot in the snow, his boot forgotten in his hand. Grief streaked across his features as he looked at her; an answering ache surged in her chest.

Mark—the idiot who couldn't recognize two people's worlds crumbling—was blathering on about how dangerous the conditions were for a helicopter, and how they needed to leave right away, and though Bethany couldn't respond with her every thought riveted to James, her mind was screaming, *Then leave! Leave me with him!*

James sighed, his great, big shoulders rising and falling, before stepping into his boot without even brushing the snow from his toes. He buttoned his open shirt with slow, deliberate fingers, raked a hand through his wet hair, and began to walk toward them.

It wasn't until that moment, when her vision wavered with the sting of tears, that she actually started paying attention to what Mark was saying to her.

"—couldn't believe how lucky it was that you got stuck here with Anderson's son."

She twisted her head in Mark's direction so fast, a hot little flare of pain shot up the back of her neck. She gritted her teeth as the pain lingered, but then what he was saying penetrated the fog of grief and physical discomfort. Her lips parted, and her eyes widened.

"So, Dewinter said you didn't tell her any details over the phone." Mark paused to laugh. "But we're all betting you know that system inside and out by now. Three weeks alone with an Anderson. Fucking jackpot." His eyes twinkled. "Am I right?" He ducked his head. "No, seriously. Tell me I'm right. There's a betting pool on how you learned the system's secrets, and since I know you, you know where I placed my money. The odds are huge. I'll split it with you when we win."

Thud, thud, thud. Her thunderous heart kept beating despite all probability as, to that ponderous rhythm, she dragged her gaze from Mark's beaming face to the spot just over his shoulder where James was standing still as a statue, his features blank and frozen. Frozen, that is, except for the way he kept rapidly blinking his eyes.

The mirth vanished from Mark's expression, too, as he turned to see what she was staring at. He gasped in a breath. "Ah, hey, bro."

For a scant second, James didn't respond, but then he blinked one more time—a long one—then pinned Mark with a glare that, could looks kill, would have slain Mark on the spot, brought him back to life, and killed him again.

Mark took a step back. "Shit," he muttered beneath his breath. He cast her a desperate look. "I'll wait for you in the chopper. We really do have to go, Bethany. Like, ASAP."

She didn't respond. As she watched Mark's retreating back, she knew most of what she was feeling had to be laid directly at her own feet. She should have told James about everything last night. Now, what James had overheard ...

He must think this was so much worse than it was.

My fault.

So, Mark spilled the beans? He wouldn't have been able to if Bethany hadn't handed him the can first.

James's face was an inscrutable mask. If not for the steady rise and fall of his chest, she would be hard pressed to find signs of life.

"James." His name on her lips was a whispered plea—for what, she wasn't quite sure. But she was sure she didn't deserve whatever she was asking for. "Baby, this isn't what it sounded like."

His lips parted, and his eyes focused in a way that betrayed hope.

Bethany winced. The whole reason they'd even met ... She couldn't lie to him anymore. "Well, it's a little of what it sounded like."

That small show of hope vanished from his face. Without a word, he turned and walked into the cabin.

She drew in a tremulous breath and gathered in her strength. She deserved everything he had to say to her in order for them to get past this. She turned to follow him into the cabin, glad they would at least be able to discuss this out of Mark's laser-beam gaze.

But the door slammed in her face with a resounding *crack*.

• • •

Just breathe.

In, out. In, out. In, out.

He made it through only a few normal respirations before his cursed breathing failed him, hitching as his eyes went wet.

He scrubbed at both eyes with the heels of his palms until stars dotted his vision.

This is what you get. How many times had his father told him other people equated pain? Did James think he was different? Would be an exception to the rule?

He could sense Bethany on the other side of the door. Why was she even still here? She'd got what she wanted—his water system, apparently—and now she had a way out. What in the world would cause her to linger, and how could he get her as far away as possible so he could lose what little control he was able to exert over himself?

"James."

His name drifted through the wood of the door on a whisper. She had to be awfully close to the door for him to be able to even hear it, and he launched himself away, turning and scrambling backward.

Get away from me. Get away from me!

"Please, can I come in?"

Panic gripped his throat at the very thought. His gaze lit on her pack in the corner, and like a man diving for a life raft, he pounced on it.

Fisting its handle in one hand, he stormed toward the door.

Get this over with. Get her gone. Out of his life.

He flung the door open.

Bethany's hand was still raised in midknock, and he recoiled, lest she use it to touch him.

He thrust her bag toward her. "Take ... it." He swallowed thickly. "Go."

For some reason, at this, her eyes flooded. "Baby, no." Her voice was broken. "I have to talk to you." She took a step toward him.

He flinched. He tossed the pack at her; it crashed at her feet, but she didn't ever take her gaze from his face. He shook his hair into his eyes, missing the coverage of his beard for the first time since shaving it. He stumbled back, grasping the door, ready to shut it once more.

Her delicate, booted foot planted on the threshold, keeping him from closing the door unless he was prepared to hurt her.

And, damn her, he wasn't.

"Bethany, the pilot says we've got to take off or the blades will freeze."

James's gaze snapped over her shoulder. Her friend was back, and James had never heard him approach. Great. He seemed to be losing all his faculties now.

The other man's expression was wary, and he stood off to the side, obviously reticent to interrupt them.

There was nothing to interrupt.

"Then leave without me," Bethany said, her gaze still steady on James.

James's grip on the door tightened. "No," he grated. "Get ... off my ... land."

Whatever the other man saw in his expression made him step forward and whisper in Bethany's ear loudly enough for James to hear. "Okay, that's what they always say right before they grab a gun, Bethany."

Her chin tilted up. James could tell by the set in her jaw that she was on the verge of saying something along the lines of *James would never hurt me*. Then that determined expression wavered. Her gaze scrutinized him, and he kept his features frozen, forcing himself not to betray the riot of his emotions. He wouldn't ever hurt her, but that same consideration did not extend to the sodding prick who accompanied her.

A flush of rage traveled up his neck and cheeks, and Bethany blanched. "O-okay. Then baby, come with me."

Hours ago, had she asked this question, he ... he would have jumped on it. Gone with her. Been stranded out in the world once her betrayal came to light.

Panic clawed at his throat from the inside, and he raised his fingertips to press against it. "Never," he managed to grate past the beast tearing him apart.

The chopper emitted a high-pitched whine, and Bethany's friend leapt into motion, grabbing her by the arm and pulling her away. "Now, Bethany."

Tears streamed down her pasty cheeks, and she half-heartedly resisted the pull of her coworker for a few moments before her jaw clenched. She lifted her chin, seeming to come to a conclusion.

"This isn't over." She pointed at him. "This isn't o—"

He slammed the door again, cutting her off.

He stumbled over to his chair in the corner, flopping down on its seat so hard the impact reverberated through his body. Grief, unlike anything he remembered feeling, took over his body. He slumped in his seat. Propping his elbows on his knees, he cradled his face in his palms, which grew wet as the helicopter changed sounds, taking to the sky.

Run! Go get her!

He gripped the chair's arms with all his might, just barely keeping his body from flinging itself toward the door. Toward the woman who had betrayed him.

The sounds of the helicopter faded to silence, and his ragged breathing echoed throughout the empty cabin.

So empty.

James's gaze landed on the bed. The sheets were twisted; the quilt fell precariously over the end and pooled on the floor. The pillow Bethany slept on still carried the indentation of her head.

He jerked his gaze to the couch instead. Before he could breathe easily once more, he pictured the many nights Bethany spent curled up on that very same piece of furniture, her feet in his lap as they both read a novel.

His gaze landed on the pot on the counter Bethany had used to save his life from the bear. *Save it long enough to get what she needed from me.*

He shot to his feet and launched himself over the couch, catching the top with his legs along the way and causing it to start a slow careen backward. It landed with a thud just as he reached the pan, which he swatted from the counter with a bellow. The pan crashed to the floor with a cathartic clanging that was still ringing as James turned on the damn bed. He wrenched the quilt and sheets from the mattress and flung them in the general direction of the fireplace before grabbing the bed frame from the side and heaving with all his might.

With a shout, James slowly pulled the frame upright, all his muscles straining to the point of pain. "Goddamn it!" He upended the big bed, and it flopped over, crushing the small side table and colliding with the top-side sofa.

He sprinted across the cabin, vaulting over strewn furniture. Grabbing great handfuls, he stuffed the bedding into the grate, then fumbled for the flint to set it aflame.

The fire caught immediately, and the acrid scent of burning fabric filtered into the cabin. The odor slapped some sense back into him. His chest billowing with each frantic breath, he slowly turned and surveyed his cabin.

Utter destruction.

In an instant, all the anger he'd managed to buoy himself with evaporated, leaving behind the mess he was. The mess Bethany had left behind with her calculated actions.

"Bethany." His voice broke on a sob, and he shoved the back of his forearm against his mouth, worried he might be sick.

This is what you get.

He swallowed thickly until he was sure he would keep what little he held in his stomach. Then, straightening his shoulders, he strode to the door and stepped outside. He sucked in lungfuls of untainted air, clearing his head slightly. His heart rate slowed, but each beat still ached. With leaden feet, he walked to the water shed, where he gathered a hammer and some nails.

He would fix this. Repair this. He would start with the damage he'd caused to his cabin, and then he would work on himself. He would never—*never*—put himself in a position to be hurt again. Those dreams of rejoining civilization? Replaced with dreams of a hurt-free life.

Nothing sounded better than that.

Chapter Twenty-Three

Bethany shoved past the lab techs who swarmed the chopper to retrieve the equipment the search party had left in the woods all those weeks ago. The pilot had stopped there before getting her, a perfect demonstration of where Delaney's loyalties truly lay.

"Out of my way," she muttered to a particularly dense young scientist as she focused on the stairwell with intent.

She had a meeting with her boss. Dr. Dewinter didn't know it yet, but she would soon.

Bethany made the stairwell in record time and trotted down, taking two steps at a time and nearly breaking her neck in the process. When she reached the main building housing Delaney Science, she forced herself to walk like a normal person and not an avenging harpy intent on a blood kill.

Something was rotten in the state of Denmark, and she wanted answers.

She didn't quite manage a normal walk, but she knew that wasn't the reason she was garnering veiled glances as she made her way to the boss's office.

Everything she'd be fighting against her entire career—her nightmare—was staring at her through these same recriminating eyes as she passed each titillated coworker. She was the scientist who had "lifted tail" for her job. A moniker she would never shed.

So, why did being separated from James hurt worse than their stares?

Bethany lifted her chin, determined to fake the usual ever-present confidence that had abandoned her the moment she'd watched James's heart break.

She walked right by the boss's secretary, ignoring the man's pointed, "Do you have an appointment?" Instead, she snatched open the door and let it close behind her with a quiet click that belied the rage brewing in her gut.

Her boss sat behind a huge mahogany desk, her head bent over a file. The gold nameplate reading Dr. Dewinter glinted in the overhead lights. At the sound of the door closing, she raised her head and her brows rose above the frames of her chic glasses. She placed her pencil carefully on the desk, tucked a strand of her salt-and-pepper hair behind her ear, and folded her hands over the file.

"Bethany?"

"Why retrieve me now?" Bethany fisted her hands behind her back to keep her boss from seeing the shaking. They were going to have Dewinter's lies out now. If it was "too dangerous" to rescue Bethany three weeks ago, it was too dangerous now. Conditions hadn't changed.

Dewinter had slipped up. Why had she gotten careless?

Her boss's lips formed a perfect *O*. The other woman was nervous. Some of Bethany's suspicions were immediately confirmed.

The *O* disappeared, replaced with a grim line before Dr. Dewinter raised her brows again. "I'm sorry, I must be confused. Didn't you beg me to get you off the mountain?" Her lips twitched as though she were barely holding back amusement. "You didn't get ... attached to this scientist, did you? Taking a career hit for romance?"

Bethany couldn't help it: she flinched. Before meeting James, she would never have put a romantic relationship above her success, and what was worse, she made sure everyone knew it. Before Bethany could think of a retort beyond *you bitch*, Dewinter spoke again.

"We happened to need your help building the system, that's all." Her boss shrugged with one shoulder. "A very motivated buyer got a look at Eugene Anderson's original schematics, and he's ready to move. We really couldn't make him wait any longer. We deemed the payoff worth the risk of retrieving you under less-than-ideal conditions."

Now Bethany's brows rose. A "big payoff" in corporate science was …

No wonder Dewinter had abandoned the "too dangerous" façade.

"You will," Dewinter continued, "of course, be fairly compensated for your work in this endeavor." Dewinter shifted the file beneath her fingers and finished, almost negligently, with, "And given credit for the project that will most likely net a Nobel."

Bethany refused to blink. Her eyes started to sting.

Everything I've ever wanted.

She wasn't even tempted.

"What about James's credit?"

The slightest tinge of color stained Dewinter's cheeks. *This* was what she was nervous about. "Oh, James?" she asked in an off-hand matter. She rapped her fingers against the desktop. "I see no reason to involve him."

Gotcha.

Bethany felt so stupid for not seeing the big picture that she could have punched herself.

Straightening, she said, "Oh, my God. The system doesn't belong to us! It was James who finished the system, not Eugene. James Anderson never worked for Delaney Science. Delaney has no rights to this technology." Dewinter was trying to steal someone's work. Jesus, this was huge. End-of-Dewinter's-career-if-anyone-found-out huge. "I wonder how your buyer would respond to such news."

Dr. Dewinter's eyes narrowed. All pretense vanished from her countenance and body, the difference so sudden and obvious that Bethany found herself shrinking back against the door before she could stop herself.

"You need to think very carefully," Dewinter said, articulating every word as she leaned forward, "about how this is going to proceed."

Bethany gulped. The message was clear: Keep your mouth shut and career made; go public with Dewinter's and Delaney's actions and career over.

Her chest ached. She bit into her bottom lip. *That destroyed glint in James's eyes as I had to walk away ...*

One simple word would take her life exactly where she'd always hoped it'd go.

She gasped. *Oh, my God.*

Dewinter's eyes narrowed as Bethany straightened.

I love James.

Completely. Passionately. Irreversibly.

She loved him. Wanted him more than anything. Definitely more than this.

There was only one path open now.

She reached behind her for the doorknob and sucked in a breath, holding it and praying for courage. "I'll pack my belongings then." She twisted the knob as Dewinter's eyes widened. "And considering I'll be going public with this, you should pack up as well."

Bethany ducked out the door, closing it behind her in the middle of her ex-boss's desperate, "Bethany, wait."

The secretary met her gaze warily.

She tossed her hair over her shoulder. "Shit's about to go down, kid. Might want to update your LinkedIn profile."

His lips parted, and his face blanched.

That's right, bitches. She'd fucked up. Badly. But she damn well was going to do whatever she could to fix it, even though she was pretty sure she'd lost James forever.

Her eyes stung at that, but she thrust her shoulders back, lifted her chin, and began the long, public walk to her locker.

Either word traveled quickly or everyone already knew what was going on, because even more people clogged the hallways. They watched her as she snagged an empty box from outside a lab and made her way to her meager stash of personal effects.

Mark was waiting for her by her locker. She stopped in her tracks, the box she held bouncing against her thigh. He smiled sheepishly at her, and she barely resisted the urge to bare her teeth.

She pinched the bridge of her nose, sighed, and walked over to her locker. Opening it by rote, she snapped, "What do you want?" She tried to juggle the box and put a crumpled picture of her mother in it simultaneously, and within a heartbeat's span, she was ready to punch somebody in the face.

Maybe myself.

"Give me that," Mark said. He snatched the box from her hands—*without asking first*—and held it out for her.

She glared at him. "Is my eye twitching? I feel like my eye is twitching."

He rolled his. "Stop being a diva. Load up the damn box."

After a second, she saw the logic, shrugged, and reached for the heaviest item next: a 700-page reference book. With an overly pleasant smile, she pitched it into the box as hard as she could.

Mark grunted, but then he raised his eyebrows at her as though to ask, *That the best you got?* "Want to talk about it?"

She snapped, "What are you doing here again?"

"I came to apologize, actually. But I think you cracked my sternum, so I'll need a minute to recoup."

"Ha-ha," she deadpanned, dropping her myriad sets of goggles into the box.

"Bethany," he said in a tone that made her pause. "Seriously. I'm really sorry for what I said. For what I, apparently, ruined."

Her shoulders fell. She dropped a lab coat onto the top of the box. "You didn't say anything that wasn't true," she admitted. James wouldn't have been able to take anything out of context if she'd confided in him last night. Or, hell, days ago. "I did this. Not you."

She cast a final glance over the interior of her locker. Empty. She shut the door quietly, pocketed the padlock, and reached for her belongings.

He shook his head. "Let me walk you out."

Too emotionally exhausted to argue, she shrugged. They were quiet as they made their way through the halls of Delaney and out to the staff parking lot. It wasn't until they got to Bethany's Volvo, parked next to Mark's ancient Chevy station wagon, that she noticed a box, similar to the one Mark already held, brimming with his personal items and sitting in the back of his car.

"Oh, yeah." He set the box of Bethany's items on her trunk. "Dewinter's secretary may be a terrible kisser, but he's A+ in the gossip department." He leaned against her car and crossed his arms over his chest. "Called me as soon as he heard what you were yelling at the boss lady through the door. I packed up directly."

She frowned. "I wasn't ... yelling."

He narrowed his gaze at her. "I didn't even have to be there to know you were yelling, Bethany. Your fuse is pretty short, and I imagine someone trying to rob your man of billions of dollars set it off in record time."

She acknowledged his point with a dip of her head. "I ... honestly don't know what to do now," she confessed, her voice wobbling. "I was so strong in her office, but I don't know shit about this kind of thing. Who do I even call to report her?"

Mark reached into his back pocket and pulled out his cell phone. "That's where I come in. And we aren't reporting her; we're destroying her. I know just who to call. He works at *Popular Science*, and he *is* a good kisser. This has *win* written all over it."

As Mark scrolled through his contacts, she stood on her tiptoes and pressed a quick kiss to his cheek. "Thank you, Mark." She choked up and couldn't continue, though his show of loyalty and support deserved freakin' sonnets of gratitude.

His gaze met hers, his gray eyes hard. "I'd do this even if it wasn't you, honey. This is wrong."

Honey.

The same endearment James called her. Bethany pressed her fingers over her lips, trying desperately to keep herself together. She'd never hear James call her *honey* again.

She turned from Mark as he placed his call, leaned against the side of her car, and let the tears fall.

Chapter Twenty-Four

A month later

James stared at the snare in which he'd first found Bethany and felt pinpricks behind his eyes. Maybe, just maybe, he'd made a mistake.

He was living in a classic manifestation of "cutting one's nose off to spite one's face," and with every passing day, he missed his damn nose more than he'd ever thought possible the day before.

The snare was empty, and with a huff, he prepared to turn back to his cabin, but the thought of going from empty snare to empty cabin did odd things to his gut.

He scratched at his scraggly beard, which even after a month's growth, itched like chigger bites all the time, something he'd reveled in adding to Bethany's list of misdeeds at first. Mentally reciting that long list had lost its draw, though; it had been a couple of weeks since he'd scratched his jaw and, with a scowl, envisioned Bethany's face.

More and more, he imagined the way her beautiful eyes were a different shade of aqua in the morning light versus the firelight when he laid her down in bed and set to touching her before they slept. The way she tipped her head back when she laughed, her elegant neck exposed and that jet-black hair he missed fisting tumbling down her back and around her shoulders. The way her brain worked as she puzzled out a solution to whatever she was working on. Her quick sense of humor and even quicker acerbic wit.

"Damn it," he muttered to the snare. He missed her. Missed the life he'd had when she was here. Missed who he'd been when she was here.

Lately, he didn't like himself, and considering he'd only gone back to the James he'd been his entire life, his self-loathing seemed to compound daily.

Why hadn't he let her talk? Would she have said something that would have convinced him to forgive her?

The question plagued him. Granted, he couldn't think of anything she could have said that would have made what she'd done better. Actions speak louder than words, and such. But maybe if he'd let her try ...

He was finally able to pull himself from the gripping sight of the empty snare, and he began a distempered stomping toward the cabin. Damn this weather. He couldn't remember the last time a blizzard had affected his ability to travel for so long. He hadn't been able to empty his post-office box in months, and his lack of reading materials chafed. He knew several periodicals awaited him as well as a shipment of novels.

Before Bethany crashed into his life, he'd been contemplating rejoining society with a hopeful naivety. Now the naivety was gone. So was the hope for that matter. But—and he couldn't believe this—the idea of rejoining society had resurfaced lately. As though he hadn't learned his lesson.

Ridiculous.

It was boredom that was lending time for these thoughts. He needed his periodicals!

With a vehemence that would have been out of the norm for James two months ago but was all too common now, he slammed the cabin door behind him. He dropped his string of rabbits on the cabinet and paced the cabin with a heavy tread.

His breaths came quicker with the exertion, and though it had been a month, the acrid scent of smoke still tinged the interior of the cabin. He wrinkled his nose.

"Going to ... lose it," he bit out as he paced. His halting speech only exacerbated the situation. Since Bethany's betrayal, he seemed to have regressed to his terrible Tarzan-like speech patterns. It was embarrassing; he didn't talk much as a result. Which was, no doubt, a healthy development as he lived alone and was really only a step or two from crazy hermit as opposed to just hermit.

Who was he kidding? Steps? He was already there.

He stopped his pacing so quickly, he practically skidded.

If he died in a fiery truck crash as a result of his idiocy or of hypothermia when the truck bottomed out on a snow drift, well, it really wouldn't be much worse than what his life was right now.

He was going into town.

He jerked a nod and strode to the door. Just as he was reaching for the doorknob, he paused. For some reason he did not want to closely examine, he turned back and shaved before he left.

Chapter Twenty-Five

James gripped a crumpled copy of *Popular Science* in his fist as he stormed through the front door of Delaney Science.

He hadn't slept in ... God, he didn't know the last time he'd slept, but it had absolutely been longer than the twenty-four hours since he'd left the cabin. And he'd certainly had a few close calls on his drive through treacherous conditions from the cabin to the nearest town and then in the harried drag race that had ensued after reading through his cache of *Popular Science*, having read them before his other periodicals in the parking lot because they amused him.

But the sight of the feature story on the groundbreaking gray-water system and the major name in science trying to steal it—well, lack of sleep wasn't the only reason his mind was hazy.

"Can I help you, sir?"

James's attention snapped to a gentleman wearing a polite expression, sitting behind a desk that James had managed not to see even though it was only a few feet away. James jumped a little, his fist tightening around *Popular Science*, before he cleared his throat.

"Where's ... Bethany?"

His words grated across the tile floor with the same spine-tingling effect of nails on a chalkboard. The man's polite expression morphed into a grimace, and he leaned away.

A flash of movement to James's right drew his attention. A security guard straightened away from the nearby wall and stepped forward. The guard's hand rested on a black shape on his belt that

James couldn't recognize. Surely not a gun. Did science security guards carry guns?

James took a step back and directed his wary attention to a spot between the two men—one seated, one standing—so he could detect movement from either.

The first to break the stalemate was the receptionist. "Do you have identification?"

James frowned. *What?* Oh. Those tiny, plastic cards. A driver's license.

He had no driver's license. He'd learned to drive by putting around the mountain. These men were wasting his time!

"Where ... is Bethany?"

"Okay, let's go." The security guard took several quick, menacing steps toward James, his hand outstretched, the intention to remove him bodily from the premises clear on the guard's face.

James shuffled his feet wider. If this man touched him, it would be a poor decision on his part.

The distant, alien sound of a ringing reached James's ears, and he held out a hand to the guard and raised his eyebrows in silent warning.

For some reason, it worked: The guard stopped his forward progress, and James turned his head to the sound. The receptionist was on the phone. That faint ringing ceased, and a male's voice faded over.

"You told me to call you if anyone came looking for Bethany," the receptionist said into the phone.

His interest fully piqued, James shot one final warning glare at the guard and walked over to the desk.

The receptionist saw him coming, turned his chair slightly, and whispered into the phone, "I will not call you sir!" A pause. The voice on the other end said something James could only define by tone as lascivious. "That was one time! Look, what should I be doing with this guy? Frank, here, is about to boot him out."

The voice on the other end was so loud this time, James could hear the voice ask, "A guy?" More unintelligible babble.

The receptionist cast a glance his way and perused him up and down. "Flannel and an obvious chip on his shoulder." A few moments later, the receptionist ended the call. He nodded to Frank, the guard, who stepped up to James's side. James braced for the guy to grab him, but he did nothing.

"Take him to Dr. Sexton's office."

The guard's lips pursed together, but after only a slight hesitation, Frank acknowledged the receptionist's instructions with a nod. Turning his disapproving glare James's way, Frank said, "Follow me," and set off across the lobby.

Some of the tension in James's shoulders dissipated. It appeared he was not going to be bodily forced from the premises. How fortunate.

The guard stopped in front of two shiny, metal doors, and when they opened with a ding, James realized they were an elevator. Despite his mood, he felt a thrill of excitement. He'd studied them extensively, of course, and knew how they worked, but if he'd ridden any elevators as a child, he didn't remember them. As he stepped inside next to Frank, it took all of James's power not to act like a giddy child riding his first roller coaster—another experience James looked forward to.

His head jerked back. Looked forward to? As though he were planning to stay ... out in civilization?

Was that why he'd come here? Because, honest to God, he wasn't quite sure why he had. He only knew that he hadn't truly had a choice in the matter. He'd seen the article, and next he knew, he had to be here. Had to see Bethany. Had to know if that scathing piece had anything to do with her.

Had she gotten caught stealing his invention? Or had she blown the whistle?

The second one, please.

So, he was here for her. Even after all she'd done, he wasn't done with her, apparently. He was back for more, actually traveling into civilization, a punishment in and of itself, to seek more punishment.

He was supposed to be smart.

There was a *ding*, and the elevator doors parted, revealing a lush lobby filled with leather furniture, potted plants, and an overwhelming sense of condescension.

Before he knew what he was doing, James was backing into the corner of the elevator, his shoulders curling in.

His nice, comfortable cabin was free of all this ... this ... *humanity.*

Bethany is a part of "humanity."

With effort, he pulled away from the corner. When his eyes focused, it was to find Frank staring at him with rounded lips and a raised eyebrow.

James tried to give him what he thought resembled a "normal" smile. It didn't feel successful, and the security guard confirmed that when his lips twisted, he rolled his eyes, and then turned his back on James with a terse, "Come on."

James avoided his reflection in the golden-framed mirror they passed, not wanting to see what, no doubt, were wild eyes in a pale face.

Frank stopped in front of an enormous door bearing a brass nameplate that read Dr. Sexton: Head of Delaney Science.

James frowned as Frank knocked. Of course, it made sense that Dr. Dewinter would no longer be the head of Delaney after the article James read, but it hadn't clicked until that moment that someone else would have taken her place.

When there was a muffled "Come in" from inside, Frank opened the door and then quickly retreated, as though he'd been dying to escape since clapping eyes on the crazy mountain man.

James peered into the office and froze.

It was *him*. The man who'd come to the mountain and taken Bethany, but not before completely destroying everything in James's soul first.

He did not want to see him. He did not want to be here.

He took a step back, but the other man shot to his feet and stretched out a supplicating hand. "James, please. Don't run." He skirted the desk and strode toward him. "*Please.*"

He was so surprised by the sincerity in the man's plea, James stayed planted to the spot.

Dr. Sexton stopped in the doorway, looked James over, and blew out a breath. "She'll just die that you're actually here."

A Pavlovian rising of hope bubbled through James's chest, and he scowled as soon as he realized it.

Undaunted by the scowl, Dr. Sexton reached out, plucked a part of James's sleeve, and pulled him into the room. James was too shocked to resist. He hadn't expected a perfect stranger to touch him. Is that what people did?

Dr. Sexton closed the door behind them and continued pulling until they arrived at a small seating area in the corner of the office. "Sit." He accompanied the order with a small shove that sent James tumbling into an armchair.

James straightened and tried to show a dignity that sprawling into furniture belied. "Where's ... Bethany?"

The other man took a seat on the couch cushion closest to James's chair and leaned toward him. "She quit. Immediately after she arrived via helicopter."

Dr. Sexton's gaze was roving his expression so intensely, James knew he was looking for a reaction. The question was *why*? Why in the world would this man care what he felt for Bethany?

A sudden and cataclysmic rush of envy flooded him. "Is she yours?" The question was quiet, but so suffused with emotion as to punch out into the space between them. It was also said without the slightest hesitation or hiccup.

Something lit in Dr. Sexton's eyes, and James clenched his fists against the foreign urge to wrap them around the man's throat. "Would that matter to you?"

James gritted his teeth and refused to answer.

Dr. Sexton smiled and patted James's knotted fist where it rested on the chair's arm. "She's not mine."

Before James could fully relax into the relief that rushed his system, Dr. Sexton continued. "Bethany belongs to no man. Never will." He folded his hands in his lap as James's shoulders tightened. "But if she was going to choose a man lucky enough to share his life with her, it'd be you, James."

His head kicked back. Had he understood correctly? "What ... was that?"

Dr. Sexton rolled his eyes, a startlingly immature move for the head of a science corporation, in James's opinion. "Bethany quit for you, you fool."

After a moment, James felt the left corner of his mouth curl up.

Maybe he should have allowed her to stay. Talk things out with her. James looked toward the door. "Why did she ... quit?"

Dr. Sexton pulled in a large breath, held it for a moment while he surveyed James, and then puffed it out, as though resigned to a decision. "She protected your invention. That's why she quit. Dewinter told her to steal it from you for the company and the buyer or get out. She got out." The man flashed a dimple. "And went straight to the press."

James's jaw slackened. "She did ..." *All of that?* For an invention that would have been used to do the great things Bethany had envisioned for it? Protecting it for a man who hadn't even cared about its potential when he'd created it, making it for his own personal gratification?

"She chose you over her career, James." Dr. Sexton leaned forward, his eyes suddenly grave. "And a smart man would recognize all that means to Bethany."

Her career had been everything to her. Her dream, she'd told him. And she'd had the magic bullet—the water system—in her possession. All her goals, professional and personal, were about to be reached, and she'd passed them up.

For him.

James shot to his feet. "Where is she?" His words were firm. Quick.

"So you *are* smart." Dr. Sexton got to his feet as well. "Can you follow a map?"

James glared at Dr. Sexton's back as the man walked to his desk and began rummaging. "Of course."

"Good." He started scribbling. James shifted his weight back and forth, the desire to run to his car and speed to Bethany nearly overwhelming.

Dr. Sexton turned, a piece of paper held in his fist. "I'm trusting you with this," he said, not yet extending the map. "Don't fuck this up. You do, and she'll hand me my ass for telling you how to find her."

James jerked a nod. "Anything. Just give it to me."

Dr. Sexton smiled slowly. "I like the desperation. It might help your cause."

Finally—*finally*—Dr. Sexton handed James the map. He snatched it and spun toward the door, lurching his way out of the room.

"I'll expect a wedding invitation," Dr. Sexton called after him. "With a plus one!"

Wedding? Oh, dear God.

James wanted that. He wanted to wed Bethany. Always had, as a matter of fact. The moment he'd clapped eyes on Bethany swinging upside down in his snare, he'd wanted her for his own.

That feeling had only grown. Had continued to grow after he'd cast her aside so he wouldn't have to suffer. Like an idiot.

He'd made a mistake. A truly big one. He only hoped that he could convince her of that as well.

James froze. He couldn't turn up on her doorstep, hat in hand, with nothing to offer her. He was a hermit, for God's sake! Granted, he was a hermit with a fortune in inherited money, but he'd done nothing to earn that. He did have one thing, though.

Turning back to the door, he tucked his head back into the office. "Dr. Sexton, I'll give Delaney the water system if they hire me." He narrowed his eyes. "And give Bethany your job."

The man's brows rose, but then he surprised James when he readily nodded. "Agreed." Before James could react, he continued, "She deserved it anyway, and the interoffice dating policy is chapping my ass."

Well, that had gone much better than planned, even though he'd only hobbled together this plan in the last handful of seconds.

"I'll need that in writing. After Bethany agrees to all the terms, of course."

Dr. Sexton smiled. "Of course. I'll have the paperwork drawn up while you win back your lady."

Was this guy for real? He took the stairs two at a time. *Where are all the evil people my father warned me about?* So far, people had been ... *nice.* Even the security guard who had looked at James as though he were crazy.

Could his father have been wrong about this in addition to all the other things he'd been wrong about?

Absolutely.

James burst out of the front doors of Delany to the cheerful tune of the receptionist wishing him a good day. He was smiling to himself in cautious hopefulness when he spotted his truck.

As it was being pulled down the road by a tow truck.

He skidded to a stop, sliding a bit on the icy sidewalk. His heart thundered in his chest.

There. There is the evil in humanity.

"That yours?"

James turned and spied good ol' Frank standing beside him and jerking his chin toward the quickly disappearing truck.

James's brow furrowed as he contemplated how he was going to get to Bethany now. He grunted.

"'S'what happens when you park on the gol-darn sidewalk."

James jerked from his mind to glance at the guard. Had he done that? Looking at the sidewalk on which they stood, he spied the melted snow tracks of his tires. Right down the center of the sidewalk.

James sighed and pinched the bridge of his nose.

Frank had the gall to chuckle. "Come back in where it's warm, and I'll call you a cab. Should only take an hour or two in this weather."

James's eyes widened. *An hour?* Why not days? A week even! Bethany was here, in this town, and this man wanted him to wait over an hour to see her.

You're not being rational.

He knew that. It was unhelpful of his psyche to argue such an obvious and—darn it—valid point in the middle of a crisis.

James stared down at the map he held in his fist. Though wrinkled, he could see that the square marked as Bethany's place was only a few turns away. How far could it be? He'd hiked miles through snow on a mountain. He could handle a soft, urban environment.

Five minutes later, he was dodging two cars at once as both blared their horns at him. He leapt back onto the sidewalk, his body shot tight with tension, and the two cars whipped around the corner, one driver shaking his head, the other thrusting his middle finger into the air with all the vehemence of King Arthur with Excalibur.

"Young man, you must wait for the crosswalk signal."

The croaky voice caused James to jump. He placed his hand over his chest and spun around to find a small, elderly lady sitting on a nearby bench. She raised a gnarled finger and pointed at something over his shoulder.

As he turned, there was a chirping, like a sad, robotic bird, and his gaze landed on the white, lit silhouette of a man in midstride in a small, yellow box.

"Now you can go."

"Thank you," he muttered while launching into motion.

"And you need a coat, young man!"

Though the thirty-degree temperatures down here felt balmy in comparison to the mountaintop, James waved over his head in acknowledgment as he jogged to the other side of the street.

Just one more turn and he'd be on ...

Her street.

Trees dripping with ice lined each side of the street, and cars parked at regular intervals on both sides. Cheery, brick buildings with charming stoops whizzed by as he started sprinting, scanning the numbers on the doors only as closely as needed to illuminate the houses as not Bethany's.

When the numbers started getting closer to the correct one, James picked up speed. He passed number eight, reached number ten, and slid to a stop. Craning his head to see around the parked cars, he spotted number nine across the street.

His heart leapt, and he was grinning like an idiot before he even realized it. He stuffed the map in one pocket with numb fingers and took a step out into the road.

Just as he did, the door of number nine swung inward.

The woman he loved stepped outside, and James rocked back on his heels, palming his chest at the ache that lit there with startling intensity. She was wearing a cream, knitted cap that caught the winter sun and seemed to spin it off her sleek, dark hair. She was pressing her slender fingers into a set of gloves, so her face was downturned, but even from this distance and without the glory of her full expression, he could tell that she looked ... *sad.*

His heart panged. "Bethany!" he called, taking another step toward her.

Her head jerked up, and her gaze unerringly found his, locking tightly with it. For a moment, her expression didn't change, and he suffered a thousand, tiny deaths.

Then, her eyes widened. A second later, her lush lips spread into the biggest grin he'd ever seen on them. She dropped her purse at her feet, grabbed the railing, and started down the stairs, her gaze never leaving his face.

James broke into a run. Skirting around a car parked on the curb, he leapt the final few feet, meeting her at the bottom of her stairs.

She launched herself at him, wrapping her arms around his neck, and—God help him—her legs around his waist. Her gloved fingers threaded through his hair, and her lips crushed his.

"James," she whispered against his lips. Her legs squeezed his hips. "Oh, God, I'm dreaming again." She pressed several more nearly violent kisses against his lips, then pulled back.

Her delicate eyebrows drew together. "Why aren't you naked? You're always naked in my dreams."

He lifted a brow. "Am I now?"

"Fuck it." She squeezed him with what had to be all her might. "We can get to the naked part soon enough."

She went back to kissing him.

With a groan, he parted his lips, sucking her bottom lip between his teeth and giving it a nibble. *About to lose myself.*

With more strength than he should have possessed, he pulled from her kiss, releasing her bottom lip with a regretful *pop*.

She blinked up at him, her face falling. "Not a dream?"

He swallowed hard. Shook his head.

Unexpectedly, her eyes brightened. "You're really here?" She cupped his cheeks with both hands. "Oh, my God. You're really here!"

And I thought she was excited to see me before. She wiggled in his arms. When he nearly dropped her, he quickly set her on her feet, holding on to her elbows to make sure she kept her balance.

Covering her lips with one gloved hand, she giggled. "Better than a dream." But then, she sobered. Eyes grave, she lowered her hand and took a step back, her heels meeting the bottom step.

He wanted to reach for her, the slight distance she put between their bodies making his stomach uneasy.

If the flash of something in her own eyes was any indication, it affected her, too. That made his shoulders straighten.

This isn't over.

Not by a long shot. Just like he'd hoped.

"Why are you here, James?" she asked, her voice so infused with hope, he nearly reached for her all over again.

For good measure, he took his own step back. He'd touch her soon. But, for now? "That morning before you ... left ..." He cleared his throat. "What were you going to tell me?"

She tucked a strand of hair behind her ear. Gazing up at him through her lashes, she said, "What I should have told you the second I knew who you were that morning after the blizzard."

He braced himself, shuffling his feet wider. "Which was?"

She thrust her hand between them. It trembled. "Hi," she whispered. "I'm Bethany Morgan. I work for Delaney Science, and I'm looking for your father."

He stared at her hand for several long moments. Was that all? The only thing she had been hiding from him? Peering at her face, he drew his brows together.

Her cheeks lost most of their color, and she slowly lowered her hand back to her side. "Uh ..." She exhaled a shaky breath, then straightened her shoulders, though she wasn't quite meeting his gaze anymore. "When I found out your father passed away, and you had improved on the original water system, I called my boss."

Now her gaze met his. Her normally brightly colored eyes were dark. "I told her about you."

There it was. "What about me?" he asked through tight lips.

She frowned. "That you existed. That you were a brilliant scientist who had continued his father's work."

He couldn't take much more. "Just tell me, Bethany. What did you tell her about the water system?"

Her eyes widened. "Nothing! I promise." She stepped toward him. "James, I never spoke a word about the water system to her. I still haven't."

What? He shook his head, taking a step backward himself to keep a safe distance between them. If she got much closer, he was going to touch her. Pull her into his chest and bury his nose in her hair. Just breathe. "What about what Mark said?"

"About ...?" She swallowed hard, her delicate throat bobbing. "Sleeping with you to steal your system?"

That would be it, yes. He gritted his teeth. Jerked a nod.

"James." She broke off, reached for him. Her fingers curled, and she winced before crossing her arms over her stomach. To keep from touching him? "James, you need to know something. I've never dated anyone I work with. Never said *yes* to any of the inappropriate propositions I've had in the workplace. Never once put my professional integrity into question when it came to a man." She licked her lips. "Not once. Not until you."

His gut clenched. "Then ... why?" His voice cracked.

"Baby—" She winced. Her lower lip quivered, and despite everything, he had to fight himself not to close the distance. "Because," she said softly, "I never cared about a man more than I cared about my career." Her eyes began to sheen. "Not once. Not until you."

His lungs clenched around the air left in them. He wavered on his feet.

"James, I did not sleep with you because of the water system." She enunciated each word carefully. "From the first time I touched you—" Now her voice cracked. "Until the night we made love ... Everything I did, I did because I wanted you more than I wanted anything else." Her eyes lowered. A droplet fell from her cheek and landed on her crossed arms. "Even things I'd fought my whole life to achieve."

He was gut-punched. His fingers twitched, needing to be on her. Anywhere.

But she wasn't done. "It tore me up inside, not being able to figure that out while I was on the mountain with you. I was selfish. I handled the situation badly. I hurt you."

Another tear fell, and he couldn't stop himself this time. He stepped toward her.

Her chin lifted once more, though it trembled. Her watery gaze locked him in place. Shot down to his heart quicker than a current. "I am so, so sorry, James."

And just like that, the last of his anger faded. "I believe you," he whispered.

Heck, if he'd paused for just one second that fateful morning and expected something different from Bethany than his father had indoctrinated him to expect from everyone ...

Well, she would have told him this then. And he would have believed her then. Because, he knew her. Knew her kind heart.

In fact, all throughout this day, people had surprised him. Every unkind act had been followed immediately by a kind one. A stranger looking out for him.

The world—people—may not be all good.

But they were certainly not all bad.

As though she hadn't heard him, words continued to pour from her lips. "Every day since returning, I've been trying to get back to you." She sniffed. "No one seemed to understand how important it was. I know you'll never be able to forgive me—"

He laid a finger across her lips. They were so soft, so lush beneath his touch, he almost lost his cool entirely. "I forgive you."

She blinked several times. A few of those blinks displaced more tears. They sparked against her dusky cheeks like the purest water.

Both of them seemed frozen in place.

Then she sobbed.

Chapter Twenty-Six

Bethany broke, launching herself into James's chest. "Oh, my God." Another sob tripped over her lips.

I forgive you. James had only said one other phrase that had meant more to her. She pressed her forehead into his sternum, her fingers curling into the muscles of his stomach. "I love you so much."

He stiffened against her.

She sucked in a breath, stiffening herself. Had she misread this?

His chest shuddered beneath her brow.

No. Her lips curved into a wavery smile. She hadn't misread this.

"What did you say?" His tone was far away. Hopeful.

She raised her head, smoothing her palms up his torso and over his pectorals until she could wrap her arms around his neck. "James Anderson, I love you. More than I could ever love anyone or anything."

His brows drew together sharply. "You love me?"

She bit back a grin. Rising to her tiptoes, she pressed a soft kiss to that dimple in his chin. "I adore you." Another kiss. "Can't live without you." Another. "I need you."

A groan rumbled from his chest to hers. Before she could say anything, his arms banded around her back. He lifted her, a fortunate turn of events since the effect of his flexing muscles against her cheek was making her weak-kneed.

She wrapped her legs around his waist, where they belonged, damn it. His enormous hand palmed her ass, and he squeezed, a shudder wracking his body as he took the stairs to her front door two at a time.

With his free hand, he jerked the knob. She was too busy pressing kisses to the underside of his jaw to notice he tried to turn the knob several times before a grunt drew her from his delectable skin. "Locked, baby," she murmured, then dived in for another taste of him, sucking on his neck until she achieved it.

Her back met the door with enough force to jar her bones. She gasped, her head falling back and meeting the door with almost the same strength.

His gaze roved her face, the look in his eyes wild and hot.

And then he was kissing her. Deeply. Her eyes slid closed as she twined her tongue with his and widened her knees, digging her heels into his ass.

He rocked against her, shoving an erection that made her want to weep right against where she needed him most, and she cried out into their kiss.

He broke away, his breathing frantic. "We need to go inside, Bethany." He rocked against her again. "Now or I'm going to"— he squeezed her ass, canting her hips into his next thrust—"leave a lasting impression on your neighbors."

She breathed a laugh, fighting to keep her eyes from closing as the feel of him hot and hard against her clit nearly drove her senseless. "In my purse." She pointed to his feet. "You have to let me down, babe."

He groaned, shook his head, and dipped down for another kiss. She pulled him close, giving as good as she got for several heated moments before she unwound her legs from his waist.

He made a protesting noise in the back of his throat, his grip on her ass tightening.

"I'll make it worth it." God, would she. "I promise."

He swallowed hard but loosened his grip.

She rocked on her feet as she stood on her own power, her sex so swollen she wondered how she was going to walk.

Before she could blink, James scooped down, gathering her abandoned purse and shoving it toward her. She sent him a grateful smile and dug around for her keys, finding them in half the time it usually took her to.

Her hand shook so badly, she had to try several times to make the key slide home. The heat from James's chest pressed against her back as she turned the key and pushed the door in.

In a swirl of limbs, James had them inside with the door closed. First her purse and then her keys hit the floor.

And then she was right back where she'd been seconds ago, only this time, they were on the proper side of the door.

Her head fell back as he licked his way down her neck. She cradled his head against her as he sucked softly on her collarbone, then began tugging at her sweater.

Naked is such a good idea.

She grabbed fistfuls of his shirt, trying to pull it up and meeting the impediment of her legs cinched around his waist.

With a growl, he pulled back, letting her legs fall but keeping her pinned upright between his hard body and the door at her back.

Buttons pinged off every surface as he wrenched his shirt off, then reached for her sweater. Her hat and gloves went flying, her hair cascading into her eyes. She brushed it away just in time to see his chest ripple as he shoved his jeans and boxers to his ankles—as far as they would go with his boots still on his feet.

She kicked her shoes off and began attacking her own pants while James's heated gaze drank her in, his hands reaching for and kneading her breasts.

She flung her pants and panties away with a kick of her ankle. She had to do no more than open her arms before he pressed against her once more. Skin met skin this time.

Bending to the right, he wrapped calloused fingers around the back of her knee and wrenched it up, pinning it against his side with his elbow and palming her ass.

She kissed every part of him she could reach—his chest, his biceps, his shoulder—as he fumbled between their bodies, his breaths so quick and shallow, she tightened her arms around him.

No sooner had the broad head of his erection met her slick entrance than he thrust home, entering her to the hilt in one, smooth glide.

His fingers tightened on her ass; his other palm met the door by her head with a slap. "Fuck." He gulped air. "Bethany."

Her mind was screaming nearly the same thing, but with her teeth lodged in the flexing muscle of his shoulder, the words couldn't make it out of her mouth. Instead, she spoke with her body, undulating her hips and grinding against him to take him impossibly deeper inside of her.

With a grunt, he withdrew sharply, and she braced herself for a teeth-jarring thrust that would send her right to the edge of orgasm.

Instead, he rolled his hips, entering her again so sweetly as he pressed a soft kiss just beneath her ear that tears sprang to her eyes. He nuzzled her hair, and she could hear him inhaling her scent.

Again, he withdrew and filled her, and as his body came flush with hers, he whispered into her ear, "I love you, too."

She cried out, the noise closer to a sob than the pure joy that rushed through her body, but she was already so close. So desperate.

As though he sensed just that, his thrusts picked up speed, though they remained just as tender. Within seconds, she was squirming against him, seeking the pressure she needed against her clit to send her that final inch over the edge ...

On his next thrust, he ground against her, rotating his hips.

Her orgasm crested over her in a wave. Crying out his name, she held him close, her body squeezing his over and over.

A broken breath passed by her ear as he stiffened in her arms. Wet heat flooded her just as he began to dissolve against her.

In moments, they were a tangled mess of limbs on her foyer floor. He still pulsed inside her as she lay sprawled atop him, her head tucked beneath his chin and his arms securely banded around her back.

When her breathing had regulated enough that she could talk, she lifted her head, propping her chin on his sternum. He gazed down at her, bending his arm and tucking a palm under his head. His biceps bulged, and if she weren't so boneless, she'd slide up his body and lick him just there.

Maybe in a minute.

"We ... uh, didn't use a condom," she began slowly.

He froze but only for a moment. His fingers spread across her back. "I'm so sorry, I should have ..."

She covered his lips with her fingers. "I went on the pill as soon as I got back." She stared down at his chest. "I was hoping for the best once I was able to get back to you."

His finger curled under her chin, lifting. When her gaze met his again, he asked, "You were coming back for me?"

She blew a strand of hair out of her eyes. "Turns out rescue is one thing. Voluntary trips up a mountain in the wake of a blizzard are another. Couldn't find anyone with the means to get me to you who wasn't a verifiable coward." She shook her head. "But that's beside the point."

Her gaze slipped from his again. "I was hoping, maybe ..." She traced a circle around the hollow of his throat with her pointer finger. She cleared her throat. "We could ditch the pill at some point. Soonish."

There was extremely loud silence above her head.

Suddenly, she was flipped over to her back. James was still wedged deeply inside her body, but he was hardening again quickly. His brown eyes were slightly wet as he gazed down at her, a crooked smile spreading his lips. "We could ditch the pill now. Head straight to the courthouse."

God, that sounds perfect. She shook her head. "We still have a lot to figure out. Where we're going to live—"

"With each other."

Her hips wanted to tilt up so badly. She held them still. "Where we're going to work."

"With each other."

She bit her bottom lip. "What we're going to do about the water system," she said softly.

His smile softened. "Whatever we decide together." He cupped her cheek. "Honey, I'm a simple man. There's only one thing I need. The rest we can figure out as it comes." The grin returned. "Right after we head to the courthouse."

She chuckled. "Baby, we can't get married so fast!"

He cocked an eyebrow. "Says who?"

He had her there. "I think ... everybody?"

He shook his head. "I don't listen to everybody."

Huh. Her either. "One year?" That'd be enough time to make sure this was what he wanted.

"One year?" he asked in the same tone he'd ask "Five decades?" He breathed a disbelieving chuckle. "No way." Then, his brows drawing together as if the concession caused him physical pain, he offered, "Three months."

Sounds reasonable. "Six months," she countered.

He narrowed his eyes. "Two weeks."

A laugh bubbled through her lips, and she wanted to clasp him to her chest and never let go. "Okay, baby, sometime between two weeks and six months."

God, it would be a miracle if they weren't dragging each other to the courthouse by next Thursday.

She didn't need any more time. This was the real thing, no doubt in her mind. And though she wanted to give James as much time as she could, he knew his mind, too. She didn't need to offend him by assuming otherwise for society's sake.

It was as though he could feel her defenses crumbling. "Honey," he said, stroking her cheek with his thumb. "We're going to be so happy."

She sniffed. *I am not going to cry again!* "Yes, but, James, this isn't going to be easy. We still have so much to figure out. We're going to argue. Disagree—"

This time, it was he who covered her lips with his fingers. "Good," he said with a shrug of one shoulder.

She'd draw back if her head wasn't already against the floor. "Good?"

"Seems to me that if it's easy, you're not doing it right."

She thought for a moment. "Sounds legit."

He pressed a kiss to her brow. "I often get things right." His kiss traveled to her temple, the bridge of her nose. "Like how long we should wait until we get married." His next kiss was pressed to her lips.

She touched the tip of her tongue to his, then wrapped her legs around his waist. He groaned as she squeezed him with her inner muscles. His hips started to roll.

She gasped, her head tilting back. "Who am I to argue with someone who is always right?"

He licked her neck. "You're the woman I love."

Her chest tightened. *Then I'm the luckiest woman alive.* "James," she moaned when he thrust into her. "God, I love you, too."

He thrust again. "Should really take my boots off this time," he murmured near her ear, though his movements picked up speed.

She grabbed his ass, meeting him thrust for thrust. "We even have a bed."

His heart thundered against hers. Reaching between their bodies, he found her clit with his thumb and circled it.

Oh, fuck. "Maybe next time."

He buried his face in her neck. "Definitely next time."

They didn't make it to the bedroom for another two hours.

But they did make it to the courthouse sometime much sooner than six months later.

About the Author

Micah Persell lives in Southern California with her husband, 1.7 children, and menagerie of pets. She writes romance with strong women, smart minds, and scorching love. She loves connecting with readers. You can find her at www.micahpersell.com, on Facebook at www.facebook.com/MicahPersell, and on Twitter @ MicahPersell.